A MASTERPIECE OF MURDER

"Professor, I understand how long you've wanted to see this painting, but this is not the time," Gus said. "After we clear your name, you'll be able to study it as much as you want. But now we've got to go."

"That's the problem," Shawn said. "That painting is the only way to clear his name."

Kitteredge looked at Shawn as if revising an earlier opinion of him. "The painting is the reason Filkins was killed," Kitteredge said. "I'm convinced it contains essential clues to the identity and purpose of this global conspiracy. . . . They knew I would be able to decipher its secret message. They had to shut me up, so they killed poor Clay and framed me for it."

"The picture's a hundred and fifty years old," Gus said. "Even if it does have all those clues in it, how is it going to help you identify the actual murderers?"

"I'll know when I have a chance to study it," Kitteredge said. . . .

THE PSYCH SERIES

A Fatal Frame of Mind
Call of the Mild
Mind Over Magic
A Mind Is a Terrible Thing to Read

psych

A FATAL FRAME OF MIND

William Rabkin

TO MILES,

[signature]

AN OBSIDIAN MYSTERY

OBSIDIAN
Published by New American Library, a division of
Penguin Group (USA) Inc., 375 Hudson Street,
New York, New York 10014, USA
Penguin Group (Canada), 90 Eglinton Avenue East, Suite 700, Toronto,
Ontario M4P 2Y3, Canada (a division of Pearson Penguin Canada Inc.)
Penguin Books Ltd., 80 Strand, London WC2R 0RL, England
Penguin Ireland, 25 St. Stephen's Green, Dublin 2,
Ireland (a division of Penguin Books Ltd.)
Penguin Group (Australia), 250 Camberwell Road, Camberwell, Victoria 3124,
Australia (a division of Pearson Australia Group Pty. Ltd.)
Penguin Books India Pvt. Ltd., 11 Community Centre, Panchsheel Park,
New Delhi - 110 017, India
Penguin Group (NZ), 67 Apollo Drive, Rosedale, North Shore 0632,
New Zealand (a division of Pearson New Zealand Ltd.)
Penguin Books (South Africa) (Pty.) Ltd., 24 Sturdee Avenue,
Rosebank, Johannesburg 2196, South Africa

Penguin Books Ltd., Registered Offices:
80 Strand, London WC2R 0RL, England

First published by Obsidian, an imprint of New American Library,
a division of Penguin Group (USA) Inc.

First Printing, August 2010
10 9 8 7 6 5 4 3 2 1

PUBLISHER'S NOTE
This is a work of fiction. Names, characters, places, and incidents either are the
product of the author's imagination or are used fictitiously, and any resemblance
to actual persons, living or dead, business establishments, events, or locales is
entirely coincidental.
    The publisher does not have any control over and does not assume any re-
sponsibility for author or third-party Web sites or their content.

If you purchased this book without a cover you should be aware that this book is
stolen property. It was reported as "unsold and destroyed" to the publisher and
neither the author nor the publisher has received any payment for this "stripped
book."

The scanning, uploading, and distribution of this book via the Internet or via any
other means without the permission of the publisher is illegal and punishable by
law. Please purchase only authorized electronic editions, and do not participate
in or encourage electronic piracy of copyrighted materials. Your support of the
author's rights is appreciated.

Prologue

1988

There had to be a way out of this. Shawn was only eleven years old. His life couldn't be over already. There was so much he hadn't done yet. He hadn't even kissed a girl. Not that he felt any sense of loss over that particular nonexperience, but it was only one of a million things he'd been told he'd get to do "when he got older."

That was back in a more innocent time, when he could peer into the future and see something other than four blank walls and a barred door.

Shawn rolled off his bed and went to the window. Cracking open the blinds, he peered out.

The man in the gray suit was still standing in front of the house. His government-issued sedan was still parked across the street. His jacket still bulged with the outline of his gun. There was no way Shawn could get past him.

And now Shawn's life was about to get even worse. Because his father's truck had just turned the corner and was pulling into the garage. In a couple of seconds Henry Spencer would walk to his front steps, and he would stop to talk to the man in the gray suit. If he had been a kind father, a considerate father, a loving father, he would have simply ignored the fact that a federal agent was standing guard over their house until Shawn had had a chance to explain. But Henry was a cop long before he was a dad, and Shawn knew that the law enforcement officer part of him would always take over in moments of crisis.

Shawn watched in mounting horror as Henry walked up to the man in gray, then looked up at his window. Shawn ducked behind his blinds, but not before he saw a look of panic flash over his father's face.

Shawn stared around the room, praying that a trapdoor or a secret panel or a transporter chamber had materialized since he'd gone to school this morning. But there was no escape route, and he could already hear Henry's heavy steps pounding up the stairs to his bedroom.

Before Shawn could begin to formulate a plan, his door blasted open and Henry was in the room. But this was a Henry he'd never seen before. Shawn expected his father to be angry. Or furious. Or so filled with rage that his skin was turning green and his muscles bursting out of his clothes.

But this was worse than anything Shawn had ever seen. Henry Spencer looked scared.

"Are you all right, son?" he asked, getting down on one knee and hugging Shawn close.

"I'm fine," Shawn said, wishing desperately there was some way to ease his father's fear. "This is really all a big misunderstanding."

"That's not how Calderone is going to see it," Henry said. He gave Shawn one more squeeze, then marched to the closet and pulled out his suitcase.

"I'm just a kid," Shawn said. "Calderone isn't going to do anything to me."

"You're damn right he's not," Henry said. He tossed the suitcase on the bed and started pulling clothes out of Shawn's dresser. "Because he's never going to find you."

"He's not even looking for me," Shawn said.

Henry crammed clothes into the suitcase. "As soon as word gets out, he will be," he said. "And I've seen what Calderone does to informants. I'm never going to let that happen to you."

"Dad, it's really not a big deal," Shawn said.

Henry forced the suitcase shut, then got back down on one knee so he could look Shawn in the eye. "I wish that was true, son," he said. "But you overheard two of Calderone's lieutenants describing a deal that's about to do down. That makes you a threat to the biggest drug kingpin in the Northern Hemisphere."

"I'm not that big a threat," Shawn said.

"You could take down his whole operation," Henry said. "And he'll stop at nothing to make sure you never have the chance. Which is why you have to go with Agent Wenzel."

Henry took the suitcase off the bed and handed it to Shawn. Then he went to the window and waved at the man in the gray suit, who nodded back at him and headed into the house.

"Go where?" Shawn said.

"I can't know," Henry said. "I can never know. Because that way, when Calderone's men come looking for you, I won't be able to tell them. No matter what they do to me."

There was a rap on the door. Henry opened it to reveal the man in the gray suit standing there. "Is he ready?" Agent Wenzel said. "Jet's waiting."

"Jet?" Shawn said.

"To take you to your new home," Henry said, and then his voice cracked. "To your new family. I'm sure they'll love you every bit as much as I do."

Henry turned away to hide his tears. Agent Wenzel came into the room and grabbed Shawn's arm. "Hope you packed for the snow, kid," he said. "Gets mighty cold where you're going."

Agent Wenzel started to drag Shawn out of the room. "Wait!" Shawn shouted. "This is all a mistake!"

Henry couldn't bring himself to look at his son. "If only it were," he said. "If only you hadn't overheard that conversation."

"I didn't overhear anything!" Shawn said. "I made it all up!"

There was a moment of silence in the room. Then Shawn felt Wenzel's grip tighten on his arm. At the same moment, Henry turned back to him, a gleam in his eye.

"Can this actually be true?" he said "If only I could believe it."

"I left campus to get lunch at BurgerTown," Shawn said. "I was late getting back to history class, and I forgot we had a test. So instead of taking an F, I told Mrs. Grisby I had used the bathroom in the public library when I went there to study and I couldn't leave because I overheard two guys making a drug deal and didn't want them to know I'd seen their faces."

For a moment, a look of hope passed over Henry's face. Then it was gone. "That's a good try, Shawn, but I just can't believe it," he said. "Your description of the deal was so precise, you couldn't have made that up." He looked up at Agent Wenzel. "Take him away, Agent Wenzel. Take him before I change my mind."

Wenzel dragged Shawn towards the hall. He grabbed the doorknob and held tight. "I got it all from *Miami Vice*," Shawn said. "Don't you remember? We watched it together last week. That's why I used it on Mrs. Grisby—it was the first thing that came to mind."

Henry thought that through. Then he nodded. "You know, son, I think I can believe that."

"Honestly, I just wanted to get out of failing the test," Shawn said, a wave of relief rolling through him. "I never thought anyone would take it so seriously they'd call the Feds!"

"One thing you have to understand," Henry said. "The bigger and more ridiculous the story, the more likely people are to believe it. Because no one could ever imagine you'd make up something so crazy."

For the first time since he'd seen the government-issue sedan roll up outside their house, Shawn was able to inhale easily. But for some reason, the gray-suited man was still clutching his shoulder.

"So I guess I don't have to go with this guy and meet my new family, right?" Shawn said, trying to extricate himself from the agent's grip.

"Oh, no; you do," Henry said.

"But there is no drug deal," Shawn said. "There never was."

"Which is a good thing, because Curtis here wouldn't do much good if a drug kingpin was really after you," Henry said. "Shawn, I'd like you to meet Agent Wenzel of the Santa Barbara School Police, Truancy Enforcement Squad. He's going to take you to your new home."

"You're going to like it there," Wenzel said. "We call it 'permanent detention.'"

The last thing Shawn saw as Agent Wenzel dragged him out of his room was Henry's face splitting into a broad, wicked grin.

Chapter One

"Are you sure this is absolutely necessary?" Shawn examined himself in the full-length mirror that had appeared in the Psych offices earlier in the day along with the two tuxedos.

"Absolutely," Gus said. "Are you ready yet?"

Gus slipped the rental studs through his French cuffs and flicked them open, locking them in place. He yanked his cummerbund into position, then slid into his dinner jacket. Even though the clock was ticking down and there was no time to waste, he took a moment to wonder why he didn't wear a tuxedo all the time, like Dean Martin or the maitre d' at Cappy's Steak and Stein. He looked that good.

"I was born ready," Shawn said. "Of course, I was also born naked, and that tells me there's no actual reason for dressing up."

"It's the social event of the season," Gus said as he smoothed his hand over his already smooth hair. "We were incredibly lucky to get an invitation. And that invitation specifically called for black tie."

"I don't wear ties," Shawn said, flicking open his un-buttoned collar to emphasize the point. "And even if I did, I don't see what that has to do with the rest of this ridiculous outfit."

"Black tie is a dress code for semiformal events," Gus said.

"I definitely agree that this event is semiformal," Shawn said. "Because it's only Ponyboy. I can't imagine what we'd have to wear if Sodapop was going to be there, too."

Gus hesitated. He'd been putting off telling Shawn the truth for so long he had begun to believe he'd never have to. "Ponyboy. Right. Look, there's something I need to tell you about the C. Thomas Howell Film Festival," Gus said.

"If you're going to say that the man's career is too vast to be shoehorned into one evening, I'm well aware we're coming in partway through," Shawn said. "Last night was his formative work from the eighties, when he grew from sensitive man-child into a solid, if still sensitive teen lead. Tonight, of course, is his timeless nineties' material, which saw him mature into the hard-boiled hero of neo-noir classics like *Jail Bait* and *Teresa's Tattoo*. And tomorrow is truly special, since so much of his work in this millennium was made for DVD and is being shown for the first time on the big screen. Or anywhere."

"Glad to hear you won't have to miss the best part," Gus said.

"Miss?" Shawn said.

"We've got to go," Gus said. "We're going to be late."

Gus scooped his car key off the coffee table and let it drop into the surprisingly roomy pocket of his rental pants, then headed for the street. Normally Shawn would have pushed past him just as he reached for the knob, showing a need equal to any golden retriever's to be first through a door. But when Gus glanced back to see what had happened to his partner, Shawn was still sitting behind his desk.

"I don't think you're taking me to the C. Thomas Howell Film Festival at all," Shawn said.

This was the moment. The absolute last second Gus could tell Shawn the truth before his small deception turned into a big lie.

"We're going now," Gus said.

This time Gus didn't look back to see if Shawn was following him. He stepped out into the cool evening fog and crossed the curb to his waiting Echo. By the time he'd walked around to his door and slid behind the wheel, Shawn was already buckled into the passenger's seat. Gus put the car into gear and pulled away from the curb.

Chapter Two

The Echo cruised down State Street. Gus glanced over at Shawn to see if he was getting suspicious. But the Bijoux Theatre, where C. Thomas Howell was being feted, was in the same direction as their real destination, and Gus figured he had another minute or two before the truth became apparent. And Shawn seemed to be completely oblivious to the deception.

Gus felt a momentary thrill of triumph at successfully fooling his best friend and partner. At least he tried to feel it. This was a huge moment for him, one of the few times he'd ever gotten away with lying to Shawn, whose ability to see through other people's lies was surpassed only by his skill at spinning his own.

But instead of victory, Gus felt ashamed. He'd lied to Shawn to get what he wanted, and now he was afraid that he'd ruined the evening for both of them. And maybe more than the evening. It was possible Gus had done ineradicable harm to their friendship.

"I can't tell you how much I'm looking forward to this film festival," Shawn said. "You're going to think I'm crazy, but it could be the high point of my existence."

"I'm sure it won't be," Gus mumbled. "Just a bunch

of crummy movies you could get from Netflix any day."

"It's not just the movies; it's the sense of community," Shawn said. "To know for once in my life that I'm not all alone in the world. That I'm not a freak."

"You're not a freak, Shawn. And you don't need a C. Thomas Howell Film Festival to—" Gus broke off, suddenly hearing his words echoing in his head. "How long have you known?"

The puzzled look on Shawn's face was so pure and innocent that a Renaissance painter could have used it as the inspiration for one of the cupids hovering around the corners of his painting, if there had happened to be any Renaissance painters hiding in the backseat of the Echo and they were able to get over the shock of being transported in a coach with no visible means of locomotion in time to pay attention to their model.

"Known what?" Shawn said.

"You know what," Gus said. If he'd felt lousy at having tricked Shawn, it was only fair that he should feel better, now that he realized Shawn hadn't been fooled. Instead, he felt even more annoyed at himself.

"That you're not taking me to the C. Thomas Howell Film Festival?" Shawn said. "That in fact you never intended to take me to the C. Thomas Howell Film Festival and instead have duped me in some cruel and manipulative manner?"

"Yes."

"Since you went out to get the tickets a week ago," Shawn said. "And when you came back to the office and I asked to see them, you said you'd dropped them off at your apartment. If you'd wanted to make this halfway believable, you could have at least bought a couple of tickets."

"If we'd had tickets, you would have found a way to use them," Gus said. "I had to make sure you thought we had seats until the thing sold out."

"And in case hell didn't freeze over, what were you planning on doing then?"

"I'm doing it." Gus pressed his foot on the gas, and the car zipped past the Bijoux, where either a small crowd had gathered to salute their favorite actor or the number three bus was going to stop soon.

"At least you could tell me where we're going," Shawn said after a few silent blocks. "You owe me that."

"You mean I could tell you where we're going *again*?" Gus said.

Shawn looked confused. "Why, did we already go there?"

"Go where?" Gus said.

"I don't know," Shawn said. "That's why I'm asking."

It took Gus a moment to run through the conversation and figure out where they had gone off track. "When I said 'again,' I was using it to modify the first half of the sentence, not the second."

"Can you say that in English?" Shawn said.

"That was English," Gus said. "In fact, it was more than English. It was specifically a point of English grammar, so you don't get much more English than that."

"What about Gwyneth Paltrow?" Shawn said. "She got pretty English. Madonna, too, although I think Guy Ritchie took the accent back in the divorce settlement."

Gus slowed for a yellow light and stopped with his front bumper precisely above the limit line. "What I meant was not that we were going someplace we'd already been, but that this was not the first time tonight's destination had come up in conversation, and that in previous discussions I had told you where I wanted to go, asked if you wanted to come along, and been denied."

"Okay, that's how Gwyneth would say it," Shawn said. "Now put it in your own words."

"We're going to meet a client," Gus said. "And after we meet with him, we are going to take his case."

Chapter Three

Shawn stared at Gus in disbelief. "You went through all this just to get me to take a case?"

"Yes," Gus said.

"Why didn't you just say, 'Hey, Shawn, here's a case; let's take it'?" Shawn said. "You know me: I love cases. I never turn a case away. In fact, I'm still waiting for that free case of Doritos they owe me for publicly endorsing their product."

"You're not getting any free Doritos," Gus said. "Not for standing in the chips section of the Food King and shouting 'Boy, I like Doritos.' That's not a public endorsement."

"It's as public as I'm going to get about a cheese-flavored corn snack," Shawn said. "But I'd do much more for a real case."

"Except for this case," Gus said. "You did turn this one away."

Shawn scrunched up his forehead as he tried to summon up the entire contents of his memory into his forebrain. "Sorry," he said finally. "Just doesn't sound like me."

"You said you'd rather spend eternity being waterboarded with lime Jell-O than even meet with our client," Gus said.

"Now that does sound like me," Shawn conceded. Then he remembered. "Oh, no. You're dragging me to see that Crispix guy."

"His name is Kitteredge, as you well know," Gus said. "Langston Kitteredge. And he's not a guy; he's a professor. And the single most brilliant man I've ever met."

"Turn this car around right now," Shawn said, clutching at the door handle.

"I will not," Gus said. "We are going to meet Professor Langston Kitteredge at the Santa Barbara Museum of Art. And while we're there, you will act like a professional."

"Great," Shawn said. "Maybe I should act like a professional waiter, because that's how I'm dressed."

"There's a gala event tonight," Gus said. "Professor K is the guest of honor. It's the only time he could meet with us."

"So now we have to listen to him make a speech?" Shawn said. "Instead of watching C. Thomas Howell as a renegade cop trying to stop a sex-slavery ring from kidnapping innocent teenage runaways, we're going to listen to some droning hack go rabbiting on about brushstrokes?"

Gus tried to keep from getting angry. After all, he had lied to Shawn. But this was the kind of case Gus had dreamed of since he and Shawn had gone into business as psychic detectives. Not just another dead body or looted mansion, but something of historical significance. A chance to make a real difference to the entire world.

At least, he assumed that's what it was. Professor Kitteredge's letter requesting the meeting had been brief and completely without details. But Gus was sure the professor wouldn't bother with anything that came in at less than earth-shaking on the importance meter.

"I don't know why you're making this so difficult,"

Gus said. "It's not like I drag you to museums every day."

"Yes, it is," Shawn said. "It's exactly like that."

Gus gaped at the injustice of Shawn's accusation. "When was the last time you were in any museum with or without me, except when you were on a case?"

"I'd have to say that would be when I was ten and my father decided I needed some culture, so he took me to this traveling Van Gogh exhibit. But in the third gallery he tripped over an art student who was sitting on the floor copying some picture of sunflowers, and the student acted like it was my dad's fault. So he arrested the kid for interfering with a police officer and copyright infringement, at which point we were politely invited to leave the museum."

"So how can you say I drag you to museums every day?"

"I didn't," Shawn explained calmly. "I said it's exactly like that. This one moment alone is exactly like you dragging me to museums every day of our lives, except Monday when they're closed."

Gus pulled the Echo up behind a long line of cars, any of which was worth at least fifteen of his. "If it's that painful for you to come with me to something that has great meaning in my life, then go," he said. "Go see C. Thomas Howell. Hell, make him your new partner."

Gus threw the car door open, nearly knocking over the small man in a red jacket who had been reaching for the handle when Gus burst out. The valet handed Gus a ticket and slid behind the wheel. He was about to drive off when he noticed that Shawn was still sitting in the passenger's seat.

"Don't let him slow you down," Gus said. "In fact, there's an extra five in it for you if you take this car to the Bijoux Theatre with that guy in it."

The valet stared at Gus blankly until the passenger's

door opened and Shawn got out. As soon as he'd closed the door, the Echo disappeared around the corner.

Shawn stepped up to Gus on the sidewalk.

"I meant what I said," Gus said. "You don't have to stay here with me."

"What, you want me to miss the social event of the season?" Shawn said.

"What do you mean?" Gus said, not quite believing that Shawn had found the spirit of the evening.

"For one thing, check out the valet line." Shawn gestured at the row of cars waiting at the curb. "It looks like half the guests brought their own police escort."

Gus glanced back at the street and saw what had been hidden by a large SUV when he'd pulled up: the first seven cars parked in front of the valet sign were flashing blue and red lights.

"And the party's so popular they can't even fit all the guests inside," Shawn said.

Gus looked up at the broad steps that led to the art museum's neoclassical façade. They were crowded with men in tuxedoes and women in gowns and jewels. If someone had pulled the fire alarm in the middle of the Social Register, the result would look like this.

"The reception was supposed to start half an hour ago."

"That makes sense," Shawn said. "Half an hour ago all these people went into the museum. Then Lamont Cranston started talking, and they all fled outside until he was done."

Gus was seized by the sensation that something was seriously wrong here. It must have been related to Kitteredge's call for help. If only Gus had insisted on acting faster, maybe he could have prevented whatever had happened. True, Professor Kitteredge had specifically asked him to meet at this time and place, but Gus could have insisted they talk earlier. It was only a couple hours' drive to Riverside, where Kitteredge taught art history at the university. He could have taken half a day off and gone down there. And then maybe none of this would have happened—whatever it was that had happened.

Gus started to push his way through the crowd. But the people on the steps were Santa Barbara's donor class—the richest and most powerful of the elites. And they weren't used to being moved out of the way. They formed a solid wall as immovable as if they had actually been made of gold.

"Excuse me," Gus said hopelessly. "Please, I have to get inside."

"We all have to get inside, young man," snapped a gray-haired woman cocooned in silk and diamonds. "And if we have to wait, you can, too." The murmur of assent that came from everyone around her assured Gus that none of them would move out of his way as long as there was the tiniest chance the old woman might still rewrite her will to include them.

Gus could feel his heart trying to pound its way out of his chest, as if it was hoping to get to the top of the stairs even if it meant leaving the rest of him behind. He needed to get up there. He needed to find Professor Kitteredge and find out what was wrong. But there was no way he was going to get through this crowd, not before the statute of limitations on whatever crime had taken place up above had run out.

He was about to give up and search for a side entrance when the people around him began to move aside. Before he could figure out what was going on, Gus heard a voice coming from the bottom of the stairs.

"No need to worry—it's not contagious," said the voice, which Gus quickly realized belonged to Shawn. "Not unless you get within thirty feet of the victim, that is. And even then, it's so quick you'll never know what hit you."

Gus turned and saw the crowd parting as if it had been Charlton Heston coming up the steps. It was Shawn, his mouth and nose covered by a surgical mask. "No need to move away from me; I've been around this plague all day, and I don't feel a thing."

"What are you doing?" Gus whispered as Shawn stepped up beside him.

"Clearing a path," Shawn said.

"Where did you get the mask?"

"Amazing what you can find in the average police car," Shawn said. "The shotgun probably would have worked even faster, but they've got those things locked down tight. Let's go."

Shawn headed up the stairs, and as the crowd oozed out of his way Gus followed. It took only seconds to get to the top, where Shawn whipped off his mask. And then froze.

"Oh my God," Shawn said. "No wonder everyone ran out of the museum."

"What is?" Gus said, pushing his way to Shawn's side.

"It must have escaped from the zoo," Shawn said.

"What?"

Shawn pointed across to the museum entrance. "The bear."

Gus looked where Shawn was pointing, and felt a huge surge of relief. Because there did seem to be a bear standing in the doorway. It stood six and a half feet tall and was covered with thick black hair. A large snout protruded from a face almost entirely hidden by fur.

But bears don't generally wear tweed coats or corduroy slacks, and this one was dressed in both. Which meant that it was not some ursine marauder come to wreck the museum and eat its patrons. It was the evening's guest of honor, Professor Langston Kitteredge, looking exactly as he had the last time Gus saw him over a decade earlier.

At least he did at first glance. But before he could walk across the plaza to meet his newest client, Gus realized there was one great difference between Kitteredge now and Kitteredge the way he remembered him.

When Gus had seen Professor Kitteredge in the past, the teacher was always surrounded by students. Students who wanted to ask him a question or transfer into his already full class or just bask in the glow of his brilliance.

But while the professor was once again surrounded by people, these weren't students. They were Carlton Lassiter and Juliet O'Hara, and they were Santa Barbara's finest homicide detectives.

And they were holding his arms like they were taking him into custody.

Chapter Four

Despite his irritation at Shawn's horror of museums, Gus hadn't actually set foot inside one in years, except for a few times when he'd had to go on a case, and then he'd spent his entire visit looking for clues, not admiring the art.

But there had been a time when he was prepared to devote his life to the study of art history. Granted, it could only be considered a "time" in the way a grain of sand can be thought of as a boulder, but for the four or five weeks of his college career during which he intended to major in art history, Gus was completely enthralled by the subject. He was already planning a career hopping the globe, revealing minor artworks hidden under major masterpieces and discovering the true provenance of pieces never before believed to be the work of the old masters, when he took his first midterm and realized that he'd been so busy astonishing the art world in his mind he'd completely forgotten to memorize the names, dates, or painters of the several dozen works of art he was expected to identify in a slide show. Humiliated by his failure, Gus dropped the survey course and moved on to a new major.

But during that period when his interest had been

riveted on art history, the prime riveter was a professor named Langston Kitteredge. Professor K, as he was known to his graduate students, was to his field what Indiana Jones had been to archeology, with the slight difference that Kitteredge was not fictional and therefore looked more like the animal on California's state flag than like a movie star. He had a love for art that spilled over into a passion for adventure, and he made the two seem like one.

It was an adventure that Gus almost became a part of. Gus had stopped by his office to ask a question one afternoon as Kitteredge was explicating the theory behind his next research expedition in hopes of persuading some of his more promising students to come along with him. The professor, an expert in the Pre-Raphaelites and their work, had been studying a painting of Hamlet's drowned girlfriend, Ophelia, by John Everett Millais, with particular emphasis on the setting. The picture, painted in the second half of the nineteenth century, was famous for its realistic depiction of the flora of the river and riverbank, and Kitteredge had hoped to prove that its setting was not, as was commonly believed, the banks of the Hogsmill River in Ewell but some other mysterious location. He was about to explain exactly why he found this so crucially important—and why he was particularly interested in the image of a water vole that had originally swum beside Ophelia's corpse but had later been painted out—when his TA brought in the test scores so that Kitteredge could discover just how little promise Gus actually showed in the field.

Gus had found an excuse to slink out of the office before his shame could be revealed, and ran directly to the registrar's office to drop the class. That was the last time he'd seen Langston Kitteredge.

But it was the rare month that went by without Gus thinking about his old professor. It wasn't that he regretted not spending his life in the study of old paintings. But

he'd rarely met anyone whose passion for life, whose de-
votion to his obsessions, was so total. He couldn't help
but wonder every now and again what he might have
done with himself if he had actually spent a few minutes
studying for that midterm.

When Gus had received the letter, he'd been stunned.
Not so much at the fact that Kitteredge was asking for
help, but at the very idea that the professor had any idea
who he was. With all the students that passed through
his classes every year, with all the yearning souls desperate to join the ranks of slavish acolytes, it was amazing
that he would have any memory of a kid who'd sat in the
fifth row of his lecture course for a half a quarter more
than a decade earlier.

Amazing or not, Professor Kitteredge had reached
out to Gus for help, and now he was in serious trouble.
It was up to Gus to help him.

"Say, exactly what is the case we're here for?" Shawn
said.

"I don't know," Gus said. "The letter only said it was
of vital importance. But now that Lassiter and Jules are
here—"

"That means it's in our wheelhouse," Shawn said.
"Although why you'd put wheels on a house is beyond
me. Unless it's just to annoy people driving behind you
on the freeway. But we should talk about traffic patterns
later. There seems to be some kind of crime here."

Shawn set off across the landing, and Gus found himself scurrying to keep up. "Wait for me!" he hissed.

"I'm going to distract the detectives so you have a
chance to talk to Lowfat Creamer," Shawn said

"Langston Kitteredge," Gus said.

Shawn waved a hand dismissively back at Gus, then
lifted it to greet the detectives.

"Jules!" Shawn called out before he'd crossed half
the distance to the detectives. "Hey, Lassie! What brings
you here?"

Lassiter and O'Hara stepped forward to intercept him before he could reach Kitteredge.

"The same thing that brings me to every crime scene I visit," Lassiter said. "The faint hope that maybe, just once, you won't be there."

"You forget who you're dealing with, Lassie," Shawn said. "After all, you're only a normal detective. You can't get to a crime scene until the crime has been discovered. But as a psychic, I can sense where the crime is going to happen and make sure to be there first. Also, I know when Happy Donuts is going to put out a fresh batch and get them while they're still warm."

Lassiter's eyes narrowed. "So you know about this particular crime, do you?"

"Is that a trick question?" Shawn said.

"Is that a trick answer?" Lassiter said. "No, don't answer that. All of your answers are trick answers." He scanned the crowd. "Isn't there an officer who can escort this man away from here?"

Apparently all the uniformed officers were occupied with keeping Santa Barbara's best and brightest from turning into a mob and storming the museum, because no one stepped up to haul Shawn away. He turned to Detective O'Hara.

"If I'd known you liked art, I would have invited you up to see my etchings a long time ago," Shawn said. "Well, not my etchings, actually, because I haven't etched in ages. But I would have shown you my Etch-A-Sketch."

She gave him a patient half smile. "Not a good time, Shawn. Things are about to get ugly here."

Shawn cast a glance down at the mob on the stairs. "I can hold the fire hose on them if you turn on the water."

"It's not the crowd, Shawn," she said. "This is a bad crime scene and you shouldn't be here. It's not going to be one of those fun murders."

"There was a murder?" Shawn said.

"No, Spencer," Lassiter snapped. "Santa Barbara's two top homicide detectives are here because we had a tip Happy Donuts was about to deliver a fresh batch to the café here."

"Let's see, then," Shawn said.

"I'll make sure to bring you back a cream-filled," Lassiter said. "Better yet, I'll have Officer McNab drop it by your office."

Shawn risked a quick look behind him and saw that Gus was still creeping along toward Kitteredge. He waggled his hand behind his back to urge him to hurry, then leaned in conspiratorially to the detectives. "You could do that," Shawn said. "Or I could just tell you the identity of the killer right now."

As the detectives leaned in to hear what Shawn had to say, Gus slipped behind them and walked up to Kitteredge. "Professor?"

Langston Kitteredge looked at him like he'd just awakened from a deep sleep. "I am Langston Kitteredge," he said.

"I know you are, sir," Gus said. "I'm Gus. Burton Guster."

Kitteredge looked blank. "Burton Guster?"

He must be in shock, Gus thought. He dug into his breast pocket and pulled out the letter Kitteredge had sent him. "You wanted to meet me here tonight," Gus said, pointing to the important parts of the letter. "There was something crucially important you needed to discuss with me. Although from the looks of things I'm a little too late."

"Why do you say that?" Kitteredge said.

"Well, generally you want to call a private detective before things get so bad the police are involved," Gus said. "But my partner, Shawn Spencer, and I will do everything we can to help you now."

A small light of curiosity shone in Kitteredge's eyes. "So you're a son of Vidocq?" he said.

If it hadn't been for those weeks in Kitteredge's class, Gus might have been thrown by a reference to someone he'd never heard of. But if he'd learned anything in the course, it was that there were huge amounts of things he'd never heard of—and that Kitteredge not only had heard of most of them but could always find ways to work them into conversation. He'd watched other students flounder helplessly as they dug for definitions of random phrases while the lecture went on above their heads. So he chose to handle this one the way he had the others—by ignoring it and moving on to the main point. "What exactly is going on here?"

"Something terrible," Kitteredge said sadly. "I fear the worst."

"And the worst would be . . . ?"

"That."

Kitteredge leveled a heavy finger at the museum entrance, where a uniformed officer was accompanying a tall, skinny man in a tuxedo out of the lobby. The man shook so hard he could barely stand up; he dabbed at the corners of his mouth with a handkerchief in a way that suggested most of his energy was going into not throwing up.

The officer marched over to Lassiter. "We've secured the scene," he said. "There's no one inside."

"Thank you, Officer," Lassiter said. "In that case, let us proceed to see the body."

Chapter Five

At the word "body," the thin man shuddered violently and for a moment looked like he was going to crumple to the ground. But Kitteredge reached out and put a comforting hand on his shoulder, and he managed to steady himself.

"Do I need to go back in there?" the thin man said. "I mean, if it will help, I'm ready to. But I don't know what else I can do. I told the officer everything I knew about poor Filkins."

"Filkins?" Lassiter said.

The thin man looked shocked, as if he assumed everyone knew the name. "Clay Filkins," he said. "He's one of our curators—this was his exhibit. That's how I found him. We were supposed to go over some last-minute details about tonight's event, and when he didn't show up I went looking for him in the gallery, assuming he was making some last-minute changes. And he was . . ."

The thin man looked like he was about to start crying.

"That's all right, Mr. Ralston," Detective O'Hara said soothingly. "We've got your statement, and we know how to contact you. There's no need to come back into the gallery."

"Except to aid in the apprehension of a murderer," Lassiter said. "Some people might consider that a priority."

O'Hara gave him a reproachful look. "I'm sure he does," she said. "But there are other ways in which Mr. Ralston can help. Someone needs to talk to these people." Her hand fluttered to indicate the socialites who thronged the steps below them.

"We've got officers taking their statements," Lassiter said. "Not that I expect it will do much good. From what I've heard so far, the only thing any of them noticed is what other people were wearing, and since all the men are wearing the same suit, that's a whole lot of useless. And it's not like any of them have been inside the gallery."

"Well, yes, of course that's right," the thin man said, then trailed off.

"I think Mr. Ralston means someone needs to calm these people down," O'Hara said. "And it would probably be best if it came from the museum's executive director."

The thin man gave her a grateful smile. "Yes, that's exactly what I was thinking."

"You know what would be even better?" Shawn said. "If I said something to them."

"No," Lassiter said.

"Well, not so much me," Shawn said. "It's the spirits who want to have a word. I'd just be the vessel."

"If you do, I'll have you and the spirits arrested," Lassiter said.

"That puts me in a terrible position," Shawn said. "Because I don't want to go to jail, but the spirits don't care at all. So they're going to speak through me, whatever happens to my earthly body."

"Not if it gets Tased into unconsciousness," Lassiter said.

Juliet O'Hara stepped between them. "Or if it comes with us to see the victim."

Lassiter stared as if he'd been the one who'd been Tased and she was still pulling the trigger. "You want to invite him to a crime scene?"

"If this turns out to be as weird as we've been told, odds are the chief is going to ask him to help anyway," O'Hara said. "This way he's here at the beginning."

Lassiter scowled. Shawn beamed back at him cheerfully.

"Fine," Lassiter said in a tone that suggested he was anything but. "Maybe he'll drop some DNA and we can arrest him for the murder."

Lassiter spun and marched toward the museum entrance. Juliet O'Hara gave Shawn a warning look, then followed. Shawn ambled over to where Gus was standing with Professor Kitteredge. "Shall we?"

"One moment," Kitteredge said. He went over to Ralston and threw his arms around him in a warm embrace. The thin man struggled for a moment, then succumbed like a drowning man to the ocean, finally putting his arms as far around Kitteredge as they would go, which was about the same degree of longitude as the professor's coat pockets.

Just as Ralston's face was turning red from oxygen starvation, Kitteredge released him and rejoined Shawn and Gus. Ralston took a couple of deep breaths, then stepped up to the front of the stairs and began speaking to the crowd in a soothing tone. "Ladies and gentlemen, please allow me to apologize for this terrible inconvenience."

Shawn held the door open and ushered Gus and Kitteredge into the museum lobby. Their steps echoed loudly on the marble floor as they walked into the empty room. "They didn't wait for us," Shawn said. "I hate when they do that. How are we supposed to know which way to go?"

Kitteredge pointed at a large banner hanging from the ceiling. Orange type stood out from a gray background, proclaiming the arrival of Rossetti's lost masterpiece. "To *The Defence of Guenevere*," he said.

"I have no idea what that is," Shawn said. "But if I have to miss the trailer for *Fatal Affair* to be here, you can wait a couple of minutes to help your girlfriend."

"It's a painting, Shawn," Gus said. "It's the reason for the event tonight."

Kitteredge beamed at Gus like a trainer encouraging the seal who'd just jumped through the flaming hoop for the first time. "Not just a painting," the professor said. "But one of the great mysteries of the art world. After Rossetti painted it in 1864, he—"

"That's a great story, Doc," Shawn said. "But maybe we should talk about something more important before we walk in on the cops. If you whacked that guy, this is your one chance to own up and let us protect you."

"That's ridiculous," Gus said. "Professor Kitteredge didn't kill anyone."

"It would explain a lot," Shawn said. "Like why he was so desperate for you to meet him here tonight. How else would he know what was going to happen?"

"He's our client, not a suspect," Gus said.

"You said that like those are two mutually contradictory things," Shawn said.

"Professor Kitteredge came to us for help, and you're doing nothing but insulting him," Gus said.

"Technically he came to you for help," Shawn said. "And he doesn't look offended to me."

Gus checked. Kitteredge didn't. He was studying Shawn with the expression of an entomologist who has just discovered an entirely new species of slug.

"You must be the other son of Vidocq," he said.

"I'm Shawn Spencer," Shawn conceded. "But if you're suggesting that my father was a space probe that was granted consciousness by an alien entity and now roams the universe eating planets, well, you're only part right."

"That's V'ger," Gus said.

The professor didn't seem to notice Shawn's misunderstanding. "Of course you know I'm referring to Eugène François Vidocq, the former French soldier, criminal, and privateer who in 1833 founded *Le Bureau de Reseignements Universels pour le commerce et l'industrie*, the world's first private detective agency," he said. "He's mostly remembered for introducing record keeping and ballistics into the science of crime solving, along with being the first to make plaster casts of shoe impressions. But what I find singular about the man was his sense of compassion. Although there is no proof that this is true, he famously boasted that he never turned in to the police anyone who claimed to have stolen out of need."

"Of course we know that," Shawn said. "I've even got it on a T-shirt. Well, not the whole thing, because that wouldn't fit. In fact, I think it actually says 'Frankie Says Relax,' but those who are in the know understand. Anyway, why'd you kill this guy?"

"I can assure you I have killed no one," Kitteredge said. Then his face darkened. "But I do fear that someone has died because of me. Because of what I've found out. I've been concerned this would happen for a very long time, but I always assumed I would be the target."

"That's why you sent me the letter," Gus said. He fished the document out of his breast pocket and shook it open. "That's what you meant when you said 'These are dark and difficult times. Events are conspiring to bring an end to those things which we hold most dear.'"

"Umm, no, not exactly," Kitteredge said. "But now that I see what's happened, I might wish it was the case."

"Then what was the urgent crisis, Doc?" Spencer said.

"It might help us to know before we start in on your case. That is, if we're going to take your case."

"Which we are," Gus said.

"Which we might be," Shawn said.

"Which some of us definitely are and others of us will be, once we get over sulking about the C. Thomas Howell Film Festival," Gus said.

Kitteredge looked from Shawn to Gus and back again like a spectator at a Ping-Pong match. He was about to say something when a glass door opened at the end of the lobby and Juliet O'Hara stuck her head through. "The crime scene's this way," she said.

Chapter Six

"**N**ow this is a crime scene." Shawn surveyed the gallery approvingly. Three walls were covered with a series of cardboard placards describing the exhibit in several languages. The fourth was hidden behind a heavy red velvet drape.

"Yes, Shawn, that's what we call the place we find a dead body," Lassiter said. "You can generally identify it by the yellow tape surrounding the area with the words 'crime scene' printed on them. At least you will once you're able to read at a second-grade level."

"Thanks, Lassie," Shawn said. "But what I meant is that this is the kind of place you want to find a body. None of those damp alleys or dismal dive bars. This has class. You'd be proud to be found dead in a place like this."

"That's a very interesting point, Mr. Spencer," Kitteredge said. "I never made the connection, but an art museum does provide the ideal circumstance for such a discovery. For one thing, the lighting and visual presentation are designed to give the maximum dramatic mood, thus heightening the already raised emotions in the situation. And on a more prosaic level, of course, the temperature will be strictly kept between eighteen and twenty degrees Celsius, while the humidity will stay at no more than four percent, which makes the forensics so much easier to read. And then of course there is the ritualistic aspect common to the investigation of a murder and the appreciation of a work of art, both of which are presented as quasi-religious ceremonies."

Listening to Professor Kitteredge, Gus was transported back to his school days. Everything he said was so fascinating that Gus would have been content simply to listen to him for days.

"Plus you've got a nifty red curtain to pull away and reveal the body," Shawn said. "Which maybe somebody should do."

"Thank you, Shawn," Lassiter said. "If it hadn't been for you, I might have completely forgotten to do my job." He walked over to the wall and pulled the curtain back a few inches, revealing a dangling push-button control like the ones for garage openers.

Gus noticed that Kitteredge was staring intently at the curtain. "You might want to look away," Gus said. "This kind of thing can be pretty shocking if you're not used to it."

"I couldn't look away if a thousand bodies lay on that floor," Kitteredge said. "I've waited so long for this moment."

"Umm, which moment would that be?" Gus said.

"Do you have any idea what's behind that curtain?" Kitteredge said. "You should, so you understand what you're looking at. *The Defence of Guinevere* isn't just a painting, Gus. It's not even just a masterpiece. It's a work of art that has gone unseen for a century and a half. But it's even more than that."

"Is it a floor wax, too?" Shawn said.

"This was the last picture Dante Gabriel Rossetti painted before his untimely death at age fifty-four on April 9, 1882," Kitteredge said, ignoring the interruption as only a man who'd spent decades teaching Intro to Art History to basketball players hoping for an easy grade could do. "For many years, it existed only as a rumor. It was never publicly exhibited anywhere, and the only references to it were brief mentions in other artists' journals. Somehow it fell into the hands of a private collector—"

"That means someone who buys a painting and then owns it," Shawn muttered to Gus. "I can't believe he missed the opportunity to explain that concept for us."

"Sssh!" Gus hissed.

"—and there it stayed for the next one hundred and fifty years," Kitteredge continued. "The owner, whose will continues to demand his complete anonymity, refused to allow anyone to see this picture, or even to acknowledge that it existed. And believe me, many scholars over the years tried to get a glimpse of the piece—no one harder than me, by the way. But the painting was handed down through the generations, and apparently each new heir was more fanatical about keeping it hidden than the last."

As Kitteredge spoke he moved out into the center of the room as if he were taking over a lecture hall.

Shawn took the opportunity to whisper to Gus. "Why does he keep doing that?"

"Doing what?" Gus said.

"Throwing in little pieces of information that have nothing to do with what he's saying, but just clutter up his speech and make it impossible to follow his point."

"He's brilliant," Gus said. "That's how geniuses talk."

"That's how the homeless guy who sits outside the Macy's on State Street talks," Shawn said. "If I'd known he was a genius, I might have dropped another quarter into his can."

Gus redirected his attention to Kitteredge, who was preparing to launch himself back onto that sea of knowledge.

"The painting's subject, as I'm sure you know, is a scene from a poem by Rossetti's friend and fellow member of the Pre-Raphaelite Brotherhood, William Morris," Kitteredge said. "It takes the form of a speech by the queen to the assembled knights of Camelot in which she explains and justifies her adulterous relationship with Lancelot while she—"

During this speech Lassiter had been walking the perimeter of the room, minutely examining the scene. Now he was back in front of the curtain. "You may be here for a painting, Professor, but we are here to investigate a murder."

Gus could have spent hours more listening to the professor talk. But that would have to wait. "I'm sure the picture is great, but you really need to prepare yourself."

"I've been preparing for this all my professional life," Kitteredge said. "It's a tragedy that there's a death involved, but that can't diminish the importance of this moment. Look—the curtain is starting to move."

It was. Lassiter had pushed the button on the control, and the drape was sliding back slowly. Maybe he'd let himself get caught up in Kitteredge's excitement, but Gus found himself leaning forward to catch his first glimpse of the painting.

"If we leave now, we can beat the line at the valet," Shawn said, leaning in to him.

Then the curtain was pulled back farther, and Gus stopped caring about the picture behind it.

Gus' first thought was that the velvet curtain had slipped off its rings and puddled on the floor. It was the only thing his conscious mind could accept as a cause of the large pool of crimson that had spread across the white marble floor.

But there was something else on the floor as well.

It was the body of a man.

And there was a sword through its heart.

Gus noticed that Kitteredge seemed to barely notice the body. He was staring at the painting as if trying to suck it into his brain through his eyes.

Lassiter kneeled down by the body, studying it closely. "Do you know this man?"

Kitteredge pulled his eyes away from the picture and looked down at the corpse. Then he reached into his jacket pocket, pulled out a worn meerschaum pipe, and put it thoughtfully in his mouth. Gus recognized the movement from his brief time in class. The professor had done exactly the same thing every time he was about to make a substantial point.

"I know who he is," he said. "As you've been told, that's Clay Filkins, the curator. But look at that sword. It's a thirteenth-century estoc—although, since it's of British manufacture, we should call it by its English name, tuck. You see, it has no cutting edge, just an extremely sharp point designed to penetrate the cracks in an opponent's armor. And judging by the inscription along the blade, it was made for Geoffrey, Earl of Norwich who lived from 1253 to 1289."

"That's very helpful, Professor," Lassiter said. "I'll send a couple of my best men to stake out the thirteenth century to see if we can catch this Geoffrey."

Kitteredge didn't seem to notice the joke. "It comes from this museum's arms and armory collection. As do many other, more appropriate weapons. There's a dirk, for instance, that was made for an assassin in the late 1500s and—"

"I don't have time for this nonsense," Lassiter said.

"There's always time for nonsense," Shawn said. "Or is that breakfast? Anyway, if you want to talk to this guy, you're going to have to make time, because there's some fascinating historical fact associated with every syllable. Apparently it's some kind of genius thing."

"You don't understand what I'm saying," Kitteredge said, an edge of urgency taking over his voice. "You have to ask why the killer chose this particular sword. It was valuable when combating an opponent in chain mail, because the blade's square cross section allowed it to be long, stiff, and extremely sharp at the tip, which is what was required for penetrating the mail. But for attacking an unarmed curator, the falx or the marmeluke, both of which are also in the collection, would have been much more practical."

Lassiter let out a heavy sigh. "You're not real, are you?" he said. "Spencer set you up for this."

"A lifetime of study and research set me up for this, Detective," Kitteredge said, drawing himself up to his full height.

"That's wonderful," Lassiter said. "Maybe I need to talk to some ignorant people for a while. Spencer?"

"Should I tell you who did it, or wait until we've got all the suspects together?" Shawn said.

"Are you actually going to pretend you know who committed this terrible crime?" Lassiter said.

"Not yet," Shawn said. "But I never know when the spirits are going to speak to me. Or what they're going to say. Right now they're so busy telling me how good I look in a tuxedo, they don't seem to have time for anything else."

"Just get out of here, Spencer, and let the grown-ups do our jobs," Lassiter said. "I promise you we'll bring you back when it's playtime."

Shawn turned hopefully to O'Hara. "It's always playtime for me," he said. "Want to come?"

"Not now, Shawn," she said. "You and Gus run along."

"You don't know what you're missing," Shawn said. "Gus?"

But Gus was still staring down at the body on the floor. And then he followed the professor's eyes back to the painting. A long-haired woman stood in the center of the picture, her arms outstretched. Behind her were a couple of knights in armor. She faced what must have been a throne, although it was seen only from behind. And leaning against that throne was a sword.

A long, wide sword.

Just like the one sticking out of Filkins' body.

Chapter Seven

In his long career on the force, Carlton Lassiter had sat across interrogation room tables from hundreds of junkies, winos, and meth-heads, and he knew all the tells. The constant fidgeting, the eyeballs shooting to the exit door, the beads of sweat appearing at the hairline: all these were signs that the interview subject cared only about getting out of the room to get his next fix as fast as possible.

But Lassiter knew Langston Kitteredge wasn't a junkie, and he wasn't jonesing for a dime bag or a dollar bottle. What he wanted—what he kept claiming he needed—was to see that painting again.

Lassiter had explained over and over again that the crime scene techs were scouring the gallery for forensic evidence, and that as soon as they were through he would personally drive the professor back to the museum and they could look at the picture together. Every time he said this, Kitteredge settled down and started back in on his story. But before more than a couple of minutes had passed, he'd start fidgeting again.

At first Lassiter had been pleased at the professor's eagerness to cooperate. Once everyone in the gallery had realized that there seemed to be some kind of connection between the painting hanging on the museum's wall and the body lying on its floor, the detective knew he needed a little background information on the picture.

Since the museum's executive director seemed to be slipping into a state of shock, Lassiter sent him off with the paramedics, who had arrived to make sure none of the museum patrons were similarly suffering, and turned to the only other person in the place who claimed to have a clue about the painting.

Kitteredge seemed happy to be asked. At least, he did until Lassiter made it clear that the conversation would have to take place at the police station. The professor would wait for him there while he finished up with the crime scene.

It was another hour before Lassiter was able to turn the museum gallery over to the techs and race back to the station to talk to Kitteredge. In that time he'd learned a few details about the crime that made it look even more puzzling than he had originally imagined. For one thing, the sword sticking out of the victim's chest was not the murder weapon. His throat had been slit with a much smaller blade, and only when he was dead had the killer used the sword. That explained why there had been so much blood on the floor, but it raised several questions of its own. Like why use a knife when you have a sword?

Even questions that should have had easy answers turned out not to. The sword was, as Kitteredge had said, part of the museum's collection, but while the museum staff were busily reviewing their records, no one could seem to figure out exactly where the weapon had been before tonight, or who might have moved it, or when. And while a major art museum is usually as well surveilled as any public institution short of an international airport, all the security cameras in this gallery had been turned toward the walls. When Lassiter asked when and why this had been done, he learned it had been earlier in the day, on the specific instructions of the victim.

The crime scene techs were scouring the gallery, but there was almost no chance they would turn up any usable forensics. Between the removal of the last exhibit and the installation of the new one, dozens of workers had tramped through the room, all dripping DNA wherever they went. The only hope was to find something on the sword, but that seemed to be as clean as on the day it was forged.

That made this interview with Kitteredge even more crucial than Lassiter had originally thought. Lassiter had asked the professor to take a little time to think through the most important information about the painting and consider any way in which it might inspire a killer. When he got back to the station, Lassiter asked the professor if he'd had any thoughts on the subject.

That was five hours earlier.

He hadn't asked another question since. He hadn't had a chance.

Kitteredge started off with the story of the painting's acquisition by the museum. Before he began, he said it wouldn't take much time, as he'd written out a brief version to deliver to the patrons at tonight's event. And it might not have, if he'd been able to stick to a single point. But early in the proceedings he'd realized he had to clarify one tiny bit of information about the nature of the art market in nineteenth-century England before he could adequately explain how odd it was that this particular picture came to be held by a private owner without ever having been publicly exhibited. And as soon as he started down that path, he discovered that Lassiter did not have a complete understanding of the place of the Royal Academy of the Arts in relation to the marketplace, and that in turn led him to a parenthetical disquisition on the question of George III's historical role as patron of the arts. And the only interruptions in the lecture came when Kitteredge suggested again that it would really help if they could continue their conversation while looking at the picture.

Not that Lassiter was sitting quietly during this entire peroration. One of the skills necessary to detective was the ability to steer any conversation toward his desired goals, and Lassiter had always prided himself on his technique in this area.

But steering Kitteredge had roughly the same effect as nudging a supertanker with a stick. He barely seemed to notice the interruption, except occasionally to say he'd get to that point in just a moment.

After a long tour through the politics of the art world in eighteenth-century England, Kitteredge finally returned to the general period of the painting's conception. Since he still had another hundred and fifty years to go before the painting would make its appearance on the wall of the Santa Barbara Art Museum, Lassiter excused himself to use the bathroom, grab another cup of coffee, and bang his head against the wall until the pain on the outside began to even out the throbbing that came from within.

He'd stayed out of the interrogation room for as long as he could possibly justify, and then kept away a little longer. He checked through phone messages on his desk, and when he couldn't find any that needed answering in the middle of the night, he checked several other detectives' desks.

Now he was out of excuses. He'd given the obvious one away to his partner when he told her to look into the victim's life, see if she could come up with any plausible motives for murder, and check his movements for the past couple of days. There were financial records to dig through; relatives, friends, and possibly lovers to contact; enemies to sniff out and track down. They'd have to interview all of the curator's colleagues at the museum, and at other museums in case there was interinstitution rivalry. It seemed ludicrous to think that someone who had spent his entire life looking at pretty pictures could have the gumption to commit a murder like this, but if the new acquisition was as significant as Kitteredge believed, was it impossible to consider that a competitor might have thought that Filkins had crossed some ethical line in snagging it and felt a need for revenge?

Of course, this was work that could easily occupy two detectives full time, and he was burning to jump onto the more useful parts of the investigation. But he needed to finish up with Kitteredge first, even if that meant spending the rest of his natural life span stuck in the interrogation room.

Lassiter took a deep breath and was attempting to brace himself for the onslaught of useless knowledge when the door to the observation room swung open and Detective O'Hara put her head out. He could see Shawn and Gus sitting behind her, smirking at his failure.

"Are you almost done, Carlton?" she said. "There's a lot of work to do on this case, and we don't have all night for chitchat with the prof."

"If you think you can do it faster, be my guest," Lassiter said.

"Not after you've spent all this time building rapport with the man," O'Hara said. "Now get moving. There's a murderer out there, and we've got to stop him before he kills again."

Chapter Eight

For the past five hours there had been nothing for Shawn and Gus to do besides listen to Kitteredge expatiate on a series of subjects, each of which managed to be less interesting to Shawn than the one before. At least, Gus kept telling Shawn there was nothing else for them to do.

For his part, Shawn could think of plenty of other things. They could go home and go to bed, for instance. Or they could swing by the Bijoux and see if C. Thomas Howell's appearance fee at the festival included sweeping up after the show. Or, as Shawn suggested after a particularly riveting aside detailing the chemical composition of oil paint and how it had remained remarkably unchanged over several centuries—unless it had changed equally remarkably over that same period, Shawn thought he'd dozed off somewhere in the middle of this passage—they could throw themselves off Santa Barbara Pier and see if they washed up in Japan before Kitteredge finished talking.

When Lassiter stepped out to take his break, Shawn was ready to drag Gus out of the observation room even if it meant clubbing him over the head with a chair first. But his mood changed when he saw the detective heading back into interrogation. Lassie looked so defeated, so close to cracking, that Shawn knew whatever happened next was going to be good.

Shawn pulled his chair up to the glass next to Gus' and lowered the volume on the speakers as O'Hara stepped out to start making calls to museums on the East Coast, which would be opening for business about now.

"Don't tell me you're finally going to admit this is interesting," Gus said.

"Don't worry. I won't," Shawn said. "But maybe it will be in a minute. I think Lassiter got his gun during the break."

A look of concern flashed over Gus' face, but he quickly dismissed the thought. "You just watch," he said. "Professor K is going to tie this entire case up in the next couple of minutes."

"Professor K couldn't tie his shoelaces without explaining the entire history of footwear," Shawn said. "He hasn't even begun to talk about the last century, let alone the current one."

"That's his genius," Gus said. "He talk and he talks, throwing out more fascinating facts than you think any one man could ever hope to know. And then, just when you think you're going to float forever on an aimless sea of knowledge, he comes up with the one tiny piece of information that pulls it all together. It's kind of like what you do in your summations."

"Except that my summations are never longer, duller, and more pretentious than *The Matrix Revolutions*," Shawn said. "In fact, until tonight I didn't think anything could be."

"Pretentious?" Gus was astonished. "Professor K doesn't have to pretend anything. He's the real deal. Everything he says is valid and important."

Shawn didn't say anything. He reached over and flicked the volume back up again. Professor Kitteredge's voice filled the small room. "You have to understand that according to the "Fifteen Discourses" that Reynolds delivered to students at the Royal Academy, the only way for a young artist to learn to create works of high moral and artistic worth was to copy the old masters and to sketch from—"

Shawn flipped the volume down again. "Valid and important," he said.

But Gus was leaning forward in his chair, eyes lit up with excitement. "This is it," he said. "Watch."

"Watch what?" Shawn said. "Is Lassiter finally going to use his nightstick?"

"Kitteredge is about to make his point," Gus said. "The one that's going to tie this whole thing together. And probably even unmask the killer."

Shawn stared through the glass. All he saw was Kitteredge talking while Lassiter held his head in pain. "How do you know that?"

"Didn't you catch his tell?" Gus said.

Shawn looked again and this time noticed that Kitteredge's hand was fishing around in his left coat pocket. After a moment, he pulled out his old meerschaum and knocked it gently on the table.

"You mean the pipe?" Shawn said.

"Every time he makes a significant point, he takes that pipe out of his pocket," Gus said. "In class, all the students knew they'd better write down whatever he was saying when it came out. Once he moves on to details, the pipe goes back into his pocket. I'm surprised you didn't catch that."

Gus turned the volume back up to hear Kitteredge's voice reaching a crescendo. "In fact, one of the core beliefs of the founding Pre-Raphaelite brothers was that everything Reynolds taught at the Royal Academy was corrupt. They believed that art had to draw its inspiration not from other artists but from truth, from nature, and from the beauty of the world."

Shawn stifled a yawn. "I did see him playing with the thing," he said. "It just never occurred to me that any one of his endless sentences was supposed to be more important than any other. Of course now that I understand that the plebiscite brothers hated Reynolds Wrap, or whatever he just said, it all becomes clear."

"So much for the brilliant powers of observation," Gus said.

"Observation has nothing to do with it," Shawn said. "It's a matter of authorial discrimination. Simply spewing out every stray bit of information lying around is not a sign of wisdom."

"There is nothing stray about what Professor K is saying," Gus said. "Something important is about to happen here and now."

"Wait. You mean something even more exciting than what we just heard?" Shawn said. "I have a hard time imagining what that could be."

Gus felt a momentary flash of pity for his partner. Shawn was so talented in so many areas, so brilliant about so many subjects, but he was also so completely blind to anything that didn't fit into his narrow set of interests. He could, as he had attempted to prove earlier in the evening, spend hours discussing every aspect of the cinematic career of a former child star whose major claim to fame was that he'd managed to become a has-been without ever actually having been anything. But there was so much that simply never grabbed him, and he refused to put any effort into anything that wasn't immediately appealing.

And yet there was so much in life that offered rich, full rewards only after you'd put in a little work. Russian novels were like that, or so he'd heard. Expensive wine and smelly cheese—not that Gus had much of a taste for either type of delicacy. Foreign movies, if the critics were to be believed. And most of all, the study of art history.

But this didn't seem to be the time for Gus to give Shawn a lecture on the sophisticated pleasures of life. For one thing, Shawn had already sat through the longest lecture either of them had ever heard, and the experience didn't seem to be inspiring him to study further.

For another, this lecture was about to reach its climax. Gus moved his chair closer to the glass. "This is it," he said.

"Yes, I can see Lassiter is about to fall over dead from boredom," Shawn said. "I only hope I can hold out one second longer than him."

Again, Gus had to repress the desire to educate Shawn. "The pipe comes out whenever Kitteredge has a substantial point to make," Gus said.

"It's amazing how much more interesting that is the second time you tell me about it," Shawn said. "Oh, wait; it isn't."

"That can happen easily a dozen times in a normal lecture," Gus said. "But he's got another tell, too. When he's about to make his ultimate point, when he's about to utter the words that will tie everything he's said together and astonish you with his brilliance, only then does he bring out his lighter and light up."

"Which is good, because then Lassiter will have an excuse to throw him in jail forever," Shawn said. "The no-smoking statutes here are tough."

"If you'll apply your justly praised powers of observation, you'll notice that Professor K's hand is moving toward his right jacket pocket," Gus said. "That means the lighter is about to come out. And that means—"

"That he's almost ready to stop talking?" Shawn said.

"That he's ready to make his point," Gus said. "I think we should listen in, don't you?"

"Why don't you listen in?" Shawn said. "You can take notes, and then in the morning you can write it all up in a big report. And then I can use that as a pillow in case we're ever stuck in an observation room all night again."

Shawn dropped his chin to his chest and pretended to be falling asleep. Gus turned the volume back up.

". . . wasn't afraid of the public's opinion," Kitteredge was saying. "He refused to exhibit at a new gallery opened by his friends simply because members of the Royal Academy had pictures there. To him, the only thing that mattered was the truth of the painting itself."

Shawn mumbled as if in sleep. "Oh, yeah, definitely worth waiting for."

Gus ignored him and focused all his attention on his old professor. "If Rossetti refused to allow this painting to be shown in public, there had to be a reason," Kitteredge said. "And it clearly wasn't an aesthetic issue. We've all had a chance to look at the work now, and we've seen that it might be his masterpiece. So the only reason it's been hidden away from sight for one hundred and fifty years is because it contains a truth so powerful, so dangerous, he couldn't afford to let anyone see it outside a select few."

Even if Kitteredge's right hand hadn't been plunging into his coat pocket, Gus would have known this was the moment they'd all been waiting for. He jabbed Shawn in the side with his elbow. "This is it," he said. "This is the moment where it all comes together."

Shawn roused himself sleepily. "As long as it doesn't involve talking, I'm in," he said.

"Just listen for one more minute and I promise you we'll learn something important about this murder," Gus said.

"I can't listen for one more minute," Shawn said. "Because that would require that I'd listened to any of the rest of it."

"Then listen for the first time," Gus said. "Because something big is about to happen."

Reluctantly, Shawn turned his attention to the professor. If there was about to be a breakthrough in the case, the momentousness of the moment was escaping Lassiter, too, who was using his index fingers to prop his eyelids open.

"I have been working up to this slowly and cautiously, Detective, so that when I reached the incredible truth you would have no choice but to believe. Because that truth is the key to a conspiracy that reaches across the seas, across the centuries, and that is without a doubt behind the murder of poor Clay Filkins." Having delivered this final, determinate statement, Kitteredge proudly pulled his hand out of his jacket pocket.

But when he held his lighter to his meerschaum, his thumb couldn't find the trigger. It slid down the sticky, wet handle. Kitteredge thumbed it again, then realized something was wrong.

If Lassiter hadn't been using his eyes to count the holes in the acoustical ceiling tiles, he might have been faster to notice what Kitteredge was holding.

Gus did see, but it took him a moment to understand what he was looking at. He expected to see that flame-jet pipe lighter sparking as if it had been newly forged, the same way it had so many times in class. Instead, the professor was holding what looked like a metal tube that had been sloppily dripped in wet paint.

Then Kitteredge's thumb found a button, and a long, thin blade shot out of the handle with a *snik* sound so loud that even Shawn had to look up.

Look up and see that Professor Kitteredge wasn't holding his lighter. Instead, he was holding a switch-blade knife covered in blood.

"What's that?" Gus said, even though he recognized

the thing in the professor's hand. His mind simply refused to accept what his eyes were seeing.

"I've got to give it to you," Shawn said. "I didn't think he could make it happen, but when he got to the end, he really did tie up the entire murder."

Chapter Nine

"**S**hoot him!"

Carlton Lassiter tensed his muscles and waited for the lead to slam into his flesh. If he was going to die, let it be at the hands of his fellow officers.

Because he was going to die. There was no way around it. This was the kind of situation no one walked away from. Professor Langston Kitteredge had him pinned against his body with one of his massive arms; the other was pressing the bloody switchblade against his neck. Facing them was a line of guns, each in the hands of a member of the Santa Barbara Police Department. Either Lassiter was going to be brought down in a storm of police bullets or the knife at his throat was going to slit him open.

"Hold your fire!"

Lassiter tried to turn his head to see who was speaking, but the blade dug into his flesh, stopping him. It didn't matter—he'd know that voice anywhere. It belonged to his partner.

"Don't listen to her!" Lassiter shouted at the assembled police. "Take him down!"

"Hold your fire!" O'Hara commanded again. "We are going to end this with no bloodshed."

Not a chance, Lassiter thought. There was going to be blood, and lots of it. His and his captor's.

Lassiter didn't mind dying. Well, that wasn't exactly true. In fact, he had lots of things to live for. First up, he had tickets to see the newly re-re-reformed Journey in a week, and he was hugely curious to see if new lead singer, Angel Pineda, could fill the shoes of Jeff Scott Soto, who had failed to fill the shoes of Steve Augeri, who had in turn failed to fill the enormous vocal shoes of Steve Perry.

But though he yearned for life, Lassiter knew that death was preferable to the alternative—that a murderer go free because of him.

This was entirely his fault. There was no other way to look at it. He'd had Langston Kitteredge in his custody. He should have cuffed him to the table and forced the truth out of him. But he'd been lazy. Weak. Foolish. He'd ignored the first law of the homicide detective— to treat everyone as a suspect until proven innocent. Instead, he'd assumed that Kitteredge was a friendly witness, and failed to notice the warning signs until it was too late.

How could he have been so blind? The way Kitteredge had droned on and on, avoiding the slightest trace of useful information while drowning him in a sea of historical trivia—in retrospect, it was so obvious that this was the professor's way of lulling him into complacency, or even into a coma. But Lassiter had treated it as if it were nothing more than an irritating tic. Now he was paying the price.

He'd had his chance to act. There was that one second when Kitteredge pulled the bloody knife out of his pocket and flicked open the blade. Lassiter hadn't been wearing his gun in the interview room, of course—that would have been an unforgivable breach of protocol. But he was trained in hand-to-hand combat, and he had no doubt that if he'd acted swiftly enough he could have disarmed the professor. Especially since Kitteredge had spent the first couple of seconds staring down at the blade in feigned surprise, as if he'd originally hoped to convince the police that he had no idea how it had ended up in his pocket.

But before Lassiter could leap into action, the professor did. He grabbed the detective and jammed the knife's blade against his throat.

"You did this to me!" Kitteredge whispered savagely into his ear.

"Drop the knife!" Lassiter commanded, but the professor didn't seem to hear him.

"I know who's behind this," Kitteredge said. "You're just a pawn. It's Polidori. It's the Cabal!"

Before Lassiter could come up with an answer, the door to the interrogation room flew open. For one brief second Lassiter's heart leaped at the thought that SWAT was coming to take Kitteredge out. Then those idiots, Spencer and Guster, burst in.

"Professor Kitteredge, what are you doing?" Gus said.

"He's part of it!" Kitteredge shouted.

"If you mean part of the reason American policemen have such a bad reputation, I can't argue with you," Shawn said. "Beyond that, I don't think he's part of anything."

"He's part of the conspiracy," Kitteredge said. "They killed Clay Filkins and now they're framing me for it. And he knows who's behind it."

"Lassie?" Shawn said. "He doesn't know who's behind anything. The music. The green door. The *Valley of the Dolls*."

"I think that last one is beyond," Gus said.

"He doesn't know any beyonds, either," Shawn said.

"In fact, he really doesn't know much of anything. Which he'll be happy to demonstrate if you'll let him go."

"I can't!" Kitteredge said. "I've gotten too close to them, and they'll do anything to stop me. But I won't let them." Kitteredge's blade dug deeper into Lassiter's throat. "I don't want to hurt him, but I will if I have to."

"Get out of here, Spencer," Lassiter said, feeling the air pressing back against the knife as it struggled up through his constricted throat. "I can handle this."

"Yes, I can see you're right on top of things," Shawn said. "Sorry we interrupted."

Shawn turned back toward the door. Gus grabbed his arm. "We can't just leave them here."

"You heard what Lassie said," Shawn said. "He's got it under control."

"But this is all a terrible mistake," Gus said. "Professor K thinks Lassie framed him, Lassie thinks the professor is a murderer, and unless we can convince them they're both wrong, somebody is going to get hurt. Or killed."

"That's why I said we should have gone to the C. Thomas Howell Film Festival instead of the museum," Shawn said. While he was talking he started to move around the edges of the room. "Very few people have ever died watching *CyberMaster*, and those who have all worked on the film and realized only while they were watching the credits that they forgot to request to be listed by their pseudonyms. Whereas everyone knows that nine-tenths of the murders in the free world happen in art museums."

It took Gus a moment to figure out what Shawn was doing, but then he realized. He was trying to get behind Kitteredge.

"What are you talking about?" Gus said. If there was any chance for Shawn's plan to work, Gus had to keep the professor's eyes on him. "This isn't about museum crime. This is about a global conspiracy—one that's already claimed one victory tonight and is about to take two more. We can't let that happen."

Kitteredge turned to Gus with gratitude in his eyes. For a moment, the hand holding the knife seemed to relax.

"Now!" Gus shouted. Which might have been exactly the right thing to say if Shawn had been the only one in the room planning to make a move. Because at Gus' command, Shawn leaped across the room to tackle Kitteredge.

Unfortunately, Shawn wasn't the only one in the room planning to make a move. Lassiter was, too. And as he felt the knife slacken away from his throat, he drove an elbow straight back into Kitteredge's stomach. The professor doubled at the point of impact—and Shawn flew right over him, crashing onto the table, then sliding off and landing hard on the floor.

Lassiter struggled to free himself, but even as he gasped for breath the professor wouldn't let go. He jammed the knife back against the detective's throat as he pulled himself upright again.

Kitteredge dragged Lassiter to the interrogation room door. "We're getting out of here," he said. Then he turned a baleful eye on Gus. "You don't understand the forces you're dealing with."

Kitteredge shoved Lassiter to the door, pulled it open, and dragged him through, making sure it closed behind them. From inside, Lassiter could hear Gus, and then Shawn and Gus, pounding to be let out.

The squad room was still only about half full as the night shift filtered out and the day watch began to check in. But there were at least twenty police officers and detectives between Kitteredge and the front door. And there was no way Lassiter was going to allow him to get away. Not even if it cost him his life. "He's got a knife!" Lassiter shouted.

From across the squad room, guns flew out of holsters,

of drawers, of lockers. They were all pointed directly at Kitteredge—and at him.

"Put down your weapons," Kitteredge said. "No one needs to get hurt."

"Don't listen to him!" Lassiter commanded, bracing himself for the sweet sting of lead. "Shoot!"

"Hold your fire," O'Hara said.

She stepped into Lassiter's line of sight. She wouldn't look at his face, though. No doubt she was as ashamed of what he'd allowed to happen as he was. She stared directly over Lassiter's shoulder into Kitteredge's eyes.

"Professor Kitteredge," she said as calmly as if she were going to offer him a stick of gum, "I need you to drop the weapon."

"I can't do that," Kitteredge said. "They're coming for me."

"And we can protect you," O'Hara said.

"Like you protected Filkins?" Kitteredge said. "He was killed right under your noses."

"We didn't know about the conspiracy before," O'Hara said. "Now we do, thanks to you. And with your help, we can shut it down for good."

"Stop talking to him," Lassiter barked. "Move away and shoot him."

"You're not helping, Carlton," O'Hara said. "Besides, Professor Kitteredge needs you alive, because you have special knowledge about the conspiracy. If you die, it dies with you."

"There is no conspiracy," Lassiter nearly shrieked with frustration. "There's just a lunatic with a knife at my throat—and you can't let him get away!"

O'Hara shot him a brief, chiding look, then turned her attention back to Kitteredge. "We can help you, Professor," she said. "We can work together to figure out who killed Filkins, and who put that bloody knife in your pocket."

For a moment, Lassiter felt the blade's pressure ease on his throat. Then it was jammed back into place.

"I can't trust anybody," Kitteredge said. "You might have planted the knife."

"But I didn't," O'Hara said. "What can I do to convince you of that?"

"Don't convince him," Lassiter said. "Shoot him."

"Quiet, Carlton," O'Hara said. "Professor Kitteredge, I swear to you that I am no part of any conspiracy, and neither is my partner. I will do whatever it takes to make you see that as long as you don't hurt him. So tell me now, before things get ugly—what is it you want?"

"I've got to get out of here," Kitteredge said. "You've got to let me go."

"Don't do it!" Lassiter shouted.

"You won't get far," O'Hara said. "Every police officer in this city will be looking for you."

"At least this way I have a chance to find out the truth before they get me," Kitteredge said.

Lassiter stared at O'Hara, mentally sending the order for her to shoot. Astonishingly, she managed to ignore it. Instead, she did the one thing Lassiter dreaded more than anything else in the world. She nodded.

Then she held up a hand to the officers. "Weapons down," she commanded. Some of the officers complied immediately. Others just stared at her, keeping their guns leveled at Kitteredge. "I said weapons down!" she said. "Now!"

This time there was no questioning her intent. The other officers stood down.

"Let him go and run," O'Hara said.

"Other way around," Kitteredge said. "I take him with me, and I leave him in a safe place once I know I'm not being followed."

"Don't do this, Detective," Lassiter said.

She thought it over for a moment, then nodded again. "If anything happens to him—"

"Then you'd better find the moles in your own department," Kitteredge said. "Because I don't want to hurt anyone."

He took a step toward the front door, then stopped, waiting to see if anyone was going to come for him. But the police officers were frozen in place. He took another step, dragging Lassiter with him, then moved swiftly toward the front door. He kicked it open and disappeared through it.

Chapter Ten

"**O**kay," Shawn said as Gus piloted the Echo back to the Psych office. "From now on, we're going to have a few rules. To start with, I choose the evening's entertainment."

"We didn't go to the museum for fun," Gus said automatically. He had no interest in the conversation, but he knew if Shawn didn't receive a response he'd keep repeating his original statement until he did, or until they were both dead. "We went on a case."

"That's rule number two," Shawn said. "I choose our clients, too."

A dozen different arguments flashed through Gus' brain. He could, for instance, have pointed out the times Shawn had agreed to take on a client who turned out to be guilty. Or the instances when Gus had brought in a case that turned into a great success for the agency.

But Gus didn't have any strength left for arguing. He barely had any strength left at all. If it hadn't been for the Echo's power-assisted steering he might have simply kept going straight down Santa Barbara Street until he'd driven into the ocean.

It wasn't just the fact that they'd been up for more

than twenty-four hours that had sucked all the energy out of him. Although it wasn't as easy as it had been when they were teens, Gus and Shawn still routinely pulled all-nighters when they were working on a case. And it wasn't the grueling interrogation they'd received from Detective O'Hara after she'd allowed Kitteredge to escape with her partner as a hostage, or even the huge sense of relief when Lassiter had been found half an hour later locked in the trunk of a stolen patrol car, furious but unharmed and definitely alive.

What had worn Gus out so completely was his sense of utter failure. Professor Kitteredge had reached out to him, reached out to the one person he had thought could help him, even though they barely knew each other. And not only had Gus been unable to help; he had stood by as things had gotten immeasurably worse for his old professor. Gus didn't know exactly what Kitteredge had wanted help with, but whatever it was it couldn't have been as bad as his current problem. He was a wanted fugitive, hunted not only for a cold-blooded murder but for taking hostage a Santa Barbara police detective. His career was ruined, his life changed forever—that is, if he managed to survive this day. Santa Barbara's police were professional above all else, but when they were chasing a criminal who'd dared hold a knife to one of their own, Gus knew that following the letter of the law would not seem as important as bringing down the felon.

"Rule number three is a no-brainer," Shawn said after checking to make sure that Gus was actually awake to hear him. "No cases that require formal wear."

Gus briefly considered responding to that, but he decided to allocate all his available strength to turning the steering wheel sufficiently to execute the right turn that would head them in the general direction of their office.

"Now, rule number four might seem a little controversial at first," Shawn said. "But when you think it over, I'm sure you realize it makes sense. If you ever get French fries when we break for food on a case, you have to give me two for every one you eat, even if I've got my own order. And if there are any soggy fries in my bag, you have to let me trade them for your crispy ones at a rate of three of your crispies for every one of my limps."

Of all the rules Shawn had laid down, that struck Gus as the one that he'd most likely insist on, ludicrous as it sounded. If he didn't object now, he knew, Shawn would not only bring it up on every case they worked in the future, but find ways to build on it so that he'd be entitled to every bit of food Gus ever ordered. Still, he couldn't get up the energy to argue. "Whatever," he said.

Shawn eyed him suspiciously. "You're making this too easy," he said.

"You could stop," Gus said.

"When I'm getting everything I want?" Shawn said. "Like that's going to happen. I haven't even gotten to the most important rule yet."

Gus didn't know what that rule was going to be, but he knew his partner well enough to imagine. No doubt Shawn was going to insist that Gus donate all his income from his pharmaceuticals sales route to Psych, or demand that Gus call him "sir" whenever they were in public, or let Shawn use his legs as a pillow if he got sleepy on a stakeout.

If he'd had any more energy, Gus might have once again muttered "Whatever." Instead, he shrugged. Let Shawn make any rule that amused him. They'd be in force only as long as Gus stayed with Psych, and after tonight's fiasco he wasn't sure how much longer he wanted that to be. He'd been playing at private detective for a few years now, and he'd been having fun. He'd even done a pretty good job from time to time.

But now he saw that whatever successes they'd had were nothing more than luck. He clearly had no idea what he was actually doing, and when his luck ran out he had no way to compensate for it. People got hurt. Maybe people even got killed, all because they trusted in him.

"Okay, here it comes," Shawn said. "The most important rule of all. The one that's going to change Psych forever, whether we like it or not."

"Why?" Gus was surprised that his tongue had bothered to form the syllable, but apparently some of his reflexes were even more powerful than his exhaustion.

"Why what?"

"Why will it change Psych forever, whether we like it or not?" Gus said. "There's no one at Psych besides us, so if we don't like one of your rules, we can simply ignore it."

"You can't just ignore rules," Shawn said.

"You do it all the time," Gus said. "And when I hesitate before breaking a rule, you get mad at me."

"That's completely different," Shawn said. "Those are other people's rules. Man-made rules. I'm talking about the laws that are set out by the universe, like gravity or entropy or the way it's impossible to get the last bits out of a shampoo bottle no matter how hard you shake it."

"Okay, fine," Gus said. "Let's have it."

Shawn started to speak, then turned around and reached toward the backseat.

"What are you looking for?" Gus said.

"A couple slabs of granite," Shawn said. "Marble, if you've got it. It just seems like the kind of thing that would sound better if it was carved on stone tablets. Although if you don't have any stone, I guess we could use aspirin tablets, as long as one of us can write really small."

"Shawn . . ." Gus said, hoping that a good set of ellipses would convey all the words he was too tired to use.

"Okay, fine," Shawn said. "Here's the most important rule: When one of our clients flips out and takes Lassie hostage with a knife because he believes that there's a global conspiracy out to frame him for murder to keep him from discovering the truth of their evil cabal, even though he's incapable of explaining what they want or why they want it—"

"I get it, Shawn," Gus said. "I was stupid to take Professor Kitteredge seriously. You don't have to make a big deal about it."

Shawn held up a finger to stop him. Gus briefly considered yanking it off his hand and throwing it out the window, but that seemed like far too much effort.

"Anyway," Shawn continued, "back to that rule. When all that stuff happens that I just laid out and don't feel like going through again, then it is our obligation to find that client and solve the murder before the police get him."

It took a moment before Gus could make sense of the words. He'd so completely expected to hear Shawn say the exact opposite that at first his brain simply wouldn't process the new information.

"Find him?" Gus said finally. "You mean Professor Kitteredge?"

"Unless you've got another client who took Lassie hostage and you haven't told me about him," Shawn said. "In which case, this would probably be a good time to bring it up, so we can prioritize."

"But you said he was crazy," Gus said.

"I said he was boring," Shawn said. "Which he was when he was droning on and on about subjects no one could ever possibly pretend to care about."

"He was talking about art," Gus said. "And history and literature."

"Exactly," Shawn said. "But it's amazing how much less boring he became when he held a knife to Lassie's throat, started screaming about a global conspiracy, and escaped."

"Even I thought he was crazy then," Gus admitted. "That's what made you like him?"

"There are three kinds of people who believe in conspiracy theories," Shawn said. "The first kind is the average guy who listens to George Noory when he should be sleeping and has decided that there are aliens in Area 51, trilateralists in the government, and Illuminati in the drinking water because it's much easier to blame all your failures on a vast global network that exists only to keep you down than it is to accept that maybe you're just a loser. These are the guys you get stuck next to when you're waiting in line at the post office and they recognize the Garfield T-shirt you pulled on because everything else was dirty as a secret welcome sign between believers. They will talk for hours about the dark forces arrayed against them, but they're completely harmless. If they actually had the gumption to do anything in the first place, they wouldn't be the kind of loser who has to blame faceless conspiracies for their own lack of success."

"That's not Professor K," Gus said.

"Definitely not," Shawn said. "Then there's type number two. This is the hard-core conspiracy freak, the guy who knows exactly who killed Sonny Bono and why."

"Sonny Bono?" Gus said. "I thought he skied into a tree."

"That's exactly what they wanted you to think," Shawn said. "And it worked so well they did it to Natasha Richardson, too."

"That doesn't make any sense at all," Gus said.

"Not to you or me, but to him," Shawn said. "This kind of conspiracy nut can take seemingly random bits of information from anywhere and weave them together

into one long narrative. And it will always make sense—
at least, to him. Once you expose it to real-world logic,
it falls apart. But these people see real-world logic as
another part of the cover-up, and they accuse anyone
who tries to talk them out of their delusion of being part
of the plan."

"So you're talking about crazy people," Gus said.

"Not just crazy," Shawn said. "Crazy and dangerous.
These are the ones who are so convinced they're right
that they're willing to act on their beliefs. They'll do
anything to fight off the conspiracy, including commit-
ting violent acts."

"You're not saying that Professor Kitteredge is one
of them?" Gus said, trying to imagine his old teacher
crouching in a basement rec room wearing a tinfoil hat
to keep out the mind-rays.

"No, because these people are so paranoid they're
completely incapable of functioning in normal society," Shawn said. "You can't spend your days finding
ways in which Brandon Lee's death is connected to the
space shuttle explosion and the mysterious two-year
disappearance of Wonder Bread from Southern California grocery shelves and still convince a university
to let you talk in front of teenagers. Unless you teach
economics, of course, and even then the tenure com-
mittee is going to look at you funny when you come up
for review."

"You said there were three kinds of people who
believe in conspiracy theories," Gus said. "I guess that
makes Professor Kitteredge type number three."

"That would be my guess, too," Shawn said. "These
are people who are on the surface indistinguishable
from you or me. They seem intelligent, well-spoken,
thoughtful. They've got meaningful jobs—or even ca-
reers. They've got rich, full social lives and the respect of
their peers, and they seem to be normal, or better than
normal, to the outside world. But one day they stumble

on a piece of information that doesn't make sense to them, and unlike everybody else, they decide to follow it. And so it leads them to another piece of information and another, and soon they're weaving them all together into a grand narrative of dark deeds."

"Wait a minute," Gus said. "How is that any different from the last guys you described?"

"Because these people," Shawn said solemnly, "are brilliant. And the connections they come up with are brilliant. So brilliant, in fact, that any intelligent person who hears them could immediately see how they might be true."

The words hit Gus like a fist. "Are you saying that Professor Kitteredge really has stumbled across a global conspiracy and they've framed him for murder to shut him up?"

"It's possible," Shawn said. "In the same way it's possible that the car we're in could actually be an alien transforming robot and you could be Megan Fox. But either way, he's a danger to himself and everyone around him. Because his belief is a black hole that can suck in everything in its path."

For the first time in hours, Gus felt strength flowing back into his limbs. He could actually do something to help his old professor. Better yet, *they* could do something.

Except for one small problem.

"Don't get me wrong," Gus said. "I'm thrilled that you've come around to this way of thinking. And I'm delighted that you're willing to help Professor Kitteredge. But how are we going to help him when we don't have any idea where he is?"

"You mean when *you* don't have any idea where he is," Shawn said.

"You do?"

"I know exactly where he is," Shawn said. "And if you turn this car around, I'll take you to him."

Chapter Eleven

The lemon–poppy seed cake was even better than it looked. The citrus flavor was mild, yet sharp enough to ameliorate the richness of the huge amounts of butter. The black seeds scattered not only on top of the icing but throughout the crumb provided an appealing crunch with every bite.

The only problem with the lemon–poppy seed cake served by the café in the Santa Barbara Museum of Art, as far as Gus could see, was that it provided no clue to the whereabouts of Professor Langston Kitteredge.

"Tell me again what we're doing here." Gus leaned across the small table until his mouth was almost pressed against Shawn's ear. "Because there's no way Professor Kitteredge is going to stop in for a sandwich when every cop north of Los Angeles is hunting for him."

Shawn ran his fork through the last traces of chocolate icing on his own plate and licked off the tines. "I wouldn't be so sure," he said. "It's a pretty good sandwich. Just look at this place."

Gus glanced around the room. The café was certainly popular. Every table was filled with art lovers here to check out the collection of European paintings, young parents eager to expose their small children to the joys of culture, and tourists determined to see every last attraction in the Santa Barbara area before they headed back to Minneapolis.

Even in this large crowd, however, Gus couldn't help feeling conspicuous. Because while the room might have been reaching its fire department–sanctioned occupancy limit of one hundred and twenty-nine people, only two men in the entire crowd were wearing tuxedos. And every one of those hundred and twenty-nine had taken a moment to stare at Shawn and Gus as they'd walked past carrying their trays.

"I have been looking at this place almost as much as this place has been looking at me," Gus said. "It's hard to be inconspicuous when you're the only one wearing formal wear in an informal setting."

"We don't need to be inconspicuous," Shawn said. "The police aren't looking for us. No one is."

"What about that guy?" Gus said. Across the room, a burly man in a "Ski the Big Potato" T-shirt and khaki shorts that strongly suggested he lived in some area that rarely saw the sun kept looking up from his mousy wife and two squabbling toddlers to stare at them.

Shawn glanced over at the man and *saw*. Saw the darker tan on his left arm. Saw the way the kids turned only to their mother to plead their case. Saw the faint traces of bruising around his right eye.

"He's a long-haul trucker," Shawn said. "Spends twenty-three days of every month on the road, and then he's forced to go home to that lovely family. His wife made him take them to Santa Barbara on vacation in hopes of bringing the magic back to their marriage, but when they went to the beach he spent the whole time staring at young girls in bikinis, and the missus has been furious with him ever since. Now all he wants is to take the family back to Idaho, get in his rig, and drive as far from home as he can possibly get."

"You can't know that," Gus said.

"Can't I?" Shawn said.

"No, you can't," Gus said.

Shawn cast another glance at the man, who was now glowering openly at them. "Well, there is another possibility," he said.

"What's that?"

"That he isn't a trucker at all," Shawn said. "And that isn't really his family. It's all part of an elaborate cover."

Gus felt his throat tightening. He knew the answer to his next question, but he couldn't stop himself from asking it anyway. "Cover for what?"

"For his role in Kitteredge's conspiracy," Shawn said. "He knows the professor is going to have to come back here, and he's waiting to take him out. But he also knows that we're here to help. And he's going to do whatever it takes to stop us."

Gus felt the lemon–poppy seed cake re-forming into a solid slab in his stomach. "Do you really think that's possible?" he said.

"I don't know," Shawn said. "But we can ask him when he gets here."

Gus looked back over to the trucker's table. The man was gone. He scanned the room and found him heading straight for their table.

"What do we do?" Gus said.

"The question is, what can *he* do?" Shawn said. "This is a public place, and we're surrounded by one hundred and twenty-six other people, not counting the members of his fake family. And statistically, it's highly unlikely that they're all members of the conspiracy. If he tries anything, there are going to be lots of witnesses."

Gus felt a pulse of relief surge through him. "So the only thing he can do is reveal himself to us," he said.

"Exactly," Shawn said. "Unless he doesn't care about

his own safety, in which case he could kill us both and then take himself out. That's the kind of thing crazed conspirators do, isn't it?"

Gus could have sworn he'd eaten only one piece of that cake. But now it felt like there was an entire bakery's worth hardening in his gut. He thought about jumping up from the table and running for the exit, but if this man really was a crazed killer sent by the conspiracy, there was no chance he'd be able to get away. Not if the assassin didn't care about his own life.

There was only one chance—to stay and fight. He slid his hand onto the tabletop and felt for the knife he'd put on the tray out of habit as they went through the serving line. The blade flexed under his fingers—it was made of thin white plastic, and it would snap in two if it ever hit the slightest obstacle, like a piece of lettuce. But Gus knew from painful experience that when it did break, the larger piece would have a jagged point. It couldn't possibly penetrate anything harder than pudding, but Gus could always aim for the killer's eyes and hope at least to cause the same level of pain as a piece of dust on the eyeball.

As Gus tightened his grip on his weapon, the man stepped up to their table and glowered down at them.

"It's over," he said in a voice filled with menace.

"On the contrary," Shawn said. "I think it's just beginning."

"I've been watching you for a long time," the man said.

"Since last night?" Gus said, trying to inject a little steel into his voice. "Or before? Did you start when Professor Kitteredge sent that letter? Or have you been watching since I first took his class?"

The man's brow furled in confusion. "I've been watching you two lazy jerks sitting here for twenty minutes while my wife and kids have been waiting for someone to take their order. Or even give us a menu. A break's nice, but you've got customers waiting, and we're hungry."

Gus tried to understand what the man was talking about. Was this some kind of code? When he talked about his wife and kids waiting for someone to take their order, did he really mean he was holding off any action until his superiors in the conspiracy told him what to do?

He glanced over to see if Shawn had any idea what was going on. And then he understood. When they'd arrived at the gala function in their tuxedos last night, they looked like elegant gentlemen of breeding. In the light of day and surrounded by tourists in T-shirts and shorts, they looked like something else.

"There is no table service here," Gus said. "It's self-serve. Didn't you see the line of people standing at the counter carrying trays?"

The conspiracy's undercover agent did the last thing Gus would ever have expected. He blushed. "That's what I told the missus," he said. "But she said if there were waiters here, there must be service as well. And you don't know my missus, but she's not one to accept second class when someone else is getting first."

"Sorry to disappoint you," Shawn said.

"Not me," the man said. "I don't mind waiting in line. But my wife—she hates it when she thinks other people have it better than her. Like when we were in that gallery with all the paintings and all we had to explain it was that prerecorded thing. Sorry I bothered you two."

"No bother at all," Gus said, feeling the cake dissolve again in his gut.

"Guess I'll go wait in line," the man said. "Unless . . ."

"Unless what?" Gus said.

The man stared down at his sandals in embarrassment. "Well, I was thinking maybe I could slip you some money and you could get some food and bring it over to us. I know it's a big thing to ask, but it would make my wife awfully happy."

"I wish we could help," Gus said. "But we're here—"

"To be of service to our fellow man," Shawn said. "That's why we're dressed like this."

"It is?" Gus said.

"Give us your order, and my friend here will bring it over to your table," Shawn said.

Gus stared at Shawn, trying to figure out what he was doing. "I will?" he said.

"You will," Shawn said. "Because this nice family has suffered enough today. Like when they were back in that gallery and all they had to explain the paintings was that prerecorded thing."

"That's right," the man said.

"When there were other people in the gallery who didn't pay anything more than you did who not only had the prerecorded tour, but also got a personal introduction to every painting in the room."

"That's right," the man said. "It wasn't like he was leading a tour or anything. There were these people looking at a painting right next to us and this giant tweedy guy came up to them and started talking about the guy who did it and where he was born and what kind of paint he used."

Now Gus understood what Shawn was after. "And did he stop talking?" he asked.

"Not as long as we were in that room," the man said. "Honestly, I don't know why the missus cared so much. At least the recorded thing runs out of batteries at some point. This guy was never going to."

"We'll get your food," Shawn said. "But then we need you to tell us exactly where you saw this man."

Chapter Twelve

Gus had never actually believed they'd find Professor Kitteredge at the museum. He'd let Shawn talk him into looking there because he couldn't think of anywhere else to start the search. But it simply didn't make any sense that the professor would be hiding out in one of the only two places in Santa Barbara where he would be quickly recognized and caught.

Not that there was any good place for him to hide. He couldn't go back to his hotel, which was undoubtedly under constant surveillance by the police. He might try to make a break for home, but he had to know the Riverside police would be hunting for him. Gus was sure the local airport, bus station, and train depot were all being watched, and there was an Amber alert out on his car, the license plate flashing on giant signs over every stretch of freeway in the state.

But he'd been here at the museum just last night; as a guest of honor he must have been introduced to many of the staffers. And while Gus had no idea how popular Clay Filkins had been, he had to imagine that most of those staffers would be overjoyed to finger the man who had killed their colleague.

Gus had considered pressing Shawn for an explanation of his thinking, but every time he'd done this in the past he'd ended up with a blasting headache. Shawn's mental processes were like string theory—knowledgeable people insisted they were actually valid, and when experiments were performed the results ended up confirming the predictions, but it was impossible to describe precisely how or why they worked.

Even though he remained dubious, Gus felt his heart beating faster as he followed Shawn through galleries of European paintings segregated by century. And as they reached the end of the 1800s and moved on to the 1700s, he was thrilled to hear a familiar voice.

"There are those who believe that Fragonard tired of these scenes of lust and licentiousness, and that's why he turned to neoclassicism in his later years," the voice was saying. "But that denies a key element of biographical research which became evident in—"

Gus quickened his pace, nearly running into the next gallery. There he saw Professor Kitteredge standing next to a young Japanese couple and gesturing toward an ornate painting of three young girls in period dress playing in a fountain. The professor kept talking to the young couple despite the fact that they both had earphones clamped over their heads and in fact were looking at a different painting.

Gus rushed over to Kitteredge. "Professor, what are you doing here?"

Kitteredge jumped, then realized who it was who had come up to him. "Mr. Guster?"

"Yes," Gus said. "Gus. The police are searching for you."

"They're not the only ones," Kitteredge said. "I don't have much time."

"I can't believe you've made it this long," Gus said. "Somebody is going to report you."

"I'm safe for the moment," Kitteredge said. "No one ever notices a museum docent."

"But the staff all know you," Gus said, checking the gallery doors to make sure none of them were closing in.

"Museum staff particularly never notices a docent," Kitteredge said. "Because the docent's favorite trick is to introduce the staff member to his tour group, and then ask him to take over the lecture. Whenever a staffer sees a docent in a gallery he'll cover his head and run out as quickly as possible."

"What happens when the museum closes?" Gus said. "We've got to find a place for you to hide."

"Professor Kitteredge can't leave the museum yet," Shawn said, stepping up to them. "Not until he's seen what he's come to see. And it's not in this room. Which means that hiding out here isn't doing you any good at all."

Kitteredge, who had been holding himself up proudly, deflated like a beach ball under a truck tire. "I've got to get another look at *The Defence of Guenevere*," he said.

"Professor, I understand how long you've wanted to see this painting, but this is not the time," Gus said. "After we clear your name, you'll be able to study it as much as you want. But now we've got to go."

"That's the problem," Shawn said. "That painting is the only way to clear his name."

Kitteredge looked at Shawn as if revising an earlier opinion of him. "The painting is the reason Filkins was killed," Kitteredge said. "I'm convinced it contains essential clues to the identity and purpose of this global conspiracy. That's why it's been held in secrecy for so many years. Now that it was finally going to be made public, they knew I would be able to decipher its secret message. They had to shut me up, so they killed poor Clay Filkins and framed me for it."

"The picture's a hundred and fifty years old," Gus

said. "Even if it does have all those clues in it, how is it going to help you identify the actual murderers?"

"I'll know when I have a chance to study it," Kitteredge said. "Last night, I was only able to get a quick glimpse. And now the gallery where it's hanging is closed and there's a police officer guarding the door."

"Just one?" Shawn said. "We're in."

Chapter Thirteen

Carlton Lassiter had never noticed just how lovely the veneer on the chief's desk was. Although he knew it was really just a microscopically thin layer of walnut glued over particleboard, it still managed to convey the sense of prestige, power, and authority that came with the office.

It surprised him that he'd never noticed this before. All the times he'd sat across from Chief Karen Vick as she gave him assignments or accepted his debriefing or just talked about the state of the department and the world with him, he'd never let his gaze drift away from her face long enough to appreciate the special quality of the wood surfacing.

But for the past fifteen minutes he'd had the chance to give the grain the kind of study it deserved, and he felt he now knew it well enough to draw its pattern from memory if he needed to.

Somewhere, in some part of his brain that wasn't completely occupied with the office's furniture, he was aware that the desk's occupant was talking to him. Apparently Chief Vick has been speaking the entire time he'd been staring at her desk. Her voice sounded sympathetic and yet with an undertone of steel, which was, he realized, not unlike the composition of that desk.

"No one blames you for this, Carlton," Chief Vick said. "As this process moves forward it's important that you understand that."

Lassiter felt his head nodding. Apparently some part of him was aware of what the chief was saying, or at least could figure out the correct response from her tone of voice.

"But it's also crucial that the Santa Barbara Police Department understand exactly what went wrong here," Vick continued. "We're not looking to point fingers or find a scapegoat. We just need to know if there are problems in our procedures that need to be fixed to make sure nothing like this ever happens again."

Whatever part of him that was controlling his muscles made Lassiter's head nod again.

"And the first tool we need to use in our study of this incident is going to be the report of the officer who was at the center of it," Vick said. She opened a file that was lying on her desk and pulled out a single sheet of paper. "That's why I need you to rewrite this."

She pushed the paper across the desk at him. His eyes, attracted by the movement, shifted up to see that it was a report form with a couple lines of type on it. He vaguely remembered having turned in a similar form a short while before.

"That's my report," Lassiter said, shifting his gaze back to the comfortingly familiar sight of walnut grain.

Chief Vick picked up the paper and sighed heavily. "This is the report you want to turn in?"

"It's the truth," Lassiter said.

"Detective Carlton Lassiter failed in his duty and allowed the suspect to take him hostage, shaming not only the Santa Barbara Police Department but every law enforcement agency everywhere in the world," she read. "The entire fault rests with him. The only mistake made by any other member of the force was in opening the car trunk in which Detective Lassiter had been locked instead of leaving him there to suffocate."

"Is there something in there you disagree with?" Lassiter said. "I think it sums up the situation pretty well."

Chief Vick let out a deep sigh and shoved the paper across the desk at him. "I can't give this to the police commission," she said. "And I won't turn it over to Internal Affairs. I will not let you destroy your career over this."

One of Lassiter's hands reached out and took the paper. "What do you want me to say?"

"You've written a million reports," she said. "You know what has to be in it. I need a complete accounting of everything that happened, starting with your arrival at the museum and ending with your rescue."

Lassiter stared down at the paper in his hand. He read the words over again. It said everything there was to say about the incident. "So you want me to pad it out?" he said.

"I've told you what I expect, Detective," Chief Vick said, the edge of steel now rising above the sympathetic tone. "And I expect it no later than tomorrow."

"Tomorrow?" He knew what that word meant—a day that would begin when this one was finally over. But he couldn't quite imagine it ever coming, because he was pretty sure that this day would never actually end.

"Tomorrow, Carlton," Vick said, her tone softening again. "Right now, what I want you to do is go home and get some sleep. The next couple of days are going to be rough. Internal Affairs will need to do a thorough review, and the press is going to be all over this. Our departmental therapists are excellent at dealing with post-traumatic stress, and I strongly urge you to take advantage of their expertise. But first you need to go home and get some rest."

"I need to work," Lassiter said. "I need to catch Kitteredge."

"You don't need to do anything but rest, Detective," Chief Vick said. "Juliet O'Hara is leading the search for Kitteredge."

"But I need to—"

"Go home right now," Chief Vick said. "You can take a personal day, if you'd like. Or I could suspend you pending review. But either way you're off this case."

Chapter Fourteen

"When a problem looks unsolvable," Shawn said, "it just means that we're not looking at it the right way."

Despite Kitteredge's insistence that the guise of museum docent provided a cloak of invisibility to rival the one elves hand out to ring-bearing hobbits, Gus and Shawn had felt that the European painting galleries were too well attended to make a safe hiding place. After a quick study of the museum map, they located the one spot in the institution that no one would ever walk into intentionally. And indeed, the Oceanic Arts and Crafts gallery was as deserted as any movie theater showing the second half of *Funny People*.

Had Gus been in more of a cultural mood he might have stopped to consider the unfairness of this. It was true that a lot of the Micronesian wood carvings all began to look alike very quickly, but some of the Melanesian works carried a sexual charge that Fragonard could only have dreamed of achieving. Granted, erotic sculptures of fertility goddesses would never replace Cinemax After Dark, but Gus was surprised not to see more teenage boys loitering around down here.

But right now, culture was the last thing on anyone's minds. Even Kitteredge, who had started a brief discussion on the destruction of traditional art forms in the Oceanic cultures after World War II when they first entered the gallery, quickly wrapped it up as they began to focus on the difficulty of the task before them.

"The problem is that we have to get into a gallery that's under constant guard by an armed police officer," Gus said. "Is there another way to look at that?"

"There's always another way," Shawn said. "For instance, we could say that the core problem is that you haven't come up with a solution."

"Me?" Gus said. "What about you?"

"I don't want to hog all the glory," Shawn said. "Especially since you were the one Professor Kitteredge asked for help."

"I'm willing to give up some glory," Gus said. "In fact, you can have it all. So solve."

"I can't yet," Shawn said. "Because we haven't come up with the right way to ask the question. Once we do that, the answer will be obvious."

"So what is the right question?" Gus said.

"That is," Shawn said. "And now that you've asked it, the answer should be obvious to you. So go ahead and answer."

The only answer that Gus could come up with seemed inappropriate to use in a museum frequented by families, even if none of them happened to be in this gallery. "What if we set some papers on fire so the alarm went off?" Gus said.

"Then steel doors would slam down on every gallery, and all the air would be sucked out to put out the fire and protect the art," Shawn said.

"That wouldn't happen," Gus said.

"It did when Pierce Brosnan tried it," Shawn said.

"First of all, you're not Pierce Brosnan," Gus said.

"I could be," Shawn said. "I am wearing a tuxedo."

"And second, that was a movie," Gus said. "No museum is going to have steel doors that slam down on galleries if there's a fire. What if there are people inside? They could suffocate or burn to death."

"They're extras," Shawn said. "No one cares about them."

"Until their survivors sue," Gus said.

Gus knew there had to be a way to get past that cop. He simply had to visualize it. He cast his gaze around the gallery until his eye fell on a carved wooden figure about a foot high. It sat in a Plexiglas box standing on a narrow pillar. A card in front of the display case described it as a Melanesian fertility symbol from the early 1600s.

"Okay," Gus said, "let's say this is the cop."

Shawn looked at the little figure, and then at the enormous priapus jutting out from its midsection. "If that's the cop, he won't need his gun to stop us," he said. "He won't even need a nightstick."

"Is this helping?" Gus said.

"It's helping pass the time," Shawn said.

"We don't want to pass time," Gus said. "Time is not our friend."

"Maybe not to you," Shawn said. "But I've always felt that Pierce Brosnan was a much more compelling actor once he got a little age on his face."

Gus fought back an image of what he could do with that Melanesian fertility symbol and tried to refocus on the problem.

"Okay," Gus said, "we're saying that this is the cop—and that's *all* we're saying on the subject. Our one goal here is to figure out how we can make him move away from the gallery he's guarding."

Shawn stared at the wooden figure. Then his face lit up in a smile. "I've got it."

"Yes?" Kitteredge said.

"I said I had the answer," Shawn said. "Not that I feel

like sharing it. Because just standing here chatting with you could be considered a felony, seeing as how you're wanted for a bunch of terrible crimes. So before we go any further down the road to helping you, I think you owe us an explanation."

Gus was about to jump in to defend his professor, but before he could speak he realized that Shawn was right.

Kitteredge looked from Shawn to Gus and saw the determination on their faces. "You're right," he said. "By helping me, you may have put yourself in terrible danger, and not just from the police. You need to know about the Cabal."

Chapter Fifteen

"But before you can understand the Cabal, we have to go back a hundred and fifty years, to when Dante Gabriel Rossetti and his close friend William Morris were brilliant young men," Kitteredge said.

Shawn let out a groan. "Are we going to get to the point while some of us here are still young men?"

Gus wanted to shush Shawn, but there was no point. Kitteredge didn't seem to have noticed the interruption.

"And as many brilliant young men have been throughout the years, they were dissatisfied with their country and their culture," the professor continued. "They joined with a group of artists and writers called the Pre-Raphaelite Brotherhood, who were attempting to reject several hundred years of art history and return to a style that was based on nature, that re-created the intense colors and abundant detail of paintings from the fourteenth century.

"But Rossetti and Morris were more radical in their approach than the founding brothers. They were appalled by the ravages of the Industrial Revolution and yearned to bring back not only the aesthetic of the Middle Ages but many of its working practices as well. Morris, in particular, was obsessed with the idea of returning to the principles of hand-crafted furniture and objects instead of the mass-produced items factories were now churning out.

"All this is accepted fact and not at all controversial." Kitteredge stopped and fished in his pocket for his pipe, and then, apparently remembering what had happened last time, pulled his hand away.

"That's really interesting," Shawn said as he stifled what Gus knew was a phony yawn. "Now I completely understand why you pulled a knife on a homicide detective."

"That was background you needed to know to understand what comes next," Kitteredge said. "Because now we are moving into my own research. And that is far more dangerous. I spent my lifetime studying the works of the Brotherhood. And as I dug deeper I began to discover anomalies and lacunae in the works that often seemed to contradict their explicit meanings. Of course this was of great interest to me; how could it not be?"

"I could explain," Shawn said.

"So I devoted myself to understanding what these little anomalies meant," Kitteredge said. "At first, they seemed totally random. But then I began to notice a pattern."

Shawn gave Gus a significant look. Gus managed to ignore it.

"It took me years to understand that the pattern was actually a code, and more years to work out what it meant," Kitteredge said. "And even when I had succeeded, I couldn't bring myself to believe what it was telling me. I went back and reworked all my research until there was no doubt in my mind."

Gus could feel his heartbeat rising with excitement. "No doubt about what?" he said. "What was the message?"

"Morris and Rossetti and a handful of others weren't simply planning to bring back the artistic standards of the Middle Ages. They aimed to bring back the political system as well. They wanted to roll back the clock to before the signing of the Magna Carta. They believed that the only way to rescue Britain from the moral decline brought about by the Industrial Revolution, from the poverty that was destroying families and killing people, from the factory pollution that was fouling the air and the water, from the migration into the cities that was wiping out the rural way of life was to bring back the idea of the king as an absolute ruler who would have command over all things political, cultural, and spiritual. That king, needless to say, would have to be someone who understood the Pre-Raphaelite way of thinking and would return England to those glory days."

"Someone like William Morris?" Gus suggested helpfully.

"Someone exactly like Morris," Kitteredge said. "With Rossetti at his side."

"Wait a minute," Shawn said. "I'm not exactly an expert on royalty, but I always thought that king was one of those jobs you couldn't just apply for. That's why I didn't bother sending an application to Monaco. Because everyone kept telling me you had to be related to the last guy."

"Inheritance is the standard way of determining the royal lineage," Kitteredge said. "But that line can be interrupted and replaced. It happened several times in England's history, usually through violent rebellion or civil war."

"So these two painters were going to lead an armed rebellion so they could make themselves king of England?" Shawn said.

"They were not violent men," Kitteredge said. "They planned for a peaceful revolution. The British people would flock to their side and demand that Morris be installed on the throne."

"Why would anyone think that?" Shawn said.

"Because they were going to have a symbol," Kitteredge said. "The one thing that would prove to the world that William Morris was the rightful king of England. They were searching for—and I believe they found—Excalibur."

Chapter Sixteen

Shawn and Gus stared slack-jawed at Kitteredge, although apparently for different reasons.

"They thought he'd be crowned king of England because he drove a fancy sports car?" Shawn said. "And one of the ugliest cars ever made, at that?"

But Gus could barely contain his excitement at Kitteredge's words. "Excalibur was King Arthur's sword," he said. "The one he pulled out of the stone. And if I remember right, on the blade it said 'Whoever wields this sword is the rightful king of all England.' "

Kitteredge nodded, pleased. "That's one of the legends," he said. "One I'm sure that Morris and Rossetti embraced."

"So these two guys figured they'd dig up an old sword and rule the country," Shawn said. "It sounds kind of nuts, but okay—let's go with it. Even if they're still alive, they've got to be two hundred years old by now, and too weak to lift the sword, let alone stick it into Filkins' chest. So how can they have anything to do with this murder?"

"They don't," Kitteredge said. "Not directly. But there were others. It took a great deal of work to ferret this out, but I don't believe Morris and Rosetti and those few of their Pre-Raphaelite brethren who joined in the search for Excalibur were working on their own initiative, nor did they come to the idea on their own. They were pawns of a greater force."

"What kind of force?" Gus said.

"Call them what you will," Kitteredge said. "The Templars. The Rosicrucians. Freemasons. Throughout history there have been shadowy forces working, and when some outsider gets a glimpse of them, they are always attributed to one group or another. I chose to call them simply the Cabal, because I have no idea with whom or what ideology they are associated.

"But rest assured, they are wealthy and they are powerful and they never go away," Kitteredge said. "They had hoped to use Morris and Rossetti to gain the sword and possibly the nation, but they failed. That doesn't mean they've stopped trying. They have a man named Polidori, who has been leading their search. He was behind Filkins' murder. I'm sure of it. But how many people are involved and where they are hiding I have no idea."

"And you think they're so powerful they've infiltrated the Santa Barbara Police Department?" Gus said.

"It's impossible to know their reach," Kitteredge said.

"Wait a minute," Shawn said. "I thought you said they found the sword."

"I believe Morris and Rossetti did," Kitteredge said. "And then they hid it again, rather than turn it over to the Cabal. I believe that is why Rossetti made sure his last painting stayed hidden for all these years. Because it contains clues to Excalibur's hiding place."

"But why kill Filkins?" Gus said.

"I can't say for sure," Kitteredge said solemnly. "But I believe they were sending me a message: Stay away from this picture—stay away from the sword."

"Wouldn't the message have been clearer if the sword had been poking through *your* chest?" Shawn said.

For a moment, all the animation left Kitteredge's face. Gus realized suddenly that the professor was much older than he'd assumed, close to sixty at least. But usually there was so much energy flowing through the man it was impossible to think of him as aging, let alone aged. Now, however, Gus could see all his years weighing on him.

"It should have been me," Kitteredge said. "I would accept death for myself before seeing an innocent killed because of my work. But I wasn't given a choice in the matter. So all I can do now is work to avenge his death. The only way I know to do that is to find the sword and make sure it never falls into the hands of the Cabal."

The three of them stood in silence for a long moment. Then Shawn nodded his acceptance.

"Okay, so my plan," he said. "How we get into that gallery."

Kitteredge looked like he was about to throw his arms around Shawn in one of his bearlike embraces. "Yes?"

Shawn walked over to the Plexiglas box housing the fertility sculpture and gave it a shove. The pedestal rocked slightly, and Shawn shoved it again. This time it tipped over and crashed to the ground.

All around them, alarm bells started ringing.

Chapter Seventeen

If Shawn had been disappointed that steel doors didn't slam down on all the galleries once the alarm went off, he didn't show it. Maybe that was because he was too busy running.

That course of action made sense for the three of them. They needed to get out of the Oceanic gallery before a squad of security guards arrived to protect the fertility figure.

But it didn't make a lot of sense for any of the hundreds of museum visitors who were also running as fast as they could for the museum exits. After all, it wasn't a fire alarm that had gone off, just the theft protection system. But while whoever had designed the museum's security had installed alarms with substantially different sounds for various kinds of disasters, he'd neglected to include a way to alert the public to the distinction. To an untrained ear the bells ringing throughout the museum might be signaling a raging inferno in the nearest gallery.

And of course, even if that thought had not occurred to them individually, the sight of two young men in tuxedos shouting "Fire!" and racing toward the emergency exits certainly would have put it in many heads. Following their directions, the tourists blasted through doors wired to set off further alarms when opened.

Moving as swiftly and efficiently as any male salmon who hasn't gotten the memo that the way upstream has been blocked by a new dam, Shawn and Gus led Kitteredge back through the centuries of European paintings until they arrived at the vestibule of the special-exhibitions gallery where *The Defence of Guenevere* had been installed. The entrance was blocked off by yellow-and-black crime scene tape, but there was no one standing in front of the door.

"Let's go," Gus said. "We've got to get in and out fast."

"Fast?" Kitteredge said. "I'm going to need some time with the painting."

"How much time?" Gus said.

"Ideally a couple of decades," Kitteredge said. "We're talking about the solution to a puzzle that has gone unanswered for more than a hundred years."

"The only way you're getting decades is if they agree to hang the picture in your cell," Shawn said. "You've got three minutes, tops."

"Three minutes!" Kitteredge said. "That's almost worse than nothing."

"Then we might as well leave now," Shawn said. "Because it's not going to take much more than three minutes to clear everyone out of this place. Then they're going to lock it down and start going room by room to make sure nothing is missing. And since you are technically missing, you really don't want anyone to find you here."

Kitteredge looked helplessly to Gus, as if hoping the higher court would overturn the verdict. "If Jean-Francois Champollion had only been able to study the Rosetta Stone for three minutes, he never would have been able to work out the translations between demotic and hieroglyphics."

"If his choice had been between looking at the stone and spending the rest of his life breaking rocks, I think we both know which way he would have gone," Gus said.

"But we have something that Champ guy never dreamed of," Shawn said. He dug in the roomy pocket of his rental pants and pulled out his cell phone. "As the new counter girl at Burger Town said to Gus, take a picture; it will last longer."

Kitteredge's face lit up in joy, and Gus was so pleased that Shawn had found a way to answer everyone's needs that he was willing to ignore the fact that the counter girl had actually been talking to Shawn, and that she had appended an extra word to the end of her sentence that had rendered her photographic suggestion even less friendly.

With Kitteredge clutching the cell phone, they started across the vestibule, heading straight for the crime scene tape. Shawn was just reaching out to push open the glass door when a gruff voice called out from behind them.

"Hey!" the voice said. "You can't go that way."

The voice belonged to the uniformed police officer who had been standing guard at the gallery door. And he was marching up to them.

Chapter Eighteen

Now what? Gus thought desperately. There was no way the cop was going to let them in to see the painting. They'd be lucky if he didn't arrest them just for trying. And if he got any kind of look at Kitteredge's face, the professor would be in prison awaiting trial for murder, and they'd be sharing a cell for aiding and abetting.

"We're just trying to get out, Officer," Shawn said in the same voice he'd been using to feign innocence when caught red-handed since he was spotted dumping a jar of green tempera powder on Suki Stern in kindergarten.

"There's no exit through that door," the officer said.

"Well, thank God you came along to let us know that in time," Shawn said, an extra coating of sugar on his tone. "If we'd gone in there, we might have been broiled alive."

As opposed to simply getting the lethal injection, Gus thought. *Which is what we'll be facing once that cop recognizes Professor Kitteredge.*

"No danger of that," the officer said. "There's no fire. But we are evacuating the building. Follow me and I'll show you the way to the exit."

"Thank you again, Officer," Shawn said.

"That is, if your friend feels like getting off the phone," the officer said.

Gus turned to see that Kitteredge was holding Shawn's phone to his left ear with his right hand, allowing him to cover most of his face with forearm and elbow.

"That's Uncle Leroy for you," Shawn said. "Anything interesting happens, he's got to tell Aunt Mabel about it right away. Come on, Uncle Leroy."

Kitteredge seemed to recognize his cue. "Don't worry about me, Mabel. You've got to see to those chickens," he said into the phone. "And when you're done, the cows are going to need milking. And the hay needs to be baled. Plus there are those pies to bake."

Shawn took Kitteredge's free elbow and started to guide him toward the cop. "That's plenty of rustic charm, Uncle Leroy," he said. "I'm sure Aunt Mabel remembers what to do."

"I'm glad somebody does," the cop said, turning and headed toward the main lobby. He was expecting them to follow, and if they didn't he'd come back fast to find out why. And the first place he'd look would be *Guenevere*'s gallery. Forget about three minutes with the painting; they'd be lucky to get three seconds.

Shawn was shuffling his feet, moving as slowly as possible while still maintaining a defensible level of forward momentum in case the cop glanced back, when there was a shout from behind them.

"Police! Help!" a man's voice shouted.

Gus turned to see the long-haul trucker from the café rushing past them to reach the officer, trailing his two small children behind him.

"What's the problem?" the cop said.

"It's my wife," the trucker said. "She's stuck in Chinese porcelain. You've got to help her."

"Is she hurt?" the cop said.

"Her feelings are," the trucker said. "And believe me,

that's bad enough. She saw you helping that pregnant woman out a couple of minutes ago."

"So?" the officer said.

"She says she's entitled to the same level of service as anyone else," the trucker said. "And if assistance is being offered, she wants some, too."

The cop stared at him, dumbfounded. "Are you serious?"

"I wish I wasn't," the trucker said. "She's sitting on the floor and won't get up until she gets everything she deserves. Even if that means burning up in an inferno and leaving our poor children motherless."

The cop looked down at the children, who stared back up at him seriously. Then he muttered something under his breath and turned back to Shawn. "Exit's that way," he said pointing in the direction he'd been heading. "Follow the crowd and you can't miss it. Don't be here when I get back."

The trucker led the officer back in the direction he'd come from. Gus let out a sigh of relief as the three of them crept back to the gallery entrance and pushed the door open. They bolted through and let the door shut behind them.

As Gus looked around the deserted gallery he marveled that less than twenty hours had passed since he'd been here. Since then the entire world had changed. The man he respected most in the world was a wanted fugitive, and Gus was helping him escape the police. He might have expected the gallery to have changed in that time to reflect the new situation, for the lights to be lower or the walls to be closing in or the floor split by a jagged fissure through which they could fall straight into hell.

But nothing looked any different than it had the night before. Sure, there were gray smudges on the walls where crime scene techs had brushed for fingerprints, and there was some dried blood etched in the grout between the marble tiles of the floor. But if you didn't know what you were looking for, you'd never know this had been the scene of such a terrible crime. You couldn't even see the tape outline of Filkins' body on the ground, as the red velvet drape had been closed over the painting again.

"Okay, Professor," Shawn said. "You've got three minutes."

Gus looked back to see that Kitteredge was frozen by the gallery door. "Professor Kitteredge?" he said.

Kitteredge seemed to shake off the spell. "Sorry," he said. "This picture has haunted me for so long, it's hard to believe that it's actually behind that curtain, even though I saw it last night."

"And we know how well that turned out," Shawn said. "We've got to move fast. If you start staring moonily at that picture, or start lecturing us about it, we'll all be caught and you'll never see it again. Get up close, take the pictures, and get out. Okay?"

"I understand," Kitteredge said. "I'll try to hold off my emotional reaction until the proper moment."

"Here's a hint," Shawn said. "You'll know that the proper moment has arrived when I'm not around."

Kitteredge nodded absently at him, and Gus went to the draped wall. He tried to move the curtain along its rings, but it wouldn't budge.

"It's stuck," Gus said, feeling a new sense of panic rising in him. "We're going to have to pull it down."

"Or we could just do what Lassie did and use the control thingy." Shawn stepped past Gus, reached into the folds of the curtain, and came up with the device. He pushed the button.

Above their heads, the small motors whirred and whined, and the red curtain began to move across the wall.

"This is exciting," Shawn said. "I'm so glad we didn't do what I wanted to do last night. Because we'd never see anything like a red velvet curtain if we went to the Bijoux Theatre. Oh, except for the one in front of the screen."

"If C. Thomas Howell is in jail because someone framed him for murder, then I'll consider the possibility that we went to the wrong event," Gus said.

"I'm sure C. Thomas Howell is perfectly capable of ending up in jail without the help of someone framing him for murder," Shawn said. "And then he could solve the crime from inside his cell with the help of the beautiful young warden's daughter, who just happens to stroll around the prison yard topless. In fact, I think that one is playing at the festival."

"Well, if we clear Professor Kitteredge's name before eight o'clock tonight, we can still make it in time for night three of the festival," Gus said. "Meanwhile, maybe we should focus on this case."

Shawn shrugged. Gus turned to make sure that Professor Kitteredge had started taking pictures instead of staring in awe at the painting.

But Kitteredge wasn't taking pictures. He was staring straight ahead, a look of despair on his face.

"Professor, we need to get moving," Gus said.

"We're too late," Kitteredge said. He raised a hand and pointed at the wall the curtain had just revealed.

Gus turned to see what he was pointing at, and his heart sank. On the wall, the ornate frame was hanging just as it had the night before. But inside the frame there was nothing but blank wall.

The painting was gone.

Chapter Nineteen

"**C**ell phone!" Gus hissed at Kitteredge. "Keep that cell phone pressed to your face."

"What's the point?" Kitteredge moaned.

"The point is not getting caught," Gus said. "And you're not making that easy."

Actually he seemed to be trying to make it as hard as he could. As Shawn and Gus led the professor through the crowd of people thronging the museum steps, he refused to hide his face behind his conversation with Aunt Mabel the way they had urged him.

"I can't hide forever," Kitteredge said. "And now that they've got the painting, I have no other choice. Because the only clues to the sword's hiding place were hidden in it. How can I ever hope to prove my innocence if I can't point at the people who framed me?"

"I don't know," Shawn said. "How about an alibi?"

Kitteredge stared at him blankly, exposing his face to a pair of uniformed police officers who were, fortunately, engaged in directing traffic around the crowd of evacuees who were spilling onto the street. Gus lifted the professor's arm and placed his left hand against his right ear, so that his elbow would hide his face again.

"An alibi?" Kitteredge said, his voice muffled by the tweed of his sleeve.

"You know, the place where you really were when the murder was being committed," Shawn said.

Kitteredge looked rattled and dropped his elbow away from his face. Gus pushed it back into place.

"I can't," he said.

"What do you mean, you can't?" Gus said.

"Well, there are two possible meanings," Shawn said. "The logical one is that no one seems to know yet exactly what time the murder actually happened, so it's impossible to pinpoint where he was at the time. But I think he's aiming for meaning number two, which is that he refuses to say where he was."

"Why?" Gus was shocked. "This is your life, Professor. What could be more important than that?"

"I was probably driving up from Riverside at the time," Kitteredge said.

"And let me guess," Shawn said. "You didn't stop, you weren't clocked speeding by a highway patrolman, and you didn't wave at any little kids who might suddenly remember having seen you right before the jury comes back."

"Nothing like that," Kitteredge said. "You see, I have a bad habit. When I have a lot on my mind, I get in my car and drive without paying any attention to where I'm going. I let my body take over the driving, and my mind focuses on my work. And when I was coming up from Riverside, I had so much to think about as I was preparing to view the painting. I can't say exactly where I went or what roads I took, but I left Riverside at seven in the morning, and I didn't arrive here until close to twelve hours later. And no, I didn't stop for gas. I have a hybrid."

"Which is not good, if it's true," Shawn said. "But there's still that other possibility."

"Which is what?" Kitteredge said.

"That there's another reason Filkins was killed," Shawn said. "It has nothing to do with the painting. It's really about Kitteredge coming home after a couple of weeks. He stops in a bar, and his old buddy Andy gives him the bad news. His new bride wasn't home that night. Since he's been gone she's been sleeping with everyone in town, including Filkins. Kitteredge picks up his gun and goes to Filkins' house, but when he gets there, he's lying in a pool of blood."

"That's ridiculous," Kitteredge said.

"That's 'The Night the Lights Went Out in Georgia,' " Gus said.

"That's the night they hung an innocent man," Shawn agreed. "All because his wife couldn't stay faithful."

"I don't have a wife," Kitteredge said.

"Sure," Shawn said. "That's one body that'll never be found, because little sister don't miss when she aims her gun."

"I don't have a sister!"

It was a good thing he was keeping the professor's arm pressed to his face, Gus thought, because it might have started beating Shawn around the head and neck.

"That does complicate things," Shawn admitted. "You don't know anyone who wanders these hills in a long back veil, do you?"

Kitteredge pulled his arm away from Gus. "What an arrogant fool I've been," he said. "All these years thinking I could best the Cabal, never realizing how powerful they really are. If I've stayed alive this long it's only because they chose to let me live. I should go up to the nearest policeman and turn myself in. Because there's nothing I can do to clear my name."

Kitteredge took a step in the direction of the cops who were still directing traffic. Gus grabbed his arm again.

"Please, Professor, don't do that," Gus said. "We will find a way to prove your innocence. You had enough faith to come to us for help in the first place. Don't let go of that, now that things look bleak."

Kitteredge barked out a bitter laugh. "I came to you for help? That's the rock I should build my faith on?"

"I still have the letter," Gus said, patting his breast pocket and hearing the crackle of twenty-four-pound bond.

"Maybe you should reread it," Kitteredge said.

"If you want me to, I will," Gus said. "But it's not safe out here. My car is parked across the street. I'll read it there if you'll come along with us."

"Now," Kitteredge said.

Gus turned to Shawn for help, but Shawn only shrugged. "Unless you want to pick him up and carry him, you've got to do what he says."

Keeping one eye on the cops, Gus pulled the letter out of his pocket and unfolded it. "Dear Mr. Guster," he read. "These are dark and difficult times. Events are conspiring to bring an end to those things which we hold most dear. And there is only one way out—if you are willing and able to help. Together we can find a way to make it through the dangers that face us. I will be appearing in your area in the near future, giving a lecture on the occasion of the unveiling of Dante Gabriel Rossetti's *The Defence of Guenevere* at the Santa Barbara Museum of Art. I would be happy to speak further about these issues if you would like to see me there. Thank you so much for your kind consideration. Sincerely, Langston Kitteredge, PhD."

Gus held the letter out to Kitteredge and then to Shawn, to see if either of them wanted to check the accuracy of his reading. For some reason, the professor's face was a mask of contempt. And even Shawn was staring at Gus like he'd reported for work wearing footie pajamas.

"What?" Gus said. He looked from Shawn to Kitteredge and back again. "What? He's asking for our help. He's practically begging for it."

"He's asking for money, Gus," Shawn said. "It's a fund-raising letter."

That couldn't be right. Gus read the letter again. And again. "But 'dark and difficult times.' You ask for my help right here."

"And the help of every other person in the Santa Barbara area who ever passed through the doors of my classroom," Kitteredge said. "I sent out similar, albeit slightly altered, letters to former students in fourteen other geographical regions."

"You said there were dangers," Gus said, his confusion turning to irritation and veering perilously close to anger.

"There are," Kitteredge said. "The state legislature keeps cutting the funding to the University of California system. Student fees have been raised much more than they should have been, and still there isn't enough money to keep all the departments open. We need the alumni to open their hearts and their wallets if we are going to survive as one of the nation's great public institutions of education."

Gus read the letter again, and this time he finally saw it for what it was. A plea for cash. How could he have been such a fool?

Shawn saw the despair on his friend's face and stepped in. "Still," he said, "you might not have needed the help of Santa Barbara's finest psychic detective agency when you wrote this letter, but it's hard to deny you're in trouble now."

Kitteredge turned his withering stare on Shawn. "Psychic?" he boomed.

It's an interesting thing about conversations in public places: sometimes two or three people can talk for hours at the top of their voices about the most intimate subjects and no one will notice. And then at other times one of the speakers will utter one simple word and the entire zip code will overhear.

That was the effect of Kitteredge's exclamation. Everyone standing on the steps around them swiveled to see what the commotion was about.

"Maybe we should keep our voices down a little," Gus whispered, pulling Kitteredge down the stairs.

Kitteredge allowed himself to be led, but he didn't take his eyes off Shawn. "This is a *psychic* detective agency?" he said, his volume still well above what any mother would consider his inside voice.

"It is for now," Shawn said. "But in about two minutes it's going to be a psychic inmates' association."

He pointed down the steps to where the two policemen had been directing traffic. But now the cars were hopelessly snarled as drivers tried to jockey their way through the crowd of pedestrians with no one to give them direction.

Because the cops weren't paying attention to the cars any longer. They weren't standing on the curb.

They were heading up the stairs toward Kitteredge.

Chapter Twenty

When he first joined Shawn in the business, Gus had often felt embarrassed at telling people whose respect he craved that Psych was a psychic detective agency. The work they did was excellent and their solve rate was the highest in town, but for so many intelligent, educated professionals the word "psychic" invoked so much skepticism that all they could hear afterward was "fraud."

That might not have bothered Gus so much if it weren't for the fact that they were, indeed, frauds. Shawn wasn't the slightest bit psychic. He simply had astonishing powers of observation and an amazing ability to interpret the tiny details that only he noticed. Gus had spent weeks trying to get Shawn to give up the pretense of supernatural powers and to simply take credit for his great skills.

But Shawn had insisted that being psychic was their brand. More importantly, it was fun. Shawn took great pleasure from the fact that so many people assumed he was a phony. That way, when he solved the case his audience would be doubly astonished.

Over the years, Gus had come around to Shawn's way

of seeing things. He, too, relished the skepticism that inevitably accompanied the announcement of Shawn's psychic abilities, because he knew they'd leave the cynics desperately grasping to explain how Shawn had solved the case without the aid of the spectral world.

But as he guided Professor Kitteredge through the throngs of people clustered on the museum steps, Gus felt that old embarrassment flooding back. Kitteredge was a noted intellectual, one of the foremost scholars in the world. Of course he'd see through the ludicrous notion of a psychic detective agency. This hadn't seemed important to Gus before—after all, he'd been operating under the assumption that Kitteredge had turned to Psych for help. Now that he knew the truth, he was doubly humiliated. He'd mistaken a form letter asking for cash for a personal plea for aid, and he'd been exposed as the kind of lowlife phony who preyed on the weak of mind.

"So you're a psychic?" Kitteredge said as Gus maneuvered him around a clutch of Danish teenagers and the mountain of backpacks surrounding them.

"Not me," Gus said. He yearned to tell Professor Kitteredge the truth, to explain that the psychic claims were just a marketing gimmick, that behind the false advertising there lay a great private detective agency. But he couldn't—and he wouldn't. "Shawn's the psychic. I'm just a detective."

"It's better that way," Shawn said. "You don't want two psychics in the same room. It's like having two homeless guys begging for change on the same corner. The spirits don't know which way to turn."

They reached the sidewalk. All they had to do now was get across the street to the parking lot and make their way to space forty-nine, where the Echo was waiting for them.

Except that wasn't exactly all they had to do, Gus realized as he risked a glance over his shoulder. They had to make it to space forty-nine before the two policemen caught up with them and beat them to the ground with their nightsticks. And the rate at which the cops were closing the distance between them made that prospect seem increasingly unlikely.

"You don't have to believe that Shawn's psychic, Professor," Gus said desperately, trying to get Kitteredge to increase his pace. "Just have a little faith that we're your friends and we're trying to get you out of the serious trouble you're in."

"At least that's what the spirits are saying," Shawn said.

To Gus' horror, Kitteredge did the worst thing he could possibly do. He stopped in the middle of the sidewalk.

"If you're psychic, then tell me one thing," Kitteredge said.

"When you were seventeen," Shawn said.

Gus could feel himself dying a little inside. The fact that Shawn was almost inevitably right, both about the question people—well, men anyway—would ask to test his prowess *and* about their age when they lost their virginity, did nothing to keep him from dreading this moment. Not every male human being thought exactly the same way, and someday Shawn would run into a man who had a different test to assess his powers. There was a good chance that Kitteredge would be the one.

Kitteredge didn't even seem to notice that Shawn had spoken. He was still in the process of formulating his question. "Do you use postcognition and psychometry, or are you simply a telepath?"

Gus was about to leap to Shawn's defense when he realized what the professor had asked. "You believe in psychic powers?" he said.

"It's not a question of whether I believe or not," Kitteredge said. "Either they exist or they don't, and my belief one way or the other can't have an impact on that at all. And if your partner does possess supernatural powers, I'd like to know which ones he claims."

Gus risked another glance back over his shoulder and saw that the officers were only a few steps back. "Unfortunately, teleportation isn't one of them," Gus said. "Can't we talk about this in the car?"

"I really need to know," Kitteredge said. "If he can truly commune with spirits, there might be a way out of this for me."

"My powers take all kinds of forms," Shawn said. "Pretty much at random. You never know how they're going to manifest themselves. It's kind of like the prize inside the Cracker Jack box."

"I've never heard of anything like that," Kitteredge said.

"Sometimes spirits talk to me," Shawn said. "Sometimes I get visions. Like right now."

"What are you seeing?" Kitteredge said.

"It's a stone room in a big castle," Shawn said. "There's a woman standing in the middle of the floor, holding out her arms as if begging for help. The rug she's standing on is woven with a pattern of leaves and flowers. And—"

Kitteredge was staring at Shawn. "That's the painting," he said. "You're seeing *The Defence of Guenevere*."

"Is that what it is?" Shawn said.

For the first time since the body had been unveiled, Kitteredge looked hopeful. "You see it in detail?"

"It's like *Avatar*," Shawn said. "I can visualize every tiny bit of the image in perfect detail. Which is good, because that way I don't have to pay attention to the crummy script."

Kitteredge turned to Gus excitedly. "Do you realize what this means?" he said. "There's hope. As long as Shawn can hold that image in his head, we have chance to decipher the clues in the painting and break this conspiracy wide open."

"Then what are we waiting for?" Gus said. "Let's get moving. And fast."

The street was still clogged with cars hopelessly gridlocked. All they had to do was weave their way through the stopped autos and they'd be free.

And better yet, Shawn had saved them. It wasn't so much that he'd restored Kitteredge's hope, although that was certainly a positive thing. Somehow he'd managed to memorize the entire painting in the one brief glance he'd gotten at it. They had a chance to solve this thing and clear Kitteredge's name.

Gus took a step off the curb, then realized he couldn't go any farther. There was a hand clutching his shoulder, and it wouldn't let him move.

Gus looked back and saw that the hand belonged to one of the cops. The other one had taken hold of Shawn.

"No one's moving anywhere," Gus' captor said. "Not until we've got a few answers."

Chapter Twenty-one

When he was little, Carlton Lassiter had, unlike any other child in the history of medicine, loved going to the doctor's office.

It wasn't the waiting room filled with toys and tattered copies of *Highlights for Children* that attracted him, although he did love studying the adventures of Goofus and Gallant. And it wasn't the lollipop or similar bribe that would be offered if he managed to make it through the appointment without bursting into hysterical screams.

What he loved about those visits was precisely what most children hated. The biting cold of the stethoscope against his chest. The invasion of personal privacy when the nurse jammed the thermometer under his tongue or any other place she might choose. And most of all the harsh jab and searing pain of the hypodermic needle.

It wasn't that little Carlton Lassiter had been a minimasochist. Even as he welcomed these insults he knew how unpleasant they were.

But he also understood instinctively what the other children couldn't begin to imagine: that the world existed in a constant state of war between the forces of order and those of chaos. And there was never any doubt in his mind which side he chose. Every indignity inflicted on him by the medical profession was actually a blow against chaos—in this case the chaos that existed to disrupt the order of the body's natural workings.

It was possible that in his preschool days Lassiter was not able to articulate this philosophy quite so precisely, and that he had come to the understanding only in his adult years. But the doctor's office was always a happy place for him, and the colder and less pleasant it was, the better it made him feel.

So even though Lassiter shared every police officer's distrust of department therapists, he felt a sense of security as he pulled his cruiser into the parking lot of the low white hacienda that housed Dr. Olivia McCormick's offices. Doctors meant order, and order was always good.

But as he stepped into the waiting room that sense of security began to slip away. Lassiter believed in changing primary care physicians every year so that he'd always have a new set of eyes to catch anything the last pair had missed, which meant he had plenty of experience with doctors' waiting rooms. And he knew what they were supposed to be like. First, there was the lighting. It needed to be the harshest fluorescent available, to render any trace of illness instantly apparent. The walls should be painted glossy white and the floor covered in matching linoleum or thin carpet to give the light plenty of hard surface to bounce off of. There should be chairs molded out of plastic that were impossible to sit in without slipping onto the floor unless you kept both feet planted at all times. Ideally the molded plastic should have cracked in several places to pinch his skin whenever he shifted position. And there should be a sliding glass window behind which sat a hatchet-faced receptionist whose only interest in life was making the patients wait as long as possible to give whatever germs they were carrying the chance to manifest themselves.

Dr. Olivia McCormick's waiting room was all wrong. It was furnished in the warmest of greens and browns. There were soft sofas against the walls, which were themselves covered with subtly colored fabrics. Blooming flowers trailed out of hanging pots, and soothing music played softly through hidden speakers. There wasn't even a receptionist to demand proof of insurance. Instead, as Lassiter came in—and even before he'd had the chance to step back outside and make sure he hadn't walked by mistake into one of the few remaining Good Earth restaurants that had escaped America's reconnection with sanity after the fern-bar-meets-sprouts craze of the midseventies—an inside door swung open and a kindergarten teacher leaned out.

"Detective Lassiter?" she said in a voice that promised juice and cookies. "Please come this way."

Although her graying ponytail and loose, flowing tie-dyed dress suggested an afternoon to be spent learning to tie his shoes followed by nap time, Lassiter realized that this was supposed to be the doctor.

Lassiter didn't have a problem with female doctors. Some of his favorite GPs had been women. But they had also been warriors in the battle against death, disease, and decay. They wore starched white lab coats and jammed their instruments in whichever orifice they chose with no consideration that they were working on anything resembling a sentient human being.

This one, he knew, was no warrior. Confronted with chaos, she'd invite it in for a chat and rap about what made it so disorganized.

But there was no way for him to leave now. The chief had made it very clear that he needed to talk to the department therapist before she'd clear him to go back to work on his case. And he would make any sacrifice if it would let him bring Professor Langston Kitteredge to justice.

Lassiter let McCormick lead him into her inner office and sit him down in a comfortable armchair upholstered in soft brown leather. She sat opposite him on what looked like an overgrown footstool.

"I want to let you know I'm here to help, Detective," she said in a voice so calming he could almost feel it smoothing his hair. "My only goal is to get you over your trauma as quickly as possible."

"In that case, consider yourself a success," Lassiter said. "Trauma was over before it began."

The smile she'd had fixed on her face since the first second he saw her wavered for a second, then came back. "No trauma at all?"

"No trauma, no drama, that's my mantra," he said. Actually, Lassiter had never had a mantra, considering such things foolish wastes of breath, but he figured it might move things along more quickly if he spoke in a language she could understand.

"But there was quite a bit of drama, wasn't there?" she said. "I read your report. An armed suspect used you as a hostage in order to escape custody, didn't he?"

Lassiter cursed under his breath. He'd known it was a mistake to write up the extended report the chief had asked for. Only for internal use, she'd said. Well now he saw exactly what "internal" meant—anyone who felt a right to meddle in the internal aspects of his life.

"All in a day's work," Lassiter said. "I admit, it was not a pleasant experience, and it left with me a bad taste in my mouth. But I also know how to get that taste out—a special kind of mouthwash called bringing the scumbag back in. So thanks for seeing me so quickly, but I'd better get back out on those mean streets."

He bounded out of his chair and headed for the door.

"We still have most of our hour left, Detective Lassiter," McCormick said in the same calm tone. "I would really appreciate it if you'd stay and talk about what happened this morning."

"Maybe we could do it another day," Lassiter said, one hand firmly clutching the doorknob. "Once the perp is in custody I'll have plenty of time to chat."

He turned the knob and opened the door. But before he could step through, he heard a voice from behind him. In certain superficial ways it sounded like Olivia McCormick. But underneath there was a tone of steel, like the indestructible armature under a Terminator's skin.

"If you walk out that door, you will never walk back into the Santa Barbara Police Department," the voice said.

Lassiter turned back and saw the skinless Terminator version of Olivia McCormick sitting where the kindergarten teacher had just been. She still had the same ponytail and hippie dress, but there was a light in her eyes that looked like it could kill from this distance.

"Excuse me?" Lassiter said.

"You are on medical leave pending my report," McCormick said. "Until I sign off on your condition, you are suspended. And believe me when I say this applies not only to the SBPD but to any law enforcement agency you can think of, including the school district crossing guard corps. So unless you want to spend the rest of your working life as a security guard in a shopping mall, you will sit down and start talking."

Lassiter's legs marched him back to the comfortable chair and dropped him in.

The steely light went out in McCormick's eyes and she leaned forward, once again the kindergarten teacher.

"So, Detective," she said gently, "let's talk about how you're feeling."

Chapter Twenty-two

It wasn't until he saw the windmill atop Pea Soup Andersen's in Buellton that Gus was able to pull his eyes away from the rearview mirror. All the way up the 101 he'd expected to see red and blue lights flashing there. He couldn't believe that the cops who'd stopped them outside the museum hadn't just allowed them to flee in order to see where they were going.

In fact, part of him believed the cops hadn't actually allowed them to go at all. It was quite possible that the three of them had been arrested and thrown into jail. That Gus had gone to trial and been convicted as an accessory after the fact and, under California's felony murder laws, had been sentenced to death. Now his body was lying in a cell on death row waiting for execution while his mind spun this elaborate fantasy of escape to keep from having to deal with the truth.

Gus checked the rearview mirror again, this time to make sure that the passenger back there was still Professor Kitteredge. If he'd turned into Mariah Carey, that would have confirmed the death row fantasy scenario. He breathed a heavy sigh of relief to see his old professor, his head resting against the window as he snored quietly.

Which meant the encounter with the police had been real, too. When Gus had turned around to meet the eyes of the officer whose hand was clutching his shoulder, he expected to see the steely stare of the hunter looking down at his prey before administering the kill shot. Instead, the eyes were twinkling, and the face was smiling.

"What can we do for you, Officer?" Shawn said cheerfully. It was a long-held theory of his that if you act like nothing is wrong convincingly enough, eventually the world will take your word for it. That long-held theory had never actually worked in practice, but he was eternally hopeful that this would change one day.

"Do you know how long I've been searching for you?" the officer said.

Gus checked the cop's eyeline. He wasn't looking at Kitteredge, who had turned his back and was now apparently fascinated by a seagull that was circling slowly above their heads. He was staring directly at Shawn and Gus.

"Umm," Gus said. "Us?"

"For weeks!" the officer said. "My best buddy is getting married next month, and I'm supposed to put together a bachelor party for him. But he's kind of a prude, so he doesn't want strippers or anything like that. I've been killing myself trying to figure out some kind of entertainment—and then I heard you talking about being psychics!"

"We're not really that kind of psychics," Gus said.

"Sure you aren't," the cop said. "That's why you're wearing tuxedos on a Sunday afternoon, because you're not on your way to a performance."

"But really we're—" Gus started, but Shawn shoved him out of the way and stepped forward.

"Available for weddings, bar mitzvahs, and bachelor

parties," Shawn said. "You have to excuse my partner—
he's afraid his mother will find out he went into show-
biz." He produced a card and handed it to the officer.
"You can reach our booking office at that number. And
just ignore the part where it says psychic detectives. It
was supposed to say psychic entertainers, but the printer
messed it up. We were going to have him redo it, but he
gave us a great price on ten thousand cards."

The officer slipped the card into his pocket without
looking at it. "You'll be hearing from me," he said. "And
say—if you happen to know any hot girls, we're not all
prudes like the groom."

Gus was searching for a way to answer that when
some sort of shoving match broke out toward the top of
the stairs. The cop gave Shawn a knowing wink, and he
and his partner headed up to deal with the disturbance
while the three of them ran to the Echo.

And that had been their last encounter with the police. They hadn't even seen a highway patrolman on the
freeway. Which didn't keep Gus from worrying for the
whole drive.

At least he was able to worry in peace and quiet.
Shawn had closed his eyes and gone to sleep as soon
as they hit the 101—less because he'd been up all night,
Gus suspected, than because his other option was to
spend the entire drive describing the missing painting in
excruciating detail. Kitteredge, too, quickly nodded off.

Which left Gus time to finally ponder the question
that would have occurred to him hours earlier if events
hadn't been moving so fast: What the hell were they
doing?

When he and Shawn had set off to find Professor
Kitteredge, it was to protect him from being discovered by a member of the force who might think him
so dangerous he needed to be shot before being ques-
tioned. But Gus had never really considered what they

were going to do once they'd found him—the task itself seemed so impossible that contemplating the next step felt like a waste of time. Then, once they had actually accomplished this, things started moving under their own impetus. Step by step, everything they did seemed to make sense at the time, and yet it didn't actually add up to a logical plan.

In fact, nothing that had happened since they first showed up at the museum made any logical sense. Unless he meant dream logic. Because while Professor Kitteredge's story about the search for King Arthur's magic sword was powerfully convincing when he'd laid it out, once Gus had had the chance to think it over, it began to sound ridiculous. They might as well be searching for Cinderella's glass slipper.

Gus knew there was only one right thing to do now. He should wake up Kitteredge and tell him he had no choice but to turn himself in. Then he'd pull into the Pea Soup parking lot and call Chief Vick to arrange the professor's surrender. That would fulfill his original intention, which was to make sure Kitteredge would be safe until he could prove his innocence.

But Gus wasn't sure he could do that from a jail cell. Not that he believed his old professor had anything to do with Filkins' murder. But as long as Kitteredge was unable or unwilling to provide an alibi, then this mysterious conspiracy was their only hope of finding the real killer. And no matter how absurd it sounded, someone had been able to steal that painting from under the noses of the cops. If not an all-powerful conspiracy, then who could have done it? And if the only clues to the Cabal lay hidden in that painting, and the only available copy of the picture was the one in Shawn's mind, then separating the professor from Shawn would present an insuperable obstacle to discovering the truth.

That meant finding a place to hide out until they

could break the conspiracy and catch the killer. For the moment that wouldn't be too hard. No one was looking for Gus and Shawn.

But they would be soon. As the manhunt broadened, it was unimaginable that one of the police officers they'd met today wouldn't realize they'd seen Kitteredge. And once they did, they'd remember who was with him. Unless it was that last cop. He wouldn't need to remember anything—Shawn had given him a card.

That gave them a few hours to find a hiding place and stock it with all the supplies they'd need until the case was over. Once their faces were on the news, they wouldn't dare show them in public.

Which brought him to one last option. Gus didn't think Professor Kitteredge would agree to turn himself in to the police. But if they stopped for lunch, there was no reason Gus couldn't excuse himself to use the rest room and call Chief Vick. He could even do it anonymously, just a loyal citizen doing his duty by reporting a sighting of a wanted fugitive. He wouldn't have to worry about Kitteredge being hurt, because the police would not risk using their guns in such a crowded public place. They'd simply surround the table and lead the professor away.

Gus hated himself for even allowing these thoughts to pass through his mind, but at the same time he knew that his self-loathing was completely irrational. Even though he was sure Professor Kitteredge was not a murderer, there was no denying he was a wanted felon. He had taken a police detective hostage and threatened to kill him with a knife that had already taken one life. Gus couldn't pretend that he was protecting a pure innocent; on one level the man was a criminal.

And it wasn't like he actually owed Kitteredge the kind of loyalty he gave his clients. After all, Kitteredge had never hired Psych. He hadn't even come to Gus for help in solving a crime, as Gus had thought when he'd felt compelled to rescue him from the police. No—he'd just sent Gus a form letter begging for a donation. If that obligated him to save the professor's hide, then he'd also have to rescue the Salvation Army, the Red Cross, the March of Dimes, and every other charity whose pleas clogged his mailbox. And at least the charities sent him personalized return address labels. They were unusable, true, because they had Ziggy on them, but they were a nice gesture. What had Professor Kitteredge ever done for him?

Gus could feel the steering wheel fighting to turn onto the off-ramp that would lead to the restaurant. It really was the correct thing to do. And he and Shawn could still help Kitteredge once he was safely in custody.

But he couldn't do it. He'd seen the fear in the professor's eyes when he realized he was being framed for Filkins' murder. He'd seen Kitteredge's passion when he thought he was about to discover the clues hidden in the painting. He knew that only Kitteredge had the knowledge to get himself out of this terrible situation, and he needed to be free to do it. Gus had to help.

Gus yanked the wheel back to the left, and the Echo zipped past the exit. He jabbed Shawn gently with his elbow until he woke up.

Shawn blinked a couple of times, then glanced out the window. "So I guess that's a no on lunch and betrayal," he said.

"You knew what I was thinking?" Gus said.

"Everyone always knows what you're thinking," Shawn said. "You should try to control your facial expressions a little more. Really, you might as well be blinking in Morse code."

"You were asleep," Gus said. "You couldn't have seen my face."

"I could hear your muscles twitching," Shawn said.

"Do you want me to walk you through your entire thought process?"

Having already sat through it once, Gus had no desire to hear it repeated back to him.

"I'd rather hear yours," Gus said.

"Okay," Shawn said. "I was wondering who would win if Julie Newmar's Cat Woman fought the Michelle Pfeiffer version. And that got me thinking about Halle Berry, and whose side she would fight on. Or would the other two team up against her because her movie destroyed the franchise forever. And then—"

"I mean about what we're going to do now," Gus said. "Since you were so avidly following my thoughts in your sleep, you must know how much trouble we're about to be in."

"Yes," Shawn said. "In fact I almost woke up to tell you to knock it off, since you were giving me bad dreams."

"Then do you have an idea where we should go?" Gus said.

"Well, we're heading north," Shawn said. "We could keep going until we cross the Canadian border."

"That's thousands of miles from here," Gus said. "Plus, Canada is a foreign country. We don't have our passports."

"Canada is a different country?" Shawn said. "That explains a lot."

"What it doesn't explain is what we're going to do now," Gus said.

"Maybe you'll allow me," Kitteredge said.

Gus glanced in the mirror and saw the professor stretching his neck as he shook off the unpleasant effects of sleeping in the backseat.

"Please," Gus said.

"We're going to see the one man in the whole world who can help us," Kitteredge said.

"If you're talking about the Wizard, I am not bringing him a broomstick," Shawn said.

Gus nudged Shawn with his elbow—harder this time.

"Who is this man, and where do we find him?" Gus said.

"To explain who he is could take a lifetime," Kitteredge said. "But in order to find him, all you have to do is take the next exit."

Chapter Twenty-three

"When the professor said that all we had to do to find this man was take the next exit, he neglected to mention that after we took the exit we'd have to drive around in circles for hours," Shawn said.

That wasn't precisely true. They had been driving in circles for only forty-five minutes. And it was entirely possible that for most of that time they had actually been going in the right direction. One low rolling hill covered in golden hay and ancient oak trees looked pretty much like every other one.

But now that they were stopped at a T-intersection where the narrow lane that had taken them up a steep hill ended with a choice of left or right turns unless he wanted to go cross-country up the rest of the slope, Gus had a chance to peer around and see a vast vineyard sprawling out at their left.

"I don't think we've been here before," Gus said. "That vineyard doesn't look familiar."

"Because last time we passed it, it was on the right side," Shawn said. "We're going back the way we came. Which might be all right, because I'm getting hungry, and pea soup is sounding mighty fine. Pea soup and everything that comes with it."

Gus knew that Shawn wasn't referring to the soup toppings Andersen's offered for an extra couple of bucks: the bacon bits and croutons and little pitcher of sherry that made a bowl into a meal. They needed to find Kitteredge's friend quickly, or Shawn would be ready to dump the professor under an oak tree and head back home. Gus turned around in his seat to see if Kitteredge seemed to know where they were going.

Judging from the smile on his face, he did. "It's a geographical anomaly that allows this valley to thrive," he said gazing out at the vineyard below them. "Because it runs east–west—the only east–west running valley in the Pacific coastal region, by the way—it gets the flow of offshore breezes and fog that temper the otherwise harsh climate and allow for the growth of the vines."

"That's fascinating, Professor," Gus said. "But this might not be the time for a discussion of the local landscape. Except for the part about where on it your friend lives."

Kitteredge waved away the objection with a sweep of his hand. "There's always time to gain a little knowledge," he said. "Because you never know when you're going to need it. For instance, in this case, you might think you don't need to know about the formation of these hills or the techniques the Chamokomee Indians used to hide from the Spanish settlers who were trying to drive them off their land."

"I might," Shawn agreed. "And so might every human being on Earth. Because we would all be busy noticing that the most important feature of these hills is the fact that the sun has gone behind one of them and it's about to start getting dark. Oh, and another one—that these hills don't have a single street light anywhere on them. So we're going to be driving around in the dark looking for a place we couldn't find in daylight."

If Kitteredge noticed the hostility in Shawn's voice, he didn't seem to be terribly concerned by it. "That's what I mean when I say you never know which bit of knowledge is the one you're going to need," he said. "In this case it turns out to be both of the ones I just mentioned."

In almost any situation, Gus would have happily listened to his old professor lecture on whichever subject struck his fancy. But he could feel Shawn's hunger-fueled frustration radiating from the passenger's seat, and it was hard not to share a little bit of it.

"I'd love to hear all about this," Gus said. "But maybe we could wait until we reach your friend's house."

"Or until Guns N' Roses finally gets around to putting out *Chinese Democracy*," Shawn said.

"They already did," Gus said. "A couple of years ago."

"Really?" Shawn said. "You'd think after all that waiting somebody would have noticed."

"I'm afraid this can't wait," Kitteredge said. "That's what I was trying to explain. You see, if we were in the Purisma Hills to the north, then we could expect to keep driving up until we reached the maximum elevation of seventeen hundred feet before we started down toward the Los Alamos Valley. If we'd gone south into the Santa Ynez Mountains we might climb as much as twenty-five hundred feet before we began to drop down toward the Pacific Ocean. But you see, we are in the Santa Rita Hills. And among the salient details of the geographical region, along with its ideal climate and soil conditions for viticulture, is the relatively lower elevations of its peaks: no more than nine hundred and fifty feet."

Shawn turned to Gus, real pain on his face. "He's going to be lecturing his executioner on the chemical composition of the lethal injection as the guy pushes the button," Shawn said. "And he'll probably still be talking after he's dead."

Gus cast a pleading look over his shoulder. "Please, Professor, we just need to know which way to turn."

"That's my point," Kitteredge said. "We are currently at an elevation of roughly the maximum for the area, as you can tell from a quick glance around."

"All I can tell from a quick glance around is that I can't see anything, because it's dark," Shawn said. "Maybe the professor wants to explain why that happens, too."

"Taking all this into consideration," Kitteredge said, ignoring Shawn as he might a student who had interrupted class without first raising his hand, "you might wonder why it is that there seems to be an enormous slope rising above us."

"I might," Shawn said. "Or I might just put my head under the front tire and beg Gus to hit the gas."

But Kitteredge's words had an impact on Gus. He stared at the looming shadow in front of them. "What about the Indians?" he said, ignoring the strangled cry from the seat next to him.

"The Chamokomee were a peaceful people, even more so than their close neighbors the Chumash, and they had neither the inclination nor the ability to fight the better armed and trained Spanish," Kitteredge said. "All they wanted was to live their lives undisturbed. So they became experts at hiding their settlements. They could construct elaborate structures to mask their villages from the outside world."

"That would explain why we haven't seen any Indians tonight," Shawn said. "That and the fact that it's too dark to see anything. But unless your friend is one of the Chappaquiddick guys—"

"Chamokomee," Gus said.

Since he didn't have a tire iron to beat Gus' head in with, Shawn ignored the correction. "—why do we care about any of this?"

"I think Gus knows," Kitteredge said.

Gus didn't. At least not quite. But there was something playing around the edges of his mind, and if he could just pull it forward he'd know which way to go.

"All we need to understand is whether we're supposed to turn left or right here," Shawn said. "So maybe the one piece of knowledge we need here is your friend's address."

Gus peered down the road to the left, then the right. And then he knew. He cast a glance back at Kitteredge, who was smiling and nodding his encouragement.

"Hold on," Gus said, taking his foot off the brake. "This may get a little bumpy."

Before Shawn could object, Gus pushed his foot down on the gas and the car lurched forward across the intersection. Straight across toward the unpaved hillside.

"What are you doing?" Shawn shouted.

"Getting us there," Gus said.

The Echo flew across the road, then shuddered and thudded as it left the pavement. Gus could feel the tires clutching for purchase on the loose dirt of the hillside. He could hear the engine screaming as it fought to haul the car's weight up the steep slope, saw the high weeds covering the windshield like a curtain. For a moment it seemed like the car was going to slide back into the intersection.

And then the tires grabbed asphalt. Flat asphalt. On both sides of them the hill angled up steeply, but they were on a level road.

"What happened?" Shawn said.

"I think it was the old Chamokomee trick," Gus said.

"An artificial hill to disguise the entry to my friend's property," Kitteredge said.

Shawn peered out the window to confirm this, but it

was too dark to see anything. "Why didn't you just say so?"

"I did," Kitteredge said. "Why didn't you listen?"

Gus glanced over at Shawn to make sure he wouldn't have to physically restrain him from leaping onto the backseat and throttling Kitteredge. But before Shawn could unbuckle his seat belt, the air was filled with the sound of an explosion. The windshield flew in their faces in a shower of glass pebbles.

"Somebody's shooting at us!" Shawn shouted. "Get out of here!"

Gus hadn't actually needed the instruction. He stomped on the brake, threw the gearshift into reverse, and jammed down on the gas.

But before he got more than a foot, there were two quick shots, and the front tires exploded out from under them. The Echo landed hard on the rims and dug divots in the asphalt.

Shawn and Gus dived for their door handles. Gus made it out first and yanked open the back door, pulling Kitteredge out of his seat as Shawn rushed around the car to join them.

"Now what?" Gus said.

"We run," Shawn said.

"Not a bad idea," a voice from out of the darkness said. "Would have been better if you'd thought of it before."

A figure stepped into the beam of the Echo's headlights. At first all Gus could make out was the double-barreled shotgun pointed directly at them. But once that had registered, he was able to make out some of the details of the man carrying it. And he wished he hadn't.

The shotgun's owner seemed to be no more than four feet tall. But Gus realized that was only because he was so hunched over from the hump on his back. His face was as gnarled and twisted as his body, with a jagged scar that started at his hairline and zigged across his face, taking out his left eye.

"Would have been much better if you'd thought of it before," the hunchback said. "Could have saved me some shells that way."

Chapter Twenty-four

This shouldn't be so hard.

After all, this wouldn't be the first time Lassiter had asked Shawn and Gus for help. When he'd been framed for murdering a suspect in his cell and suspended during the investigation, the Psych boys had stepped in and found the real killer. And when Lassiter's surrogate father, the sheriff of old Sonora, had been in trouble, he hadn't hesitated to ask them to assess and correct the situation.

But this was different. Shawn and Gus had seen him at the lowest point in his career, probably his life. They had seen him helpless, humiliated, held hostage at knifepoint. And not by some meth-crazed biker with arms like sewer pipes, but by a professor of art history. Granted, the professor was the size and shape of a grizzly bear, but that was no excuse. Now he was contemplating crawling to them for help.

Lassiter let his department Impala idle while he struggled to decide whether he should turn the corner and pull up to the Psych headquarters. At least Chief Vick had let him keep the car pending the official Internal Affairs review.

But the car was all she'd left him. When he returned from his rap session with that hippie quack, Chief Vick had already gotten a report from her. Of course it was a pack of nonsense. *Detective Lassiter is uncooperative*, it said. *He refuses to acknowledge the seriousness of the incident or the emotional impact it's had on him. Some level of denial is to be expected in this sort of situation, but Detective Lassiter's unwillingness even to begin to process his reaction to the event is so total it tends toward the psychotic.* And on and on.

In other words, a load of hogwash. Clearly this was a woman who hated strong men. She couldn't stand the thought that some people didn't allow themselves to be ruled by their emotions like little children. And she refused to let herself believe that he could have gone through that ordeal and come out stronger for it. In her world, people who had a bad experience had to curl up and weep for a month just to get over it. If she accepted the fact that he had emerged psychologically unscathed, it would destroy her entire worldview. She'd need to close down her practice and take up a career she was better suited for, like teaching kindergarten or serving at soup kitchens.

But Chief Vick didn't see it that way. At least she couldn't admit she did. Lassiter knew that the chief saw the world the same way he did—the same way any good cop would. She must have wanted to burst out in peals of derisive laughter when that quack tried to insist there was something bad about the fact that he wouldn't give in to his emotions.

But Karen Vick hadn't gotten to be chief without understanding how the system worked. And she must have had some kind of inside knowledge about McCormack's ties to the upper echelons of the city's bureaucracy. No matter what her personal feelings about this psychiatric witch hunt might be, she knew she had to pretend to take the shrink seriously. If McCormack demanded that

Vick place her lead detective on suspension until she signed off on his mental health, the chief would understand that this battle needed to be fought on another level. Because while it wasn't true that you can't fight city hall, you had to be smart to do it well. She would surrender this battle to win the war.

That's why he didn't argue when the chief asked for his badge and gun. Well, he didn't argue much. Definitely not more than half an hour. And the instant she informed him that he would be fired on the spot if he didn't hand them over and accept his suspension immediately, he did as she asked. It was all a bit of departmental kabuki. He'd fought for his rights, and she could say she had brought the full power of her office to bear on the recalcitrant detective.

The last words she'd said to him as he left the police station were to get help, get better, and come back quickly. And that's why he was coming to Psych.

Surely, this must have been what she meant when she told him to get help. For some reason, Chief Vick had a bizarre faith in Shawn Spencer's abilities; when there was a problem she thought (inevitably mistakenly) that the police couldn't solve on their own, she reached out to the Psych boys. Where else would she have wanted him to go?

But it wasn't easy for him. Asking for any kind of assistance came hard to Lassiter men. His grandfather had settled in Santa Barbara only because he'd gotten lost on the road from Boston to Chicago and refused to ask for directions. And begging for help from a couple of guys with a work ethic that would get them fired from a comic book store was particularly painful. He longed to slam the car into drive and head out to search for Kitteredge on his own.

Instead, as he always did when faced with a difficult decision, he made a mental list of pros and cons.

The negative list was filling up fast. To start with,

there was nothing Shawn and Gus could do that would clear his name. He hadn't been framed this time; he had allowed himself to be taken hostage inside his own police station. There wasn't a bizarre set of circumstances that needed to be exposed; tragically, everything had been visible to the world all along. And since the Psych boys had been present to see his humiliation, there was a strong possibility that they'd simply start laughing the instant he walked through their door.

He knew he could keep filling up the cons all day long—or all night long, since the sun was sinking quickly into the ocean. There were so many ways in which Lassiter had been humiliated, and there were a thousand variations still to be played out. Anything he did now would just make it all worse. Best to turn the car around, drive home, and stay in bed until the official investigation was over.

Especially since the list in the other column was so damn short. One item. Six words.

I'm going to get that bastard.

It was that simple: Lassiter wanted him. Wanted to see him behind bars, where he belonged. He wanted to be the man who put him there. And he knew Chief Vick wanted the same thing. Why else would she have sent him here?

That was that, then. He was going to do it. Before he could second-guess himself, he put the car into drive, flipped on the turn indicator, and pulled around the corner and up to the bungalow that served as Psych's headquarters.

But before he turned off the ignition he saw that something was wrong. The bungalow's lights were all ablaze, and its front door was partially open. And it clearly hadn't been opened by its owner. The glass half of the door had been smashed in.

Lassiter reached instinctively for his gun and cursed when he remembered that it was locked in the chief's

desk. How was he supposed to roust evildoers if he was
unarmed? What had Chief Vick been thinking?

He didn't have a gun and he didn't have a badge, but
Lassiter still had the two most important tools in his
crime-fighting skill set—his intelligence and his training.
And what they were telling him was that this was his
moment. He couldn't guarantee that Kitteredge was inside the bungalow. He was unable to swear that the professor had come back to finish off two of the witnesses
to his crime spree. But he could make an educated assumption. And his intelligence and training would back
him up.

Silently opening the car door, Lassiter crept to the
front of the bungalow and positioned himself at the side
of the doorway. He listened intently, and after a moment
he heard a rustle from inside.

That was Kitteredge. It had to be. All Lassiter had
to do was step through this door and take him down. It
would all be over.

Except that it wouldn't, he realized. He was pretty
sure he could take down the man-bear in a fair fight, but
what then? Without his badge, he had no power to make
an arrest. And what he wanted more than anything was
to see Kitteredge back in the custody of the Santa Barbara Police Department. If Lassiter launched an attack
at him without the authority of the shield, he might actually aid in the professor's defense once some commie
lawyer started screaming about brutality.

Lassiter wanted his man, but even more he wanted to
see him taken down the right way. He couldn't do this
on his own. He pulled out his cell phone and punched in
the first number on his auto-dial. He didn't know how
many friends he had on the force right now, but he was
certain that no matter what had happened his partner
would still be loyal to him.

Inside the bungalow, someone started singing. For
a moment Lassiter wondered why Kitteredge would

take this moment to belt out the chorus to "Billy, Don't Be a Hero." As soon as the thought crossed his mind he realized that the voice didn't belong to the professor but to Bo Donaldson. And he knew why Bo was singing.

It was his special ring tone on Juliet O'Hara's phone.

The song stopped, and Lassiter heard O'Hara's voice in his ear. "Carlton?"

"I'm at the door, Detective," Lassiter said and disconnected the call.

He moved in front of the open door as she emerged from the bungalow's back room, holstering her phone, her gun in her other hand.

"What are you doing here, Carlton?" O'Hara said as she reached the doorway. "If the chief knew . . ."

"The chief sent me here," he said.

She gave him a confused look. "You've been reinstated?"

"Not officially," Lassiter said. "But Chief Vick must have known my help would be appreciated. I'm only sorry I got here too late."

O'Hara studied him carefully, trying to decide if the truth he was telling matched up to objective reality. "Too late for what?"

"To protect Spencer and Guster." He pointed at the shattered glass where Kitteredge had clearly broken in. "I'd guess that the mad professor came after them. They thought they'd be safe if they locked the door and cowered in the back, but he smashed his way in and took them hostage. Or is it worse than that?" He tried to peer over her shoulder. "Did he leave their battered bodies bleeding in the back room?"

O'Hara's face hardened and she stepped up to block his view. "Kitteredge didn't break in, Carlton," she said.

"Then who did?" he said.

"I did," she said. "With the authority of a court order signed by Judge Haskin."

Lassiter tried to make sense of what she was telling him. But none of the pieces fit together. "Why?"

"Because Shawn and Gus were seen helping Langston Kitteredge escape," O'Hara said. "They're wanted for aiding and abetting a fugitive, as well as being the chief suspects in the theft of *The Defence of Guenevere* from the museum. And every police officer in Southern California is looking for them."

Chapter Twenty-five

"**A** hunchback?" Shawn whispered furiously to Gus. "We're about to be gunned down by a homicidal hunchback in a mysterious valley? When did we turn into the Hardy Boys?"

"We're not the Hardy Boys," Gus said, wishing his last words might be something more inspiring to future generations.

"You're right," Shawn said. "The Hardy Boys had a couple of chums. All we've got is *him*."

Gus reflexively glanced over at the *him* in question. But Professor Kitteredge wasn't on the ground where Gus had set him. He was on his feet, walking toward the armed man with his hands raised high.

"Not a step further," the hunchback growled.

"Not even a box step?" Kitteredge said. He stopped walking forward and demonstrated the move. "How about a grapevine? It certainly seems appropriate here."

Gus covered his eyes and waited for the rain of Professor Kitteredge's body parts that would follow the inevitable gunshot. But when no sound came, he peeled his hands away from his face.

The hunchback had lowered the shotgun. And while

Gus would not claim an ability to read expressions on that twisted face, he thought he saw something like a smile there.

"Professor Kitteredge?" he said, taking a step forward through the headlight beams.

"It's me, Malko," the professor said. "Now let's see a couple of those moves."

To Gus' astonishment, the hunchback held his gun up like a dance partner and with surprising grace executed a perfect box step. "Haven't forgotten a thing you taught me," he said when he finished.

"A dancing hunchback," Shawn said. "We're leaving the Hardy Boys and joining up with Mel Brooks."

"Malko, let me introduce you to a couple of friends," Kitteredge said, turning back toward the car. "Gus, Shawn, come over here."

Shawn and Gus exchanged a look, then stepped away from the car and toward the other two. Kitteredge waved them closer. Malko narrowed his one good eye and stared at them.

"Are these the two that helped you get away from the police?" he said. "When I heard they were last seen wearing tuxedoes, I thought the reporters were joking."

Gus felt his heart pounding. So the cops were after them now. He couldn't be surprised. He knew it would happen sooner or later. But he'd hoped that they would have time to find the real killer before they actually became wanted fugitives.

"We've been on the news?" Kitteredge said.

"You *are* the news," Malko said. "We were expecting you. Come."

Malko turned and started to walk away. Kitteredge followed.

"Wait a minute," Shawn said loudly. "You were expecting us?"

Malko stopped and glared back at him. "Yes."

"You shot at us," Shawn said.

Malko shook his head wearily. "Yes."

"What would you have done if you hadn't been expecting us?" Shawn said.

"Aimed better." Malko started to walk again.

"What do we do now?" Gus said.

"We know what's behind the curtain," Shawn said. "A long, dark walk back to Buellton, where half the police in the state will be looking for us. So we might as well go with what's in the box. And hope."

"Hope for what?" Gus said.

Up ahead, Malko and Kitteredge were about to disappear out of the range of the headlights.

"Hope that whatever is in the box isn't us."

Chapter Twenty-six

If Malko had led them to a hidden Chamokomee tee-pee village where all ten thousand tribe members had been hiding for three hundred years, Gus wouldn't have been surprised. At this point in the evening he was willing to accept anything as long as it didn't start firing shotguns at him again.

But the hunchback merely led them to a battered golf cart filled with gardening equipment. He threw the tools on the ground and told the three guests to get in. Then he took off at what felt like fifty miles an hour until they reached a high stone wall. He turned the cart and followed the wall.

Gus wanted to ask Malko where he was taking them, but the hunchback's attention was totally focused on Kitteredge, who was involved in a lengthy disquisition on the etymology of the word "foxtrot"—it was, apparently, commonly believed to be named after the vaudeville performer Harry Fox, but Kitteredge had come across a document suggesting that an earlier practitioner had actually coined the name for what he saw as vulpine movements—and when Gus tried to interrupt, Malko simply ignored him.

"There is no way this is going to end well," Shawn said.

"Since when are you so concerned about our safety?" Gus said.

"Being shot at does that to me," Shawn said. "I'm funny that way."

"We've been shot at before and you've never complained," Gus said.

"There's a good reason for that," Shawn said.

"What's that?"

"Those were cases I chose," Shawn said. "And I would never get us killed."

Until this moment, Gus had been filled with competing feelings. He was hungry, he was tired, he was in pain where his bruises from the car's rough stop were being jostled by the golf cart's rougher ride, and he was scared that he was going to spend the rest of his life in jail or shot down like Warren Beatty at the end of *Bonnie and Clyde*. But now all those emotions were swept from his mind by a tidal wave of self-righteous anger.

"I knew it!" Gus said. "You've been a complete pain all day. Complaining about the kind of stuff you do all the time."

"I haven't been complaining," Shawn said. "I've been observing."

"You observe with your eyes, not your mouth," Gus said.

"That's right," Shawn said. "What I do with my mouth is eat. And thanks to you, we haven't been able to do that, either."

Gus started to respond, then snapped his mouth shut. There was no point in taking this conversation any further. Shawn had been sulking ever since Gus told him they weren't going to the C. Thomas Howell Film Festival. But it wasn't because he'd missed his chance to see *The Thirst: Blood War* on the big screen. It was because Gus had taken the lead on this case, and Shawn couldn't stand taking second position to anyone, even his partner and best friend.

Gus and Shawn rode in silence as the cart made its way along the wall. Finally, after what felt like hours but was probably less than two minutes, they reached an opening and turned onto a flagstoned driveway into a courtyard.

At least Gus assumed it was a courtyard, although the night was so dark he couldn't see the building that enclosed it. But as the cart stopped, strings of overhead lights flickered on, bathing the area in a warm yellow glow.

It was as if they had been transported to Tuscany. Rough stone walls broken by shuttered windows loomed above them, the harshness of the building materials softened by blooming wisteria vines that drooped from every surface.

The illusion was only enhanced by the man who stepped through a large glass door into the courtyard. His face gnarled with age and cloaked in a long white beard and framed by a cascade of white hair, he looked like he had stepped out of a painting by Rembrandt. Of course Rembrandt was Dutch, not Italian, and Gus had no idea whether the painter had ever set foot in Tuscany, but then there was a reason he'd failed Professor Kitteredge's class all those years earlier.

The old man raised a hand in greeting. "I had hoped you'd come to me, Langston," he said in a voice filled with warmth.

"If only it were under happier circumstances." Kitteredge strode across the courtyard and embraced the man in a hug so hard Gus expected to hear bones snapping. "I hate the thought that I might bring the police to your doorstep."

"We'll worry about that if it happens," the old man said.

"I'm afraid it's not going to be if—it's going to be

when," Kitteredge said. "Someone's going to figure out before long that you're my friend."

"Then we have no time to waste," the old man said.

"We have a little time to waste," Shawn said. "The police are going to have to find their way in here. So maybe you can take a few seconds to tell us who you are."

Kitteredge glanced back at him as if he'd forgotten that Shawn and Gus had come along for the ride. The old man looked puzzled.

"They came in the back way," Malko said.

"Ah," the old man said. "That would explain why you arrived later than I expected. I'm afraid that when the police arrive they will simply drive through the front gate and right up to the house."

"The front gate." Shawn glared at Gus, then at Kitteredge. "Wonder why we never thought of that."

"But there is certainly time for introductions," the old man said. "I am Flaxman Low. This is my home." He waved around the courtyard. "And of course, as long as you choose to stay, it is your home as well."

"That's too generous of you, Flaxman," Kitteredge said.

"Not at all," Low said. "Perhaps you'd like to introduce me to your friends—although I feel I already know them, thanks to the TV news."

Kitteredge motioned for Shawn and Gus to join him. "This," he said, "is an old student of mine, Burton Guster."

"That explains why he was willing to risk his life and freedom to help you," Low said. "I've never met a student of yours who wasn't."

Kitteredge waved the compliment away and gestured to Shawn. "And this," he said, "oh, Flaxman; you will not believe it. This is *The Defence of Guenevere*."

Chapter Twenty-seven

"**H**e's the killer."

Gus seriously considered ignoring Shawn's declaration. All he wanted was a few minutes to close his eyes before dinner. And the room the hunchback had taken them to seemed to want the same thing. Its two queen beds were huge and firm and covered with deep down comforters. Its shutters were open, and the soothing sound of a fountain wafted through the soft air. And it was so large that Shawn's voice seemed to be coming from miles away.

Still, the accusation was so outrageous that some kind of response seemed obligatory. Gus cracked open one eye. "The old guy?"

"Who else?" Shawn said.

"What do you mean who else?" Gus said. "It could have been anyone else. There are billions of people in this world, and the only ones we know for sure didn't do it are you and me."

"That's where you're wrong, my friend," Shawn said. "Well, it's the place where you are most currently wrong. If we wanted to go back through the catalog of all the places you've been wrong, we'd have to start with Mrs.

Peyser's first-grade class, where you thought you were putting your hand over your heart and pledging your achievements to the flag. But this is the big one."

"I still think it would be better to pledge my achievements than just my allegiance," Gus said. "That way I'm actually doing something for my country. And I don't see how I'm wrong here."

"Look back on everything that's happened on this case so far," Shawn said. "Who have we dealt with? Jules and Lassie, of course, but I think we can rule them out pretty safely. That guy from the museum."

"Hugh Ralston, the executive director," Gus said.

"Right," Shawn said. "But he's pretty boring. I mean, he works in a museum. He's going to start killing people? Not on my watch. Who else does that leave? A bunch of uniformed cops, not one of whom we met more than once. And that trucker guy with the crazy wife who wanted us to wait on them. I don't think so."

Gus wanted to keep his head comfortably nestled among the down pillows. But the insanity of what Shawn was saying lifted him up like a possessed teenager levitating for the exorcist. "Those are just the people we've encountered," Gus said. "Why does the killer have to be someone we've met before?"

"There are rules to this kind of thing," Shawn said.

"You don't believe in following rules," Gus said.

"I told you, I don't believe in man-made rules," Shawn said. "But even I can't ignore the immutable rules of the universe."

"And which rule would this be?" Gus said. "Because I really don't think that the key to this mystery lies in how many French fries I give you."

"Think about it," Shawn said. "Think back on all our cases. Has the killer ever turned out to be someone we hadn't met in the course of the investigation?"

Gus cast his mind back over the hundreds of crimes they'd investigated. "What about that serial killer, Mr.

Yang?" he said. "Not only hadn't you met Yang earlier in the case—you didn't even know she was a female."

"Really?" Shawn said. "That's the best you can come up with? A serial killer I was in phone contact with for ages before she revealed herself? Of course we'd met. Just not face to face."

Gus wasn't sure that counted, but he decided to let it go. There had to be another example. He just couldn't think of one. "That doesn't mean it couldn't happen," he said finally.

"Think of it this way," Shawn said. "Let's say you're watching Scooby-Doo—and I've seen you, so don't bother denying it. Anyway, the gang tracks down the ghost that's been haunting the old circus, they set a trap, and bang! They grab him and pull off his mask. Who's under there? Well, it's the developer who wants to put a shopping mall on the fairgrounds, of course. But how would you feel if they whipped off the mask and underneath was a guy you'd never seen before?"

"This is not a Scooby-Doo episode," Gus said.

"Granted, our current adventure may lack the mastery and grace of classic stories like 'Hassle in the Castle' or 'Foul Play in Funland,'" Shawn said. "But as I've always said, aim high."

Had it not seemed so far off the point, Gus might have noted that the only time Shawn had ever told anyone to aim high was in the last minutes of a seventh-grade dodgeball game when he was unsuccessfully imploring Malachi Rabinowitz to throw the ball over, rather than at, his face.

"You can't accuse this man of being a killer just because no one else we've met has seemed interesting enough," Gus said.

"That's far from the only evidence I have," Shawn said.

"You're half right," Gus said. "It certainly is far from evidence. What else do you have?"

Shawn waved his arms around the room. "How about this secret villain's lair hidden behind a fake mountain?"

"Apparently it's only secret if you can't find the front gate," Gus said. "I don't think SPECTRE's volcano had a street address."

"Or this level of guest amenities." Shawn checked out the grooming supplies that sat on a low table under a mirror. There was a matched set of razor, bowl, and shaving brush, all elegantly carved out of ivory. "Somehow I doubt this guy keeps the TV remote on a chain so people can't walk off with it. And I looked in the robes. There's no note about how we can buy one at the front desk but if we steal it we'll get charged ninety-five thousand dollars."

"Yes, he's rich and he's generous," Gus said. "That must mean he's a murderer."

"What about his name?" Shawn said. He rapped his fingers against a framed diploma that hung on the wall, proclaiming in Latin to any guest who cared that their host had a doctorate in art history from Harvard University. Then he took a second look at it, as if noticing something interesting, before turning back to Gus. "Who names their kid Flaxman Low if they don't want him to grow up to be some kind of villain? And then there's his henchman."

"You mean his servant?"

"Whatever," Shawn said. "He's got a one-eyed, gun-wielding hunchback working for him. Apparently hiring an albino with barbed wire wrapped around his midsection was too subtle for the guy. Either that or he was afraid of the advocacy groups. After every action movie in the eighties had an albino villain, they started to get a little testy."

"If hiring the handicapped makes you a villain, then we should be focusing our investigation on the March of Dimes," Gus said.

"I would, but we haven't met any of them yet, either," Shawn said. "And that brings us back to Flaxman Low, murderer."

"You keep saying that, but you don't have any evidence," Gus insisted.

Shawn stared at him. "Haven't you been listening to a word I've said?"

"All of them," Gus said. "With a mounting sense of dread that you've gone insane."

Shawn crossed the room in a few large strides, and for a moment Gus thought he was going to attack him physically.

"Look around you," he said. "The hair, the lair, the henchman. It even fits structurally."

"What do you mean 'structurally'?"

"Look at the events of the last day or so," Shawn said. "We were there at the crime scene, we had rising tension as Kitteredge was interrogated, and then it was chase, chase, chase," he said. "Now it's twenty-four hours later, and we've got a break from the tension. We're in a safe place with a good friend. According to every movie Alfred Hitchcock ever made, this friend has to be a bad guy."

"I thought we were in a Hardy Boys book," Gus said.

"It seemed like it at the time, but apparently we've been upgraded," Shawn said. "Now we're being lured to our doom by Eva Marie Saint. Except that Eva Marie was a lot prettier and wore her hair shorter."

"Does that inflamed brain of yours have any idea of why he murdered Filkins?"

"No, but if we pay attention in the next few minutes, we may be able to put it together," Shawn said.

"How do you figure that?" Gus said, wishing he had never lifted his head from the pillows. At least that was one thing that could be easily remedied. He lay back down and closed his eyes.

Then he heard the sound of a throat being cleared. And judging from the deep growling noise that came from the throat, it didn't belong to Shawn. Gus sat up and saw the hunchback standing in the doorway.

"Dinner is served," Malko said.

"That's how," Shawn said.

Chapter Twenty-eight

As he'd said, Flaxman Low had been expecting Kit-teredge and his two friends. That's why he had arranged for dinner to be served whenever they arrived.

Judging by the amount of food spread out on the long granite table, he must have been expecting his old friend to show up with at least a platoon. Or maybe he was planning to feed all the law enforcement personnel who would no doubt start to arrive once someone figured out the connection between the men. There were three roast chickens, their skins perfectly browned, each resting on beds of crispy potatoes. There was a platter of steaks so tender they almost split apart under a harsh gaze. In case there were any Catholics at the table and they were still working on this meal by the time Friday rolled around, there was a whole barbecued salmon stuffed with herbs. There were bowls of vegetables prepared in ways that made them irresistible even to people who hated vegetables.

And that was just the entrees. The kitchen door had swung open when Shawn and Gus came into the dining room, and Gus had caught a quick glimpse of the dessert array that was being prepared. He didn't have a time to compile a list of the delights that were being laid out for them because he was so completely distracted by the centerpiece—a pineapple that had been hollowed out and transformed into a chocolate fountain.

Which might have explained why Shawn's accusations against their host brought so little reaction from Low or Kitteredge. Shawn was so hungry he started stuffing food into his mouth even before he was completely settled in his chair, and whatever he said for the next twenty minutes was completely incomprehensible, even to Gus. And he wasn't alone. For once, even Langston Kitteredge had found something other than lecturing to use his mouth for.

When Shawn's consumption had slowed down to the pace of the runner-up in a hot-dog-eating contest, Gus braced himself for the worst. But the enormous meal had had a mellowing effect on Shawn, and his prosecutorial zeal subsided to what could be mistaken for ordinary curiosity.

That curiosity extended to both sides of the table. Low had spent most of the meal picking at his food while he watched Shawn and Gus closely. When Malko came through to clear away the dinner plates, it was their host who asked the first question.

"While the two of you were freshening up, I had a chance to talk to Langston about you," he said. "I don't believe I've ever met a psychic before."

"You'd be surprised," Shawn said. "We look just like everybody else. Well, not *just* like. We've got that healthy psychic glow that makes us irresistibly attractive to all who see us. But aside from that, we're just plain folks."

"Aside from that and your extraordinary talents," Kitteredge corrected him.

Shawn shrugged modestly.

"I don't suppose," Low said, "I could ask you for a demonstration of your prowess."

Normally, Gus would have been delighted at the opportunity for Shawn to show off his psychic bona fides. Whatever he might come up with, Gus knew it would be impressive.

But after their conversation in the bedroom, Gus was afraid that Shawn's demonstration might be a little too impressive. He'd speak to a demon or read an aura or commune with the departed spirit of one of the roast chickens, and what he'd come back with would be an accusation of murder against Flaxman Low.

Gus couldn't let that happen. Not only because it was an unspeakable breach of manners to call your host a murderer before dessert was served, but also because they were all alone on his massive property and nobody knew they were there. If, by some insane chance, Shawn was right and Low was behind the killing, it wouldn't take a lot of work to do away with them in such a way that no one would ever know.

And if Shawn was wrong, it could be even worse. Because if Flaxman Low wasn't the killer, then he might be their only chance at getting through a couple of decades without bars in front of them. If Shawn were to alienate him with an accusation of murder, that chance might disappear.

"I'd be happy to," Shawn began. Gus kicked him in the ankle as hard as he could.

"But there are better uses of our time right now," Gus said as Shawn's mouth was too busy forming into an O of pain to utter the rest of his sentence.

"Better than an exploration of mysteries that have fascinated mankind through the ages?" Low said.

"It's one thing to communicate with the afterlife," Gus said. "But right now our top priority has to be keeping Professor Kitteredge from doing that in person. We need to figure out who killed Clay Filkins and how we're going to prove it."

Flaxman Low nodded thoughtfully. "It had occurred to me that the two tasks might be collapsed into one."

"I think that could be arranged," Shawn said. "Why don't we start with the killer's identity first?"

Once again, Gus' foot made contact with the same spot on Shawn's ankle with unerring accuracy.

"Which of course we can't possibly know," Gus said. "Because it's locked in that painting. And we haven't had a chance to talk about that yet."

At the mention of the painting, Low and Kitteredge exchanged a look that could almost have been called wistful. "Ah, Langston, I can't tell you how much I envy even your brief glance at that masterpiece," Low said. "Even though it has come at such a cost."

"No more than Adam and Eve paid for the gift of knowledge," Kitteredge said. "And I'm sure they would have made the same choice if given the opportunity to do it all over again."

"Yes, this certainly is fascinating," Shawn said. "But maybe we should move on to another subject. Like the identity of the real killer."

Gus kicked out again, but this time his foot sent Shawn's chair skittering across the floor. He looked up to see that Shawn was standing and pressing his fingers to his temple in the way he used to signify the arrival of a vision from the beyond.

"And that identity is obvious to anyone who has ever read a book or seen a movie," Shawn said. "Although the continuing acceptance of Dan Brown's plotting skills by the worldwide reading audience strongly suggests that there are plenty of people who don't fall into that category."

"Shawn, don't," Gus begged.

"Let him speak," Low said. "I am extremely curious about what he's going to say next."

But as adjectives go, "curious" didn't seem strong enough to describe Flaxman Low's level of interest in the subject. His voice had changed from the friendly, avuncular quality it had held into one of dark menace.

Gus cast a quick glance at Shawn to see if he had noticed the sudden change of tone in the room. Apparently he had.

"Of course, the simple fact that we could make an accusation based on experience with books and movies simply shows that truth is more complicated than fiction," Shawn said.

Flaxman Low rose to his feet. Gus knew what was going to happen next. He was going to thrust both arms straight up in the air and summon a storm. Then, as thunder and lighting crashed on the roof, he would send energy bolts out of his fingers and hurl them across the dining room.

Of course, that too was drawn from Gus' experience with books and movies. What Low actually did next was not nearly so dramatic—although to Gus it had essentially the same impact.

"The real killer's identity is known to everyone here," he said. "It is Shawn Spencer."

Chapter Twenty-nine

For a moment no one moved. Then Kitteredge pushed himself away from the table.

"Flaxman, don't be ridiculous," the professor said. "These two saved me on multiple occasions."

"Saved you from being recaptured by the police," Low said, his fiery eyes never leaving Shawn and Gus. "When you might have alerted law enforcement to the real nature of the threat we face."

"But they brought me to you," Kitteredge protested.

"To find out who else knew about the Cabal," Low said. "And then they could shut down all threats at once."

Gus managed to pull his eyes away from Low to sneak a look at Shawn, hoping to see the cocky smile he wore when he knew he was in charge of a situation everyone else thought was lost. What he saw made him wish he'd never turned away. Shawn wasn't even looking at Low. He was staring past his shoulder, toward the kitchen. Gus knew he didn't want to know what Shawn was looking at, but his neck refused to follow his explicit instructions. It swiveled until Gus' gaze matched Shawn's.

The hunchback was standing in the kitchen doorway, the shotgun leveled at them.

"How do you even know who they are?" Low said.

"He sent me that letter," Gus said. He turned to Kitteredge. "I showed it to you."

"You sent someone a letter," Low said to Kitteredge. "Do you have any evidence that this man was the intended recipient? Do you even remember a student named Burton Guster?"

Yes, Gus implored Kitteredge silently. *Think back of all those times we had together.*

"I've had so many students over the years," Kitteredge said warily. "The doctoral candidates I get to know very well. But the undergrads come and go so quickly, a hundred at a time. I'm lucky if I ever match a name to a face."

Gus felt his heart break a little, although he suspected the sensation was really just a preview of the effect Malko's shotgun was about to have on him.

"And their story about how they came to help you?" Low said. "They got a fund-raising form letter and mistook it for a personal cry of distress? Could you imagine anything more ridiculous?"

Gus saw that this last question seemed to be having an effect on Kitteredge, who sank slowly into his chair.

"I can't believe it," the professor said, although his voice didn't hold a fraction of the conviction his words were intended to convey.

"You've been set up, Langston," Low said. "From the very beginning, this entire charade has had one purpose—for the members of the conspiracy to find everyone who knows about them and wipe us out."

"Could I have been so mistaken?" Kitteredge said in a tone of utter weariness. "Could I have been such a fool?"

"It's not true!" Gus said. "All we ever wanted to do was help."

"Of that, I'm sure," Low said. "But that still leaves us with one question: You wanted to help whom? Fortunately my man Malko is extremely skilled at ascertaining the truth in this kind of situation."

From across the room Malko gave Gus a twisted leer that suggested he not only was talented at this part of his job but was going to take great pleasure in it. Gus tried to fight off the images of what kind of tortures the hunchback could come up with. And what his mangled body would look like before his interrogator would believe that he didn't actually know anything about this conspiracy.

Gus was so busy battling panic that at first he didn't notice the low moaning sound that filled the dining room. Even after the noise finally registered, it took him a moment to understand where it was coming from. Only when he saw that Kitteredge, Low, and Malko were all staring at a spot to his left did he realize it must be emanating from Shawn.

He turned and saw that Shawn was staring straight up at the ceiling, eyes wide open, hands pressed against his temples. "Hmmmmmmm," he moaned. "Hmmmmmmm."

"What's he doing?" Low snapped.

Gus felt his hopes rise. "I think he's communing with the spirits."

"Fascinating," Kitteredge said. "I'd hoped to see a demonstration of his abilities."

"You have been fooled by these spies too many times," Low said. "Do not allow them to betray you again."

"Hmmmmmmm," Shawn said. "Hooooooommmmmmmm."

"Listen," Gus said, desperately hoping to keep Kitteredge's interest in the face of Low's suspicion. "The sound of the spirits is changing."

"What does that mean?" Kitteredge said.

"Hoooooooommmmmmmm!" Shawn moaned.

"We'll have to ask him when he comes out of the trance," Gus said, hoping that Shawn would come up with some kind of answer soon.

"Malko can get an answer out of him," Low said.

"HOOOOOOOMMMMMMM!" Shawn wailed. Then his head snapped down and his eyes blazed at Low as his hands dropped away from his temples. "The spirits have a question."

"What is it?" Kitteredge said eagerly.

"They want to know what kind of pretentious clown actually uses the word 'whom' in conversation," Shawn said. "Especially when they're getting ready to torture and kill someone."

Gus felt his heart sink. He couldn't really blame Shawn for not coming up with the miracle words that would free them from danger and make everything all right. But surely he could have tried a little harder than this.

"So much for the psychic abilities," Low said. "Although I have to say I'm a little disappointed in the Cabal. I'd like to think that if they were going to make their final move to eliminate their enemies from the face of the earth, they'd send someone a little less transparently fake."

Low signaled to Malko, and the hunchback came into the dining room, the black hole in the center of the shotgun never wavering from them.

"But the spirits aren't surprised," Shawn continued, apparently oblivious to anything occurring around him on the earthly plane. "They say that's often the way with people who are desperate to cover their lack of education and fit into a class to which they don't really belong."

"That's ludicrous," Low said, his face paling a little under the white beard.

"Not according to the spirits," Shawn said. "They say

that just because a man looks like Albus Dumbledore, that doesn't mean he could actually get into Hogwarts."

"I don't understand," Kitteredge. "What are these names?"

"Great wizards," Gus said quickly. "And, umm, the wizard school."

"From a children's fantasy," Low said contemptuously.

"But a children's fantasy that comes with a great lesson," Shawn said. "Did we not learn after *The Chamber of Secrets* that if you stick enough hair on a man's head and face it doesn't matter who is beneath it?"

"What is the point of this?" Low demanded. "Malko!"

The hunchback marched over to Shawn and shoved him roughly toward the kitchen door. But Shawn simply rocked back into place.

"If a wig and a fake beard can turn the Singing Detective into a Man Called Horse, imagine what it could do for a forger and a smuggler," Shawn said. "It could give him the kind of respectability he craved."

Low took a step back, as if Shawn had slapped him. His face was ashen.

"I don't know what you're talking about," Kitteredge said. "Flaxman Low is a scholar and a great man in our field. If he were a smuggler and a forger, I can tell you there would be many museums across the world with phony masterpieces on their walls. But that's simply not the case. There has never been a hint of scandal around his name, and unless the Cabal has planted lies, there never will be."

There was no doubt in Kitteredge's eyes, Gus saw, but Low's were filled with apprehension.

"I only know what the spirits tell me," Shawn said. "But sometimes the reception is a little hazy. Let me recheck the message."

Shawn tilted his head back, pressed his fingers against his temples, and let out a deafening howl. "HOOOOOOOMMMMMMMM!" Then he snapped his head back down. "Apparently, the first time around I woke the spirits up from a nap and they were a little confused," he said.

"Confused about what?" Low said tentatively.

"The century," Shawn said. "Apparently there was another Low who lived in this house who was a smuggler. He wouldn't be any relation of yours, would he?"

"My father was a bootlegger," Low said, relief heavy in his voice. "He ran his operation out of this house until Prohibition ended, then turned his business into a legitimate winery."

Kitteredge stared at Low as if seeing him for the first time. "You never told me this before, Flaxman," he said.

"It's not the kind of family anecdote that breeds trust in a dealer of art and antiquities," Low said. "I have never told a soul."

Kitteredge silently digested this new information. Then his face lit up as its ramifications suddenly became clear. "If you've never told anyone, and if there is no public record—"

"There is none," Low said. "My father was never arrested, or even suspected."

"Then there's no way the Cabal could have given Mr. Spencer this information. And there's only one way he could have learned it."

Low nodded his assent. "He does indeed seem to have special abilities."

"Of course," Shawn said cheerfully, "if you'd like further evidence, I can check back in with the spirits. I'm sure they'd be happy to tell me much more about your father—and even about you."

Malko looked to Low for instructions, and his employer signaled him to leave the room again. Shouldering the shotgun, the hunchback glared at Shawn and Gus, then disappeared back into the kitchen.

"That would be fascinating," Low said. "But I'm sure there are better uses to which we could put your skills."

Gus wanted to reach over and give Shawn a hug. He wasn't sure exactly what Shawn had done or how he'd done it, but something he'd said had spooked Low enough accept him as a real psychic. Or at least to pretend to in front of Kitteredge.

"So now that we've gotten that out of the way, maybe we could get back to the subject at hand," Shawn said. "Which was dessert. I'm starving."

Shawn plunked himself down in his chair and scooted up to the table.

"I think there's something a little more important than food," Kitteredge said.

"If you mean coffee, I was including that with dessert," Shawn said. "Although I think I'll stick with decaf. The shotgun in my face was enough stimulation for the moment."

"I'm talking about *The Defence of Guinevere*," Kitteredge said. "It's time we all got a good look at it."

Chapter Thirty

While Malko cleared away the dinner dishes, the others moved on to Low's library, a massive room with oak-beamed ceilings and a fireplace the size of Gus' first apartment. Paintings covered the dark wood walls between the vast shelves of antique books, and while the past days' exposure to Professor Kitteredge had not greatly expanded Gus' knowledge of art history, he thought they seemed to be in the same general style as the one he'd glimpsed so briefly in the museum.

Flaxman Low settled himself in a large leather armchair facing the fire, a sketchpad across his knees and a pencil poised above the paper.

"Although he never pursued it, Flaxman is a superlative artist," Kitteredge said. "Whatever you describe he can duplicate."

"I'll bet," Shawn said.

Low glowered at Shawn, then turned to his pad. "The painting," he said. "If you can really see it."

Shawn nodded, then pressed his fingertips to his temples and closed his eyes. "I see a marble hallway," he said. "It seems to lead on forever. And a crowd of people pushing to get through."

Kitteredge looked stricken. "A marble hallway? I don't remember that."

Shawn didn't seem to hear him. "And there's something on the wall. A sign. Suggested donation twenty dollars." His eyes flashed open. "What does that mean, anyway? If you walk into the museum without following their 'suggestion,' the guards are going to haul you out."

Low looked ready to jam his pencil into Shawn's eye.

"Sometimes the spirits are not as precise as you want them to be," Gus said hurriedly, then glared at Shawn. "Or as we need them to be. Right now."

Shawn shrugged and closed his eyes again. "Okay, we're traveling down that hallway. Traveling, traveling. Pass through a door. Okay, we're in the gallery. Good thing we got here early, so there aren't any tour groups fussing around the picture. We've got a clear view."

Kitteredge leaned forward in his chair. Low, although he looked dubious, pressed his pencil to the paper.

"In the center of the picture there's a woman," Shawn said. "She's got long curly red hair and a sharp nose."

"That's Jane Burden," Kitteredge said excitedly. "Morris' wife and Rossetti's favorite model."

Low hadn't yet started drawing. "Go on," he said.

"She's standing in the middle of this enormous room. It looks like it must be in a castle," Shawn said. "The walls are stone where they're not covered with tapestries. She's wearing this big drapey dress, and she's got her arms outstretched to someone who's sitting in a big chair. Can't see him, though—just the back of the chair."

"That would be King Arthur," Kitteredge said. "He is sitting in judgment of his wife, who has committed adultery with Sir Lancelot. In Morris' poem she is defiantly stating her own defense."

Now Low was sketching quickly. "Was the throne on her right or her left?"

Shawn squeezed his eyes shut even more tightly for a moment. "Left."

Low blocked that in.

"What else?" Kitteredge said.

"There are a bunch of servants or pages or something on her right and two knights standing behind her to the left," Shawn said. "At least I assume they're knights. They're wearing chain mail and holding shields."

Low looked up sharply. He and Kitteredge exchanged an excited look. "Just two?" Low said. "Are you sure?"

"I'm pretty good at counting," Shawn said. "At least as far as two. Once we get past six it's a little tricky, but we're definitely on safe ground here."

Gus tried to figure out why Kitteredge and Low suddenly seemed so fascinated. "Is that important?" he said.

"In the poem, the entire Round Table has assembled for the trial," Kitteredge said. "If Rossetti painted only two knights, that's a major change and unsupported by any literary account of the event. I can't believe I didn't notice that detail, but there was so much to see. This could well be the key to the message he was trying to send." He turned eagerly to Shawn. "Are their shields marked in any way?"

"The shorter guy on the right—he's got a silver lion standing up on its hind legs on his shield," Shawn said. "And a gold crown."

Low filled in the shape of the shield with the images and lifted the paper for Shawn to see. "Like that?"

"Pretty much," Shawn said.

Kitteredge and Low exchanged a significant look.

"Does that mean something?" Gus said.

"The lion rampant and crown d'or," Kitteredge said, trying to put pieces together in his mind. Then they seemed to snap into place. "That's the crest of George Villiers, first Duke of Buckingham."

"That can't be what it means," Low said. "Villiers

died early in the seventeenth century. Why would Rossetti place him in Camelot?"

Kitteredge thought for a moment, then broke out in a smile. "I think it's a little pun," he said. "In *Morte d'Arthur*, Malory mentions there was a knight called Sir Villyars at the Round Table. This is Rossetti's way of labeling him."

"But why Sir Villyars?" Low said. "Does he have any significance in the poem?"

"Morris doesn't mention him at all," Kitteredge said. "In fact, I believe the sole reference to him in all the Arthurian literature comes in Malory's long list of Round Table knights."

"Then maybe we're looking at the joke the wrong way around," Low said. "Perhaps Rossetti wanted to call attention to Villiers, but needed to find a way to reference a sixteenth-century courtier in a medieval picture."

"Or possibly not the man, but his name," Kitteredge said. "There is still a Villiers Street in London, near where York House used to stand."

"If he was the Duke of Buckingham, couldn't that mean Buckingham Palace?" Gus said, getting swept up in the excitement of the moment.

Before the others could answer, Shawn cleared his throat loudly. "Spirits have a message here," he said. "They say one conversation at a time. These interether connections aren't easy on any of us, you know."

Low looked annoyed at the interruption, but Kitteredge was immediately apologetic. "Please, go on," he said to Shawn, then turned to Low. "We're trying to form a pattern from one piece of data. We need to know more."

Low nodded his agreement, then picked up his pencil again. "What about the other knight?"

Shawn squeezed his eyes shut and pressed his fingers against his temples so hard it looked like they might break through his skull and meet in the middle. "He's got a shield, too. And it's got a lion on it, although that lion is sitting."

Low and Kitteredge looked baffled. "Another lion? What can that mean?" Kitteredge said.

Low threw down the sketchpad and stalked across the vast library. He ran his hand along a shelf of books until he found what he was looking for and pulled out a large volume.

"If it existed, it will be in Fox-Davies," he said, carrying the tome back to his chair. Gus could make out the words *Complete Guide to Heraldry* on the cover. "Now, what color is the second lion?"

Shawn squeezed his eyes, then blinked a couple of times. "Gold."

Kitteredge got up from his own chair to look over the back of Low's as he paged through the book. "A golden lion," he said. "That would have been the symbol for England, which meant it would have been on Arthur's shield. But Arthur is on the throne, so he can't be standing behind her. It simply wouldn't make any sense."

Low flipped through page after page. "This is useless," he said finally. "The lion is one of the most common symbols in heraldry. Without more details, we can't tell a thing."

"Hold on a second," Shawn said. "It's not all gold."

"If it's got a red tongue and claws, that's no help at all," Low said. "They all do."

"Well, the tongue and claws are red," Shawn said. "But the spots are all black."

Kitteredge and Low stared at him. Gus didn't understand what was happening, but it must have been important because Low nearly dropped the book.

"Spots?" Kitteredge said.

"Yeah, it's got black spots all over," Shawn said. "Does that mean anything?"

"It means it's not a lion," Low said. "The only large cat with a spotted coat is a leopard."

"Although in heraldry, the animal was almost never painted with spots," Kitteredge said.

"It's possible that Rossetti didn't know that," Low said. "Not everyone has your level of knowledge, Langston."

"He knew," Kitteredge said, a tone of rising excitement in his voice. "The Pre-Raphaelites were extremely well versed in medieval decoration. If he put a spotted leopard on that knight's shield, it's because he wanted to make sure that someone viewing it would not mistake it for a lion."

"But why would that be so important?" Low said, flipping to another part of the book. "There are almost as many leopards in heraldic history as there are lions."

"But not in Arthurian legend," Kitteredge said. "There was only one knight of the Round Table who wore a leopard on his shield." His voice dropped to a whisper as he said the name. "Lancelot."

"That doesn't make any sense," Low said. "Lancelot is the one knight who couldn't be in this scene. During Guenevere's trial he was in exile, and mad with grief at the loss of his love and the betrayal of his king."

"When I was in third grade, I sat next to a kid named Bernie Schwartzman who drew airplanes all day long," Shawn said. "Maybe Rossetti was like Bernie, only he painted leopards because airplanes hadn't been invented yet."

Low weighed the book in his hand as if he wanted to hurl it at Shawn's head. "That's not a mistake Rossetti would have made casually."

"It's not a mistake at all," Kitteredge said. "It's the message. There's something about the placement of these two knights that contains a clue to Excalibur's hiding place."

Shawn dropped his hands away from his head and opened his eyes. "Does this mean you're done with the spirits for a while?" he said. "Because I still haven't had dessert."

Kitteredge and Low ignored him. And while Gus was beginning to feel a slight rumble in his stomach he knew could best be silenced with chocolate, he did, too. This moment was thrilling. They were on the verge of unraveling a secret that had been hidden for over a hundred years.

"What could Rossetti be telling us with this pairing?" Low said.

"You have the most famous knight in literature next to one who's mentioned only once, and then just in a list," Kitteredge said. "Could it be something about high placement and low?"

"Something both celebrated and unknown?" Low speculated. "What could that describe?"

"When you think about it that way, it's clear there's only one answer," Shawn said. "C. Thomas Howell. Famed far and wide as one more instance of teen heartthrob vanished into video obscurity, but who among us knows the real C. Thomas?"

"You're not helping," Gus said.

"You have to admit, it would be a great bit of symmetry," Shawn said.

Gus glanced over to see how Kitteredge and Low had taken this interruption. Fortunately, they were so wrapped up in their own theorizing that they seemed not to have heard any of it.

"I have an idea," Gus said.

This time the two older men did look up. Low only scowled at him and turned away again, but Kitteredge gave him the same welcoming smile he bestowed on any student willing to stand up and volunteer an opinion in class. "Yes?" he said.

"I know Rossetti wanted to hide his message, but would he really get so symbolic that no one could figure

it out?" he said. "Maybe it's simpler than the most famous and the most unknown. Maybe it's the name."

The contempt on Low's face made Gus want to throw
himself into the fireplace. "Although I am not as familiar
with all the details of Rossetti's life as my friend Langston, I know enough to be certain that he never encountered anyone named Lancelot Villyars."

But Kitteredge's eyes had lit up with excitement.
"Not the name, but possibly the initials. LV. What does
that mean to you?"

Gus cycled the letters through his head, but all the
associations were too modern to be taken seriously—
Louis Vuitton, Las Vegas.

"It's the Web site address ending for Latvia," Shawn
said. "Maybe he was trying to tell us that those Eastern
European brides are never as pretty as the pictures in
the advertisements."

Now it was Gus who wanted to hit Shawn with that
book. Why couldn't he see how exciting this was? "Did
Rossetti know anyone with the initials LV? Was there a
place? If there's any way to bring down the number of
possibilities so we could—"

"That's it!" Kitteredge said, clapping Gus on the
back.

"Good," Gus said, trying to figure out what it was
about his last sentence that could have solved anything.
"Glad I could help."

Apparently Low wasn't following Kitteredge any
more than Gus. "What do you have, Langston?"

"I need a copy of Morris' poem," Kitteredge said,
scanning the shelves.

Low jumped up and walked quickly across the
room. "I've got the 1858 Bell and Daldy first edi-
tion," he said, scanning the shelves. "And of course
the Kelmscott."

"It shouldn't matter," Kitteredge said. "But bring me

the earlier volume, just in case. Rossetti was dead by the time Morris founded the Kelmscott Press."

Low had the small volume in his hand before Kitteredge finished speaking. He brought it back and handed it to the professor. "What is it you've discovered?"

"It was Gus who provided the clue," Kitteredge said. "It was the word 'number.'"

Kitteredge let that statement hang as he leafed carefully through pages that were still white and supple after one hundred and fifty years. Gus tried to take pride in the assistance he'd lent his professor, but he still had no idea what he'd done.

Low did, however. "LV!" he said. "Not initials but Roman numerals. Fifty-five."

"Which must refer to the line number in the poem," Kitteredge said.

"Unless he was just agreeing with Sammy Hagar," Shawn said.

Kitteredge found the appropriate place and read eagerly. But his face fell as he said the words. "Though still she stood right up, and never shrunk," he quoted. "It means nothing. It has nothing to do with Excalibur."

The professor sank back into his chair, crushed. But Gus wasn't ready to give up yet. Not after he'd provided the clue that had gotten them this far. He looked over Kitteredge's shoulder down at the page. The poem was divided into stanzas of three lines each.

"Maybe it's not line fifty-five," he said. "Maybe it's the fifty-fifth verse."

Kitteredge looked up and smiled. "If only you'd stayed with the program," he said. "What a credit you'd be to our profession today!"

Kitteredge counted the stanzas until he came to the right one. When he read it out loud, his voice quavered with excitement. "Let not my rusting tears make your sword light! Ah! God of mercy, how he turns away! So, ever must I dress me to the fight."

"The sword of light," Low said. "Is it possible?"

"Is what possible?" Gus said.

"There are those who have speculated that Excalibur is the same weapon that was wielded by Nuada, first king of Tuatha de Danaan in Middle Irish mythology," Kitteredge said. "Also known as the Sword of Light. Rossetti is telling us where it lies."

"Where?" Shawn said.

They all turned to stare at him.

"Seriously," Shawn said. "If that poem is giving us a hiding place, tell me where it is."

"It's a clue, not a map," Low said. "It needs to be deciphered."

"If he wanted this sword to be found, why go through all this nonsense?" Shawn said. "I mean—I understand there's no reason anyone would ever write a poem or paint a picture except to send secret messages, but why not just write a letter and stick it in a safe deposit box?"

There was a long moment of silence in the room, broken only by the crackling of the fire. Finally Kitteredge spoke.

"We are talking about one of the great treasures of the ages," the professor said. "One with not only unimaginable monetary value but potentially a huge political impact. He needed to tailor his message so that only the right audience would understand it."

"And that's us?" Shawn said.

"It is now," Low said. "Do you have a problem with this?"

"Just an issue of time management," Shawn said.

"It's still early, Mr. Spencer," Low said. "We have plenty of time to discuss this."

Shawn ambled over to the window and glanced up at the full moon. "Do we?" he said. "What time does the sun set around here?"

"This time of year, before six," Low said.

"And the moon rise?" Shawn said.

"It varies," Low said with rising impatience. "I believe tonight it was supposed to be around seven-thirty."

"Okay, one more question," Shawn said. "What time do the blue and red stars come out?"

Low started to answer, then stopped, confused.

"Blue and red stars?" he said.

"You know, the ones that are casting that lovely twinkling light on the ceiling," Shawn said.

Gus looked up to see what Shawn was talking about. Blue and red lights flashed between the oak beams on the high white ceiling.

Before anyone could move, an amplified voice came from outside. "This is the police," it said. "Langston Kitteredge, Shawn Spencer, and Burton Guster, come out with your hands raised."

Chapter Thirty-one

The tunnel was barely five feet high. Shawn and Gus had to keep their knees bent with every step to keep from hitting their heads on the ceiling. And for Kitteredge it was even worse. He'd be better off crawling, Gus thought as the professor slammed his forehead into another light fixture. If the bare bulbs hadn't been caged in wire he would have smashed half of them and his scalp would have been shredded by glass.

Only Malko didn't have any trouble maneuvering his way through the narrow tunnel, and he led them at a pace that suggested it had never occurred to him that anyone else would.

"What is this tunnel?" Gus whispered to Shawn.

"Apparently one of the benefits of having a bootlegger for a father," Shawn said.

"Smugglers have long used tunnels for storing and transporting their goods," Kitteredge said. "For example, in the small hamlet of Hayle in Cornwall, there is a seventeenth-century smugglers' tunnel that runs for hundreds of yards. Of course, the seventeenth century was when smuggling really took off across Europe, thanks to huge taxes imposed by governments to pay for a series of financially crippling wars and—"

There was a dull thud as Kitteredge smacked his head into another light.

Gus wanted to turn back to see if Kitteredge was all right, but the tunnel was too narrow. "Professor?" Gus asked.

"I'm fine," Kitteredge said. "Although perhaps I should focus on the present moment for a while."

"There's a plan," Shawn said.

Gus had to agree. The present was the time to focus on. Partly because the past was becoming a blur in his sleep-addled and stress-befuddled brain, but mostly because the future was increasingly obvious. It involved arrest, incarceration, and, after some number of decades, an unmarked grave in a prison cemetery.

That had become evident once everyone realized that the blue and red lights on the dining room ceiling were the flashers from a squad of police cars. Almost immediately after the amplified voice had boomed through the house, there was a pounding on the front door. It was only fists, but Gus knew that was just an opening gambit. If Low didn't open it fast, they'd be using a battering ram.

Low knew it, too. Grabbing Kitteredge by the arm, he led them quickly out of the dining room through a long, high-ceilinged hall, and then left into a smaller corridor. Behind them, Malko scurried to keep up. Halfway down the hallway, Low stopped and threw open a door.

"Get in," Low said.

Gus and Shawn peered into the room. It was four feet wide and four feet deep. Mops and brooms hung on one wall, and the shelves on the other side were stocked with cleaning supplies.

"It's a broom closet," Shawn said. "Don't get me

wrong—it's a perfectly nice broom closet, and if we had a couple extra hours to clean this place up, we'd be really happy to see it. But if you're thinking this would be a good place to hide from the police, I've got to tell you I've been at lots of crime scenes, and they almost never forget to check in the closets."

"Get in, fool," Malko growled. He shoved Shawn and Gus through the door. Then he gave Kitteredge a respectful bow. "Please, Professor."

Kitteredge looked dubious, but he stepped into the small space, taking up nearly every available square inch that didn't already contain Shawn or Gus, and more than a couple that did.

"I'll hold the police off as long as I can," Low said apologetically. "You just run. Follow Malko. He knows the way."

"Run?" Shawn said. "I can't even lift my big toe."

Malko growled dismissively and then forced his way into the closet. Before Gus or Shawn could shove him out again, Low slammed the door. After a second there was a dreadful, final click. That could mean only one thing: Low had locked the door. There was no way out.

Claustrophobia had never been one of Gus' primary fears. Not that he wasn't uncomfortable in tight spaces; it was just that there always seemed to be something better to be frightened of.

But now, in this tiny coffin, gasping for a breath that hadn't already been exhaled by one of the others, Gus suddenly realized that there was nothing more terrifying than the prospect of being buried alive. And if the burial happened not to be under six feet of dirt but pressed up against six feet plus of art history professor's tweed, it was still the most horrible fate imaginable.

At least it was until he felt something squirming against his legs. What kind of disgusting creatures had been breeding here in the eternal blackness? Gus had a vision of hairless creatures, half rat and half slug, with white blanks where eyes should be, reaching out with their scaly talons to feel their way through the world— and through Gus' flesh, if it got in their way.

Until he heard Malko's angry whisper. "Get out of the way, you idiot. I've got to get past you."

Gus would have breathed a sigh of relief, but all the air had been pressed out of his lungs by Kitteredge's bulk. He squeezed closer to the professor. Or thought he was squeezing closer; it was hard to tell. But he felt the scrabbling move across his legs, and Malko didn't curse him out again, so he assumed he had done the right thing.

"Anyone got ideas on what we should do to pass the time?" Shawn said. "I was thinking about a game of tennis."

Gus heard Malko mutter a curse under his breath. At least, he hoped that's what he'd heard. If it wasn't the hunchback, that meant there really was someone or something locked in the closet with them. And while Gus liked to think he was generally a level-headed person immune from irrational panic attacks, he couldn't help recalling the scene from *C.H.U.D.* in which one of the cannibalistic humanoid underground dwellers reached up through a manhole and dragged an innocent passerby and her little dog to their unspeakable fate.

"Panicking isn't going to help," Shawn said. "At least not panicking about C.H.U.D.s. Because you're not going to find any here. We're not underground. And I've never heard of a cannibalistic humanoid closet dweller. If you want to panic about something useful, panic about the fact that the police are going to open this door at any minute."

"I wasn't panicking about C.H.U.D.s," Gus said. "I wasn't even thinking about them."

"Then you'd better get your facial muscles under control, because they're sending out some seriously bad messages," Shawn said.

"Both of you, be silent," Malko snapped from a corner of the closet.

"I've got to tell you: the police are going to think to look in here even if we don't say anything," Shawn said. "If your boss lets them down this hallway, it's all over."

Gus heard a noise from far above him, and he realized it was Kitteredge clearing his throat. "I'm sorry I got you two into this," the professor said. "My own research has made me a target of the Cabal, and I've long accepted that prospect. But to drag in the two of you, when all you wanted to do was help—all I can say is I will do everything I can to take all the blame if we are captured."

"We won't be, if you'll all be silent," Malko said.

Gus heard a thunking noise from the back of the closet and suddenly felt the most wonderful sensation he'd ever experienced—a fresh breeze blowing in his face. The fact that it was only as fresh as the air from an unplugged refrigerator opened for the first time in a year didn't concern him. It had oxygen in it, which put it far ahead of anything he'd been breathing since Low locked the closet door.

"This way," Malko said.

Gus couldn't imagine which way Malko was talking about, but since two of the four possible choices entailed passing through the solid flesh of either Shawn or Kitteredge and the third would mean unlocking the closet door just in time to meet the local constabulary, he chose to step toward the back wall.

Toward, but not to, as it turned out. The back wall had disappeared, and now the closet seemed to go on forever. Before he could figure out exactly what was going on, he was shoved forward by Shawn and Kitteredge.

Gus took a step, then two, keeping his arms out-

stretched in case the back wall had merely moved ahead
a couple of feet.

"Everybody out?" Malko said, and received grunts of
assent in return. "Good."

Gus heard a door closing behind him, and then a string
of lights glowed into existence overhead. Gus couldn't
believe what he was seeing in the faint illumination—a
low, rounded tunnel carved through the bedrock of the
hills. He couldn't tell where it went or how long it would
take to get there. It seemed to stretch on forever.

"Now get moving," Malko commanded, and set off
down the tunnel.

It wasn't like there were many other options at this
point. But if the rest of them had any doubts about the
course of action, they were quickly convinced by the
muffled sound of Low's voice behind the door, apparently explaining to a policeman that the room they had
just entered was indeed nothing more than a broom
closet.

So they set off. How long they'd been walking and
how far they'd gone Gus couldn't say. At one point he
contemplated counting the light fixtures they had passed
under, figuring out how many feet there were between
them and using that to calculate distance. But he kept
losing count every time Kitteredge banged his head on
a bulb, there didn't seem to be any consistency in their
spacing, and he realized he had no idea how many feet
there were in a mile, so he gave that up and just kept
moving.

Finally the tunnel walls fell away and disappeared
into the darkness outside the radius of light pumped out
by the bulbs.

"I think I understand now," Kitteredge said. "This is a
natural cave in the hills. Whoever built the tunnel started
here and worked back toward the house. I'd guess this is
an artifact of the Prohibition days."

"Mr. Low's father had it made," Malko said.

Kitteredge peered back down the way they'd come. "Truly astonishing," he said. "Even if it had been dug after 1956, when the first successful tunnel-boring machine was deployed in digging the Humber River Sewer Tunnel, a passage this long would have been an astonishing feat. But to think of the work that must have gone into construction without such a machine—it must have taken years."

"Wasn't around then to know," Malko said.

"Do you know how long it is?" Kitteredge said.

"Unless it's long enough to reach across the Mexican border, we're still in trouble," Shawn said.

"It's not," Malko said.

"So we are," Gus said.

"But it's got something just as good," Malko said.

The hunchback took two steps forward and disappeared into the darkness. Before anyone could move, another set of lights switched on, and they could see where they'd arrived.

The cave was the kind of place Gus had dreamed of as a kid. It was so vast that even with the illumination of a hundred ceiling lights, its corners faded away into darkness. Stalagmites jutted up out of the ground around the walls—unless they were stalactites; Gus could never remember which was which—but the center of the cave had been cleared and the floor had been blasted and sanded until it was a solid slab of rock hundreds of feet across. It was, Gus thought, big enough to house a 747.

Which meant it was several times larger than it needed to be, since the only plane it housed was a Learjet.

Malko walked quickly to the plane. He turned a handle on the door, yanked it open, and pulled down a flight of steps. "Get in," he growled.

Kitteredge wasted no time in racing up the stairs and into the plane. Shawn and Gus held back.

"Do you know how to fly one of these things?" Shawn said. "Because I'm pretty sure Gus doesn't."

"I don't," Gus said.

"Then you'd better hope I don't have a heart attack when we're at ten thousand feet," Malko said. "Now get in."

Chapter Thirty-two

It had occurred to Gus to worry that their takeoff might be noticed by the police. If that happened, their brilliant escape would have been for nothing. He didn't know what kind of technology was available for tracking planes these days, but he was pretty sure it was good enough to tell the cops where they were going before they got there.

If Shawn shared Gus' concerns, he didn't show it. Once he climbed into the jet's cabin, his attention was completely focused on the luxurious surroundings. Four giant reclining chairs faced one another in the center of the cabin, solid mahogany tables jutted out of the walls in front of each seat, and a flat-screen television swung out of the bulkhead above each table. In the back there was a spacious galley, although there wasn't anyone to cook in it.

Shawn buckled himself into the seat farthest away from the one Professor Kitteredge had taken, and a smile crossed his face that suggested all his troubles had just eased away. Gus took the recliner next to him and fastened his own belt, but even the softness of the leather didn't make him feel much better.

"Where are we going?" Gus said to Shawn.

"Wherever he wants." Shawn jerked a thumb at
Malko, who had latched the cabin door and then headed
into the cockpit, slamming that door behind him. After
a moment they heard the whir of jet engines starting up,
and the jet began to roll across the cave floor.

Gus winced as the plane passed through the cave's
mouth, but the wings cleared the walls with at least an
inch to spare on either side. He tried to look back to see
how the entrance was camouflaged, but he couldn't tell
in the dark.

The plane moved ahead a couple of feet, then stopped.
Malko's voice came over the loudspeaker. "Ladies and
gentlemen, we are about to take off. Please make sure
your seat belts are securely fastened."

Gus peered through the window to see if the cave led
to an airfield, but it was too dark.

"If my knowledge of smugglers' routes is any guide,
I'm going to assume that the tunnel led us through the
hill and the cave mouth empties onto a valley on the
other side," Kitteredge said. "No doubt Flaxman's father
owned this valley, too, probably under a different name
to keep investigators from looking at it too closely. Then
it's a simple matter to disguise the runway as a country
road. I suppose Flaxman keeps it hidden this way out of
a sort of sentimental tribute to his father's spirit."

"No doubt," Shawn said.

This was a side of Kitteredge Gus had never seen before. It was so obvious that everything Shawn had said
about Low was the truth—he must be the smuggler and
probably even the forger the "spirits" had accused him
of being. But the professor, who knew everything about
every subject, seemed completely blind to this obvious
truth about his friend.

Well, it was obvious to Shawn, anyway, and now that
it had been pointed out to him, to Gus as well. Not that
Gus knew how Shawn had figured it out. They hadn't

had a chance for a private discussion since it had come up.

Still, it didn't seem to be the time to school the professor on his old friend's true nature, especially since that friend's servant was at the controls of the jet they were using to escape the police. And since that jet was accelerating to liftoff down some darkened runway.

"Well, this is quite an adventure," Kitteredge said. "Once again, I apologize to the two of you for dragging you into my mess. But I think when all is said and done, you'll find it was all worth the trouble."

"Uh, no trouble at all, Professor," Gus said.

"Now you stop that right now," Kitteredge said.

"What's that?" Gus said, wondering what he had done wrong this time.

"You must stop calling me Professor," he said. "We've been through so much together that I'll be hurt if you don't call me by my first name."

Gus felt a surge of pride flow through him. Even if he had studied for that midterm, even if he had been able to name every one of those slides, he wouldn't have been offered this privilege.

"I'll be happy to ... Langston," he said. "And you call me Gus."

"He has been," Shawn said. "And speaking of hasbeens, maybe we should talk about what we're going to do now, since it's pretty clear that Langston here can't go back to teaching, and we're going to look pretty silly trying to run a detective agency from inside a prison."

"Actually, that's not a bad idea," Kitteredge said. "I imagine that with your unique abilities you could be tremendously useful to the other inmates. After an initial testing period, they would be coming to you with—"

Even Kitteredge, who frequently became so enraptured by his own thought process he had no idea what effect it was having on others, was stopped by the glare on Shawn's face. "Although I can see why you'd prefer not to be in a position to start such an enterprise," he said.

"Thank you," Shawn said. "So let's figure out how we're going to avoid that."

"It seems perfectly obvious to me," Kitteredge said. "We know the Cabal was behind the murder of Clay Filkins, so all we have to do is expose them and let the truth come out. It will be a grand adventure."

"That would be great," Shawn said. "Except that the real truth about the murder is back in Santa Barbara. And since we're climbing almost straight up, I think our flight is intended to go a little farther than thirty-five miles."

"If the proof is in the picture, why do we have to go anywhere?" Gus said. "Why can't we just figure it all out right here on the plane and then turn it over to the police?"

Kitteredge looked surprised, as if he'd expected Shawn and Gus to understand what he'd been thinking all along. "The picture, even now that we know about the crucial verse, isn't enough to convince a doubting world," he said. "We need to retrieve the sword."

"And just where would all that be?" Shawn asked warily.

"That we still need to figure out," Kitteredge said. "It's in that verse, but we may have to compare it with some of Morris' and Rossetti's other works, along with those of some of their contemporaries, to understand the meaning. Those works are scattered far and wide."

"How far?" Shawn said.

"And how wide?" Gus said.

"I believe in terms of those pieces freely available to the public at large, we'll find several of them at the Tate Gallery," Kitteredge said as he checked through a mental catalogue. "They've got both the Waterhouse *Ophelia* and Burne-Jones' *The Golden Stairs*, which I believe together announce the Cabal's manifesto. There are the Arthurian frescoes at the Oxford Union. Lizzie Siddal's grave, of course, is in Highgate Cemetery. Those are the clues that seem the most compelling, although I'm sure now that we have the key, each one will lead to a discovery previously unimagined."

As Gus listened to the list of locations, something was nagging at the back of his mind. He knew he hadn't been to any of those places, but even aside from that, he was sure he was missing a connection. Then it hit him.

"Professor," he started, then corrected himself. "Langston. The Tate Gallery, the Oxford Union, Highgate Cemetery—aren't they all in England?"

"Of course they are," Kitteredge said. "And we will be, too, in about ten hours."

Chapter Thirty-three

Even after all his years on the force, there was almost nothing Carlton Lassiter didn't like about the institutions of law enforcement. He loved the ritual of the morning briefing, the ceremonial bonding of the post-shift cop bar, the rigid adherence to standards of excellence. Unlike most of his peers, he even welcomed strictures like the ones placed on police by the Miranda rules. Working within a rigid set of restrictions only forced you to be smarter, better, and stronger.

The one thing that Lassiter didn't like about the profession was the replacement of thought with procedure. And this was a prime example, he said to himself as he pulled up a few car lengths behind the squad car sitting across from Henry Spencer's house. When you were searching for a suspect, it was standard practice to post lookouts at the homes of his family and friends, and clearly that's what was going on here. The department needed to find Shawn Spencer, and they hoped he might show up to see his father.

But one moment of thought would have made a chimp realize there was no reason to waste a team of officers and a departmental vehicle on Henry Spencer's street. Or, more precisely, on former detective Henry Spencer's street. Although he'd been retired for years, Henry was and always would be a pure cop. If a wanted fugitive showed up on his doorstep, he'd find a way to detain him and then call for backup.

Of course, the brass knew that. But he could practically hear the conversation in the chief's office. *Sure, he was a fine cop, but this is his son we're talking about.*

If he'd been there for the discussion, Lassiter would have made sure that everyone knew the truth—that would only make Henry Spencer more certain to make the call. Because he'd know that if Shawn was innocent, the fastest and safest way to prove that would be to turn him in.

Instead, they assumed that Henry was as weak and foolish as the average member of the citizenry. But if he were, would he be standing by the squad car, handing the officers frosty glasses of lemonade?

If Lassiter had been in charge of this investigation, things would be running differently. But he wasn't. He wasn't even allowed in on briefings. All because that quack of a shrink didn't understand how a man was supposed to react to a bad situation.

Well, he was going to show her what a real man did when the chips were down.

At least he would if those two cops would move.

Lassiter needed to talk to Henry Spencer. He was the only one who would understand. But if he was spotted, word would get back to Chief Vick that he'd been at Spencer's house, and she would leap to the assumption that he was trying to work the case even though he was on suspension.

Of course Lassiter could always do what Spencer was doing now—walk right up to the squad car and sweet-talk the surveillance team. In normal circumstances that would have been his first move. But he knew what he'd feel about any other cop—particularly one as high in the

command structure as he was—who'd allowed himself
to be taken hostage in his own station and been responsible for freeing a suspect wanted for murder. Lassiter
wouldn't be in a mood to do any favors for that loser. He
couldn't imagine that these two would be, either.

If only there was a burglary in the area. Or a hit and
run. A flasher, even. Anything to pull those two away
from Henry's door. But this was a good neighborhood,
and the presence of a squad car only made it safer.
There was no way Lassiter could get to see Henry without Chief Vick finding out. He couldn't even call. With
Shawn on the wanted list, the cops would have put taps
on Henry's home and cell phones.

Henry was heading back to his house. In a second
he'd be back in his comfortable living room, and Lassiter would have lost his chance. But before Spencer
reached his front door, he made a hard right turn and
disappeared into his garage. After a moment, Lassiter
saw a glow of red. Henry's truck was backing out.

Lassiter put his Impala back into drive and eased
away from the curb as Henry headed down the street,
shielding his face with his hand as he passed the two
cops in the squad car. But they didn't even glance up in
his direction as he cruised past. *If this were my case, I'd
have those two on report*, he thought. *There's no excuse
for that kind of sloppiness.*

Henry's street was residential and quiet; there was no
traffic in either direction. Which made it easy for Lassiter to keep Henry in sight, but also for Henry to spot
him. Which might be a problem. Lassiter was certain
that Spencer would be cooperating with the police in
every way possible, but he was also sure Henry would
draw the line at being followed wherever he went. If he
called Chief Vick to complain about the tail, he was cop
enough to give her Lassiter's plate number. And there
was no way he could claim this was part of his therapy.

Henry wasn't making it any easier for Lassiter to remain inconspicuous. He couldn't have been going faster than fifteen miles an hour. Any normal driver would have passed him right away, and all but the most saintly would have flipped him off as they did. The fact that Lassiter considered to dawdle along behind him had to look suspicious.

Henry did the full grandpa down the street for two blocks. Then he reached an intersection, and instead of slowing further to check for cross traffic, he accelerated furiously, taking the right turn at thirty-five. What the hell was he doing? Lassiter hit the gas and screamed around the corner.

And then slammed on the brake to keep from hitting Henry's truck. It was sitting at the curb, exhaust chugging from the tailpipe. Lassiter could see Henry sitting completely still behind the wheel.

Again, Lassiter wondered what he was doing. It was possible he'd pulled over to take a cell call, but both hands were on the steering wheel, and his head wasn't moving in the way most people's do when they're talking. He was just sitting in his truck.

And then he wasn't sitting anymore. He snapped off the ignition and opened his door. Lassiter assumed he'd come to see a neighbor, although it surprised him to see that Henry would drive rather than walk such a short distance. The cop in him wanted to watch Henry to see which house he went to, but the suspended-cop part of him won out, and he slid down in his seat so that Henry wouldn't see him.

Since he couldn't tell which direction Henry would be going in, Lassiter decided to give it a slow ten-count before rising to look out the window again. Before he could get to eight, there was a loud rapping on the passenger's window.

Henry Spencer was standing outside, staring down at him.

Lassiter straightened in his seat, then reached over

and opened the passenger's door. Henry got in and slammed the door closed.

"You wanted to talk to me?" Henry said.

"When did you make me?" Lassiter said.

"My house has this amazing new invention called windows," Henry said. "I saw you pull up behind the idiots in the cruiser. I almost brought you your own glass of lemonade."

"Did they spot me?"

Henry scowled disgustedly. "No," he said, "and don't think that isn't something else I'll be bringing up with Chief Vick."

"Something else?" Lassiter said. "Besides what?"

"I don't know," Henry said. "Maybe a level of incompetent police work that was directly responsible for my son becoming a fugitive from justice."

Lassiter's instinct was to argue. He'd take the blame for a lot, but to make him responsible for Shawn Spencer's irresponsibility was more than even his guilty conscience could take. One look at Henry's face, however, suggested that if he wanted any help at all, he'd let that go unchallenged.

"I screwed everything up, Henry," Lassiter said. "I treated Langston Kitteredge as a cooperating witness, and it never even occurred to me that he was the perp we were hunting."

"Is that all?" Henry said.

Lassiter didn't want to answer the question. He didn't want to think back to that moment. He never wanted to face it again. But he needed Henry's help. And Henry would know if he was holding something in, and then he would get out and go home without a look back.

"It's not all," Lassiter said. "Although God knows that was bad enough. But there was a moment when I could have turned everything around. When I could have apprehended Kitteredge and kept any of this from happening."

"Go on," Henry said.

Lassiter let the images from the interrogation room back into his mind. As he did, he realized how much effort he'd been putting in to keeping them out. He could feel the muscles loosen in his forehead, his temple, even his jaw. The headache he'd been fighting for days began to ease.

And he realized something else. He wanted to tell Henry Spencer about that moment.

"Kitteredge was giving his statement," Lassiter said. "I have to admit—I wasn't paying as much attention to what he was saying as I should have."

"Why?"

"Believe me, if you ever talked to the man, you'd understand," Lassiter said. "Let's just leave it at that for the moment."

Henry nodded, then gestured for Lassiter to go on.

"Anyway, the man was talking and talking and talking," Lassiter said. "And at one point he reached into his left jacket pocket and pulled out an old pipe, which he'd already done several times in the interview. He never actually lit the damn thing, just waved it around as if it added something to the conversation. Anyway, this time after he pulled out the pipe, he reached into his right pocket. And I didn't pay any attention to it. I assumed he was going for a lighter or a book of matches."

"Not unreasonable," Henry said. "But then I'd guess that no individual step here was unreasonable on its own. You're too good a cop for that."

Lassiter winced. He'd never had a compliment that stung so badly. "As I said, I assumed he was going for a lighter," he said. "So when he opened his hand and revealed the murder weapon, I was still acting on my assumption and not on what had just happened. I looked at that knife and for one second the only thing in my mind was the question of why his pipe lighter was painted red.

Just for a second, Henry, I swear. But that second was all it took. Kitteredge realized he'd exposed himself, and he grabbed me and jammed that knife against my throat. I could give you a load of excuses about how late it was, about how I'd been up all night, or that I had no reason to suspect the man. But no excuses can change the fact that I screwed up."

Henry was giving him an odd look. Lassiter didn't bother trying to interpret it. He was deserving of nothing but contempt, so he assumed that's what Henry was feeling.

But for the first time since the incident, Lassiter was beginning to feel a little better. Not about what he'd done, of course; that was still shameful. But about himself. He'd always carry this humiliation, true; but now he saw a possibility of carrying on with his life and career in spite of it.

It was, he thought, amazing how much better simply talking about this made him feel. If only Chief Vick had realized this was the way to deal with the problem, rather than sending him to that quack of a shrink.

"How did Shawn and Gus get involved?" Henry said.

"They already were," Lassiter said. "They were at the museum before we discovered the body. It seemed that Kitteredge was their client, although I never had a chance to ask what it was he wanted them to do. They were—"

Henry held up a hand to stop him. "He was their client?"

"Apparently."

"Well, then," Henry said. "You should have mentioned that earlier."

"It doesn't change anything, Henry," Lassiter said. "There's no exemption in the aiding-and-abetting statutes for private detectives helping their clients. If anything, the law is harder on those who have sworn to uphold it."

Henry scowled, and his hand twitched as if it wanted to reach across the car and slap Lassiter. "You've known Shawn a long time, Carlton."

Lassiter worked hard to keep any trace of irony out of his voice. "Oh, yes," he said, desperately hoping that he'd managed not to imply what he was feeling—that five minutes with Shawn always felt like a year.

"I know you don't approve of his methods," Henry said. "Or his manners. Or his attitude. Or his clothes. Or his sense of humor. Hell—I don't either. But there's one thing even the dumbest cop should have figured out by now—he's got good instincts. If he says someone's a good guy, he's probably right. And he's not going to take on a client if he thinks he's dirty."

"The man held a knife to my throat, Henry," Lassiter said. "A knife that was almost certainly the weapon in a gruesome murder. I've got to put that up against your son's instincts."

"It's possible the guy panicked," Henry said. "Recognized he'd been framed and reacted out of instinct before he knew what he was doing."

"A lot of things are possible," Lassiter said. "But as long as Kitteredge is out there and Shawn and Gus are helping him avoid capture, there isn't anything we can do for them."

Henry didn't take his eyes away from Lassiter's face. He just kept staring as if he could bore holes through his skull. "So what is it you want from me, Carlton?"

"I helped to create this mess," Lassiter said. "No, strike that. I created this mess. And I've got to clean it up. The best way to do that is to find Shawn and convince him to turn himself and Kitteredge in."

Henry's stare still didn't waver. "And you think I know where he is?"

"I know you don't," Lassiter said. "Because you would have done the same thing. But I thought maybe if we sat down together we could figure out where he might be hiding. And then we could go talk to him."

After a long moment, Henry pulled his gaze away from Lassiter's face. He looked out the window as if he expected to see Shawn and Gus strolling up to the car. "I've tried every place I could think of," he said finally. "We're not going to find him."

"I can't believe—"

Again, Henry held up a hand to stop him. "But I like the other half of your suggestion."

"The other half?"

"We're going to work together," Henry said. "But we're not going to waste our time looking for Shawn and Gus. We're going to do the job you would have done if you'd trusted his instincts in the first place."

"What's that?"

"We're going to find the real killer," Henry said.

Chapter Thirty-four

Rarely was Gus able to hear good news without contemplating its darker side, and when things were clearly getting bad, he always managed to figure out a way they could be worse.

But his feelings had rarely been as divided as they were right now. On the positive side, he and Shawn were on their way to England. That sceptered isle had never made his top-five list of destinations to visit, but it was hard to deny the romance of the unexpected trip.

Especially since they were flying across the globe in a private jet without a moment's notice. They were even wearing tuxedoes. You didn't get much more romantic than that, unless there was actual romance involved.

But somehow the reality wasn't matching up to the description. Which might explain why Gus was still wide awake when Shawn and Kitteredge had been asleep for hours.

There was the tuxedo, for instance. When he'd put it on thirty-six hours earlier, it had felt like a timeless symbol of elegance, the uniform for entrance into a world of glamour and wealth.

But while the rented suit still looked shockingly good after all this time, it was feeling less and less comfortable. Apparently it was woven out of some kind of super-synthetic fabric that kept it from wrinkling or showing stains even during the most extreme circumstances. But it seemed to be accomplishing that by absorbing all the dirt with which it came in contact, mixing it with Gus' sweat, and holding it all inside. Gus felt like he was sitting in a sauna whose water hadn't been changed in months.

That could be remedied once they were on the ground, he assumed. Gus didn't know a lot about contemporary Britain, but from the YouTube clips he'd seen of an audience watching some homely lady singing a sad song, he knew the Brits wore clothes that were strikingly similar to the ones worn back home. He didn't have a lot of cash to lay out for a wardrobe, and he was pretty sure he had a lot more than Shawn, but the TV commercials his credit card company ran during sporting events assured him he could charge anything he wanted anywhere in the world.

And it wasn't like they were exactly welcome in Southern California right now. The police had clearly decided that they were involved in a criminal conspiracy with Professor Kitteredge, and they seemed to be devoting a good many resources to looking for them. He'd figured for a while that the best way to clear Kitteredge's name was to learn the identity of the real killer and present that to the cops, and now the same went for himself and Shawn. If that search took them ten thousand miles out of the SBPD's jurisdiction, Gus could live with that.

But before they could start searching, they had to get into London, and maybe even out into the countryside. And that was the one part of this trip he couldn't figure out.

Shawn stirred himself up from sleep and glanced over at Gus. One look at his friend's face woke him up the rest of the way.

"You find the most amazing times to start worrying," Shawn said. "We're on a private jet over the ocean, the fridge in the back is stocked with food, and in a couple of hours we'll be in England. You should try to relax and enjoy the adventure."

"I didn't just start worrying," Gus said.

"That's true," Shawn said. "I have very clear memories of you worrying about whether we were allowed to use the swings on the upper playground or if those were reserved for the big kids in second grade. But as I read the wrinkles on your forehead, you are not fretting about access to recreational areas right now. This particular concern has something to do with our current excursion."

"It does," Gus said. "Do you remember the conversation we had when you suggested we might flee to Canada?"

"I do," Shawn said. "And I have to say I've felt much better ever since, knowing that I don't belong to a culture that accepts *DaVinci's Inquest* as entertainment."

"Do you recall the objection I raised about undertaking such an expedition?" Gus said, avoiding the opportunity to engage in yet another conversation about the lack of conflict in Canadian television dramas.

"Something about not having passports," Shawn said after a moment of thought.

"Not something about not having passports," Gus said. "But the fact itself that we don't have passports. Which means the English immigration people aren't going to let us into the country."

"What are they going to do?" Shawn said. "Shoot us down? It's not like Malko's going to radio down to the airport to say we don't have passports, so by the time they find out, it will be too late. We'll be there."

"We'll be in immigration at the airport," Gus said. "They'll let us out of the plane. They'll take us to a counter where they'll ask us for our passports. And when we can't produce them, they'll put us in a cell until we can prove our identities."

"That's easy. If they ask me who you are, I'll just tell them. You do the same for me, and we're fine." Shawn unbuckled his belt and ambled to the back of the jet, where he opened the refrigerator and pulled out a plate of sandwiches. "Looks like we've got roast beef with some kind of blue cheese horseradish sauce and a tarragon chicken salad on raisin bread. You want one?"

If the seat back hadn't been made of such soft, supple leather, Gus would have slammed his head against it. "They're not going to take my word for our identities."

"Don't sell yourself short," Shawn said through a mouthful of sandwich as he returned to his seat. "You can be very convincing."

"There are laws and procedures," Gus said. "Trying to enter the country without a passport is some kind of felony. They'll throw us into a cell. And if we're lucky enough to be able to get through to the American consulate, he'll probably e-mail our pictures back to the Santa Barbara police for confirmation—and then we'll be arrested and sent back there."

"Then you really should try one of these chicken sandwiches," Shawn said, holding out his plate with the untouched half on it. "Because it would be the highlight of a much better trip than the one you're describing."

If Gus had thought to pack his shoes with explosives, he would have definitely set them off at this point in the conversation. "How can you be so calm about this?"

Shawn took back the half sandwich and crammed it into his mouth, then returned to the refrigerator for another one. By the time he got back to his seat, he had swallowed just enough of the chicken salad to be able to talk through the rest of it.

"Because we're not going through immigration," Shawn said. "We're not going to be locked in a tiny cell for not showing our passports because no one is going to ask us for our passports."

"You have to believe me on this, Shawn," Gus said, wishing there was some way he could get through his friend's astonishingly strong denial mechanism. "Maybe there was a time a few years ago when that was possible, but after 9/11 there isn't a country in the world where you can land at an airport and just waltz into town without proving you're not some wanted terrorist."

"I'm sure you're right about that," Shawn said. "But we're not landing at an airport."

Gus stared at him. "If you think we're jumping out of this plane with parachutes, you're insane."

"Really?" Shawn said. "You want to jump out without a parachute?"

Gus resisted the temptation to shove Shawn's second sandwich down his throat and watch him choke on chicken salad. "We can't do any kind of jump out of a jet," Gus said. "We'd die. Even if we had any idea what we were doing, we'd still die."

"True," Shawn said. "Which is why it's a good thing we don't have to jump out of the jet. We're going to land."

"But you just said—"

"What did I just say?" Shawn said. "I can't remember that far back. We'd better rewind the tape." He made a series of noises that Gus assumed were meant to approximate the sound of an audiotape rewinding. "No, really, Gus isn't a complete dweeb. He just comes across that way. You should go out with him." Shawn stopped. "Sorry. Ran that tape back too far. That was when I was talking to that blond sales rep at your company Christmas party."

"I didn't invite you to that party," Gus said, the humiliation over the recent past momentarily eclipsing his fear of the near future.

"Don't I know it," Shawn said. "And let me tell you, that was one tough ticket. I think I had to walk almost all the way up to the door before they let me in."

"In fact," Gus said, as the memories came rushing back, "I didn't even go myself. We were supposed to be on a stakeout that night. Instead, I was alone, because you said you were watching the rear entrance while I was covering the front."

"I stake much better on a full stomach," Shawn said. "Besides, that was the wrong part of the tape. Here." Shawn made a slightly different set of noises to indicate that the tape was now fast-forwarding. "Here it is: 'We're not landing at an airport.' Although I can see how you got confused. Most of the time it's not worth listening to the second half of a sentence, anyway."

Gus thought through his options and decided which of these subjects he wanted to talk about the least. Eliminating both the Christmas party and Shawn's victory in the rhetorical battle, that left only asking exactly what he had meant. "So where are we going to land?" Gus said. "A petting zoo?"

"Probably something like that," Shawn said. "I'd guess it would be a farm out in the countryside that just happens to have a long paved road right through the middle leading directly to a barn with suspiciously wide doors."

"And you know this because you had a chance to study the flight plan, I suppose," Gus said.

"I know it because it's the only way a smuggler like

Flaxman Low is going to be able to get his loot in and out of the country," Shawn said. "He's probably got some people on his payroll at air traffic control, too."

"You keep saying he's a smuggler and a forger," Gus said. "But I didn't see any evidence of that."

"Sure you did," Shawn said. "You saw everything I did. You just didn't happen to notice any of it."

"Then why don't you tell me what I missed," Gus said.

"Really?" Shawn said. "You don't want to take a few guesses? Because we've got hours of flying time left, and since you won't let me sleep, you might as well entertain me."

Gus glared at him. "Forger and smuggler."

"Fine," Shawn said. "Start with forger. Perhaps you noticed a diploma on the wall of that room we were in."

"From Harvard," Gus said. "What about it?"

"Do you remember what it said?"

"It said he graduated from Harvard," Gus said. "Isn't that what Harvard diplomas generally say?"

"Yes, but this one said it in Latin," Shawn said. "And while my knowledge of that language is pretty shaky, I did recognize the numbers 1963, which told me what year he was supposed to have graduated in."

"If you're going to tell me Harvard hadn't been founded in 1963, I'm going to have to argue with you," Gus said.

"Harvard stopped using Latin on their diplomas in 1961," Shawn said. "Even though the students rioted over the change, they've been in English ever since."

"There is simply no way you could know that," Gus said.

"Unless I had undertaken an in-depth study of the history of higher education in this country," Shawn said. "Or it was a clue on *Who Wants to Be a Millionaire?*"

"Okay, fine," Gus said. "But they made that change

almost fifty years ago. You'd think he would have noticed by now."

"I'm sure he did, and he's got himself a Harvard diploma done right hanging in some prominent place,"
Shawn said. "The fact that this was on the wall in a guest
bedroom suggests he's only held on to it for sentimental
reasons, like it was one of his first forgeries."

Gus looked for holes in Shawn's reasoning but
couldn't find anyway. "And smuggler?"

"Remember the razor, bowl, and shaving brush in
that room?" Shawn said. "They were made out of ivory.
And judging by the style, they were made in the past ten
years."

Shawn didn't bother to explain further, but Gus didn't
need him to. "It's been illegal to import elephant ivory
since before 1990," Gus said. "But this could have been
a gift. Or a souvenir. Bringing a trinket back in your lug-
gage doesn't make you a smuggler."

"Except by definition," Shawn said. "But that's not
the kind of smuggler I'm talking about. Again, this is in
the guest bedroom, as if it was nothing special. I suspect
it was part of a large shipment and he decided to keep a
sample back for himself."

Gus worked through the logic and again could find
nothing definitive to suggest it was wrong. He glanced
over at Kitteredge to make sure he was still asleep. A
quiet snore assured him he was. "If this was so obvious
to you, how come Professor Kitteredge hasn't been able
to see it in all these years?"

"The same as with the conspiracy thing," Shawn
said. "Call it the Bernie Madoff effect. It's because he's
smart. He's certainly too intelligent to be taken in by
an obvious crook. So he never bothers to question his
assumptions about his old friend—because any assumption made by such a smart person must be right."

This time Gus could poke a hole in the logic. "But we
don't know there isn't a conspiracy, just like he says,"

Gus said. "Somebody killed Clay Filkins, and somebody managed to steal that painting. If it wasn't a mysterious cabal run by some shadowy characters, who was it?"

"That's an excellent question," Shawn said. "And I suggest we wake up your professor and figure it out."

Chapter Thirty-five

Waking Kitteredge turned out to be easier in the abstract than in the concrete. After several minutes of trying, Shawn was tempted to give up, assuming that the professor had drawn not only his appearance, but the ability to hibernate for months at a time, from his ursine ancestors.

But Gus remembered the way Kitteredge would walk around in the mornings with a coffee cup glued to his hands, and he had the notion of starting a pot brewing in the jet galley. Once the scent had permeated the cabin, Kitteredge stirred awake with the slightest prodding.

After Kitteredge had consumed several cups of coffee, he stood up and walked around the cabin and then returned to his seat, where Gus and Shawn were waiting for him.

"Gentlemen, we are off on a great adventure," he said. "And I want to thank you for being a part of it."

"It wasn't really our idea," Shawn said. "It kind of happened to us. Like becoming fugitives from justice. So we were thinking we could use answers to a couple of questions before we go any further."

"That's certainly nothing I can object to," Kitteredge said.

"Maybe I should have mentioned that we need short answers to our questions," Shawn said. "We've been in the air for hours, and I think we'll be landing sometime soon."

Kitteredge smiled indulgently. No doubt people had been saying this sort of thing to him for years, and he took it as a welcome joke. At least, that's what Gus told himself. Still, he felt it would be prudent to jump in with a question of his own before Shawn offered one that ended any possibility of useful conversation for the duration of the flight.

"One thing's been troubling me, Professor," Gus started before Kitteredge cut him off.

"Langston," he reminded Gus.

"Langston," Gus said, again feeling that silent little surge of pride.

"Like that's any better," Shawn said. "It's almost as bad as being named Flaxman."

"Yes, there's one thing I don't understand, Langston," Gus said quickly, before the professor had a chance to notice that Shawn was speaking, too. "We're following clues you believe Dante Gabriel Rossetti painted into his picture that would lead to the location of the sword Excalibur."

"That's right," Kitteredge said.

"But that only makes sense if he and Morris actually found the sword," Gus continued, checking his logic as he went to make sure he was on track.

"Also correct," Kitteredge said.

"So if they had Excalibur, why didn't they do what they'd set out to do?" Gus said. "Why didn't they use it to become kings of England, or if that didn't work out for them, at least sell it for unbelievable amounts of money?"

Gus shot a glance at the seat next to him and saw

Shawn was nodding his approval of the question. And from Kitteredge's pleased expression, it looked like Gus had hit on something the professor was eager to explain.

"That is an excellent question," Kitteredge said. "But in order to explain it fully, you need to have a basic understanding of the Victorian view of the Arthurian legends as exemplified by Tennyson's *Idylls of the King*. Although to be entirely accurate, it must be said that this element was certainly present all the way back to Malory."

It was possible that Shawn did not mean for his groan to be so loud it filled the entire cabin. Not probable, but there was a small chance. Either way, it served to break Kitteredge's attention away from the lecture he was about to launch into.

"Don't worry," Kitteredge said. "I'm not going to drag you down into the weeds of Balin and Balan or Pelleas and Ettare. This is just a quick introduction. And you probably know a lot of it already."

"I remember when Wart got turned into an owl," Shawn said. "And then there was something about a sword, and then his mother was raped and killed, and he spent years pushing a big log around in a circle. Although that last part might have been from *Conan the Barbarian*."

"We know the basics about King Arthur," Gus said. "Camelot, Round Table, Merlin, jousting."

"And the knights who say *ni*," Shawn said.

Kitteredge nodded, clearly mentally adjusting his lecture for his current audience. Gus hoped he wasn't expanding it too far.

"The details of the Round Table and its knights aren't important to us now," Kitteredge said. "But the Victorian approach to it is. In Tennyson's eyes, and those of so many other poets and painters, Arthur was the image of the ideal man who attempted to build the perfect kingdom of justice, beauty, and truth on Earth. But despite all his grand intentions and brilliant efforts, he failed because of simple human weakness.

"Arthur, as I'm sure you are aware, was married to Queen Guenevere. He loved her with all his heart. And she loved him, too—but only with half of hers. Because when she first came to Arthur from her father, it was Lancelot—the bravest, purest, and most beautiful of the Round Table knights—who brought her. And on that journey Lancelot and Guenevere fell in love. For years they tried to deny their feelings, but ultimately they proved to be all too human. And when Arthur found out about the adultery, it tore his perfect kingdom apart."

Kitteredge stopped as if he had finished his story and was waiting for someone else to take over.

"And this has what to do with what we're talking about now?" Shawn finally prompted.

"Oh, right," Kitteredge said. "Morris and Rossetti. I told you that I've come to the conclusion that Morris saw himself as a latter-day Arthur. Some of that comes from the clues I've found scattered in his writings, but its psychological truth is indisputable. Time after time in his life, he set up situations where he would be the benevolent ruler of a Round Table of artists, writers, and artisans. In his last years, he even set up what was essentially a small town for his laborers to live in. And as long as Morris was Arthur, Rossetti was his Lancelot—the brave, pure warrior for truth and beauty.

"But it gets really interesting once we introduce Morris' wife. Jane Burden was the model for many of the most famous Pre-Raphaelite paintings, including Rossetti's indelible *Proserpine,* and she was definitely what they called a stunner. It was Rossetti who discovered Jane when he and Morris and several of their friends were painting a series of murals at the Oxford Union. He persuaded her to sit for his portrait of Guenevere. And then he delivered her to Morris.

"Is it possible that Rossetti was in love with Jane even then? I'd say so. But he had been seriously involved for many years with Lizzie Siddal, the other significant model of the Pre-Raphaelite Brotherhood, whom he would marry within a few years. So he handed his model for Guenevere over to his friend Morris, who fell in love with her instantly and married her a year and a half later."

Gus could sense that Shawn was getting bored with the story, if only because he was fidgeting so much he was making Gus' seat shimmy. But Gus had a sense where this story was going, and he leaned in, fascinated.

"Did they have an affair?" Gus said. "Rossetti and Jane?"

"There is officially some controversy about that," Kitteredge said. "There are those who insist that their love was never consummated. But those people are, not to put too fine a point on it, fools. Of course they were having an affair. Probably from the second year of her marriage and straight through nearly until his death twenty-five years later. There was a long period where the three of them were even sharing a house together."

Now even Shawn was looking interested. "And Morris never figured it out?"

"That's another question on which there is much controversy," Kitteredge said. "I believe he chose not to know, chose to ignore the signs, because he was so focused on creating an ideal society he couldn't admit just how far from that ideal he and his colleagues lived. Instead, he focused on his schemes to restore England to what he believed it once had been—schemes that in public were focused on the political but—if my thesis is correct—secretly involved the search for Excalibur.

"And then something happened. In 1871, Morris, who had spent the past few years studying the Icelandic language, took his first trip to Iceland. Officially the purpose was to explore the country that had produced the sagas he'd spent several years translating into English. But I believe there was a second, secret reason for the voyage."

"To find Excalibur?" Gus said.

Kitteredge gave him another of those "good student" nods. "My belief is that he found clues to its location in the saga of Grettir the Strong, one of the old Icelandic texts he translated. He was gone for several weeks, and his letters from that period suggest he was on the verge of a major change in his life. They are phrased as if he's merely talking about an alteration in mood brought about by the beauty of the Icelandic wilderness, but if you read between the lines, it's not hard to see how he might have been preparing himself for the changes that would be set into motion once he returned home with the sword. Those changes were never to come."

Kitteredge paused, as if he'd timed his lecture to end on a cliffhanger at the precise moment of the class-ending bell rang.

"Why?" Shawn said. Gus glanced over and saw that Shawn was apparently as wrapped up in the tale as he was.

"You must understand that so much of this is my con-jecture," Kitteredge said. "Based on exhaustive research, of course, but so far without objective proof. Until we find that sword."

"Okay, we understand," Shawn said. "Let's have it."

"Morris returned to Kelmscott House, where Ros-setti and Jane had been living as man and wife in his ab-sence," Kitteredge said. "Who knows what happens that changes the way we see the world? Who can understand why the scales suddenly fall from our eyes? Perhaps it was simply the extended absence that gave Morris the perspective to see what he had been unable or unwill-ing to see before. But he returned home and could no longer deny the fact that was before him—that his best friend and wife were lovers."

"Okay," Shawn said, "I can see kicking Rossetti out of the king thing after that, but Morris still had the sword, didn't he? He could have sold it—or even cut his so-called buddy in half with it."

Kitteredge waited for an answer, and after a moment Gus realized what it had to be. "But it wasn't just his friend sleeping with his wife," Gus said. "It was repeating the tragic history of Camelot."

Kitteredge nodded so enthusiastically he nearly fell out of his chair. "When Arthur let his kingdom be destroyed over Lancelot and Guenevere's adultery, at least he could say he never dreamed that the accusation would have that effect," he said. "But Morris had studied Arthur, had modeled his life on the king's. He had read Tennyson's *Idylls* and could say to himself, 'We see where the mistakes were made; we can avoid them and finally build a real Camelot, one that will stand the ages.' But now he had indisputable proof that no matter how much he knew, no matter how aware he was, there was simply no escaping human frailty. It's every bit as much a part of us as is our grandeur. And so the dream of building a perfect society must always remain just that—a dream. He was no more fit to rule the Britons than any other schmuck off the street. I believe he confronted Rossetti and then told him the entire project was off. They were going to hide the sword and pretend they had never heard of it."

For a moment there was no sound in the airplane's cabin besides the low whoosh of the engines. Then Shawn shook off the mood Kitteredge's tale had cast.

"That's a great story, but it's got a lot of holes," Shawn said.

"If we had more time, I could go into the research that led me to these conclusions," Kitteredge said.

"The only conclusion I care about is the one to Clay Filkins' life," Shawn said. "There's nothing in that entire fairy tale about your Cabal or the mysterious Mr. Pollycracker."

"Polidori," Gus corrected him, then realized that the rest of what Shawn had said was right. "What about the Cabal? You said they were secretly supporting the search for the sword?"

"That is my working hypothesis," Kitteredge said. "But not just the sword. They needed a figurehead to wield it for them; that's why they chose Morris as their tool to recover it, why they gave him the initial clues to its existence and then stayed out of his way as he, too, became obsessed with the hunt."

"They must have been mighty ticked when he gave it up," Shawn said.

"You could say that," Kitteredge said. "I believe it was no coincidence that shortly after Morris renounced his claim on the sword, Rossetti took ill and began the downward spiral that led quickly to his death."

"What happened to them after that?" Gus said.

"You have to understand," Kitteredge said, "that this is a shadowy and secretive organization. They show their heads above water only when there is a matter important enough to force them to take the risk. So I have lost track of them for many years after that. They allowed Morris to live on, possibly hoping he'd change his mind and lead them to Excalibur. And I've found no signs of their activity for more than a hundred years afterward. Until I began to discover the truth about the sword. Then they came after me."

Chapter Thirty-six

Gus leaned forward in his seat as far as the belt would let him. "How? How did they come after you?"

Kitteredge let out a deep sigh. "There, too, I can point to no concrete proof that will convince someone eager not to believe. Their existence is a matter of shadows and rumors. Or at least it was until they made contact with me several years back."

"What kind of contact?" Gus said.

"Was it a phone call, or more of a 'stick a sword through a guy and leave him on the floor' kind of thing?" Shawn said.

"It was an infiltration," Kitteredge said. "Polidori sent a spy into my class. His son, or so young Chip Polidori claimed."

"Chip?" Shawn said incredulously. "The greatest conspiracy in the history of mankind, and they send an operative named Chip?"

"That was what he claimed," Kitteredge said. "I have no reason to assume it was his real name, or even that he was actually related to the man he called his father. He used his time at the university to get close to me, eventually convincing me to take him on as one of my research assistants. This was at a key point in my investigation, when I was just beginning to realize what was at stake, and I'm afraid that in my enthusiasm I was too eager to share my discoveries. I let slip to this young man that I believed I'd found a lead on the location of Excalibur."

"What did he do?" Gus said.

"He did nothing I could prove," Kitteredge said. "They are too smart for that. But when I shortly there-after made my first trip to London to locate the sword based on the clues I had discovered in several of Morris' longer poems, they started to act directly to impede my progress. One of my suitcases was rerouted by the airline and sent to Mombasa. My hotel reservation was canceled with no explanation. A pickpocket managed to steal my passport, and I spent much of my trip at the American embassy trying to have it replaced. And the day of my appointment at the British Library, there was a twenty-four-hour tube strike that essentially shut down all of central London."

"That's all?" Gus said.

"Airline, hotels, labor unions, and street crime," Kitteredge said. "This Cabal clearly had fingers in all four areas. Isn't that enough?"

Gus felt a cold chill of fear pierce his heart. It wasn't the first time he'd had a sensation like this when listening to Kitteredge talk about the Cabal, but previously it had come from imagining the global reach of the terrible conspiracy. This time it was a completely different kind of alarm.

"But that could all have been coincidence, couldn't it?" Gus said. "Airlines lose suitcases all the time, hotels screw up reservations, pickpockets steal things. And disgruntled employees go out on strike. There's no way to say they're connected."

Gus shot a panicked look at Shawn, looking for some reinforcement. But Shawn just shrugged.

"That's exactly what they want us to think," Kitteredge said. "They continue to thrive because people don't want to believe there are forces so great and so evil at work in the world. But they showed themselves to me. Oh, yes, they exposed themselves. By the time I was finally able to access the archives at the British Library, where I believed I would find my next lead in Morris' manuscript of the first part of his mammoth *Earthly Paradise*, it was clear that someone had been there shortly before me."

"The library wouldn't have those papers if people weren't interested in them," Gus said. "And I'm sure you're not the only scholar in the world to make an appointment that week."

"Not the only scholar, no," Kitteredge said. "But I was able to see the log of people who'd had access in the previous two days. And at the exact period during which I was marooned at the embassy, a man named Paul Dorrington was searching in Morris' manuscripts."

Gus stared at Kitteredge blankly, waiting for an explanation from the professor. Instead, it came from Shawn.

"Paul Dorrington," Shawn said. "A fake name, but one left deliberately to tell you they'd been there first. Paul Dorrington. Polidori."

"Exactly," Kitteredge said.

"The names aren't even all that similar," Gus said, feeling the veins throbbing in his temples. "It's probably all a coincidence."

"The second time is coincidence," Shawn said.

"*What*?" Gus nearly screamed.

"First time is happenstance, second time is coincidence, third time is enemy action," Shawn said. "And while Goldfinger never said what came next, I think we're about to find out."

Kitteredge nearly applauded; he was so pleased with Shawn's insight. He was about to speak when Malko's voice crackled over the intercom.

"We're about to start our final descent, so if you need to move around the cabin, this would be a good time to do it," he said.

Kitteredge unbuckled his seat belt and stood up, his head brushing the cabin's ceiling. "If you'll excuse me, I need to freshen up before we land," he said.

Gus waited until the professor had disappeared into the lavatory before daring to open his mouth. Then he turned to Shawn, his face ashen.

"Did you hear that?" Gus said.

"Everyone makes noises in the bathroom," Shawn said. "The polite thing is simply to ignore it."

Gus stared at Shawn, trying to figure out if the cabin pressure change had turned his brains into cream of mushroom soup. "What he was saying," Gus said. "Did you hear what he was saying?"

"I thought the story about Morris and Rossetti and the wife was quite poignant," Shawn said. "And as a parallel for the original Arthurian legend, quite a fascinating bit of literary detective work."

"Yeah, that stuff was great," Gus said. "Really hung together well. Made perfect sense. And then he started talking about other stuff, and how it all hung together and made perfect sense."

"And?" Shawn said.

"And he's insane!" Gus nearly shouted. "He's taking random incidents that have absolutely nothing to do with each other and stringing them together to create evidence that there's a conspiracy out to get him!"

"That's an interesting observation," Shawn said. "That the man who claims some museum employee was murdered in Santa Barbara by a centuries-old cabal dedicated to finding King Arthur's sword and taking over England is actually insane. How would you ever come to such a conclusion?"

Frantically Gus thought back over everything Kitteredge had said to them—and that he'd believed. Piece by piece, everything hung together. There was not a single flaw anywhere in the internal logic of the conspiracy theory.

But it was ridiculous. And Gus had been so interested about seeing where every new piece would lead that he never stopped to consider the thought that he shouldn't be letting Kitteredge lead in the first place.

"If everything Kitteredge has been saying is based on a fantasy, then we can't trust any of the assumptions we've been working under," Gus said.

"That's a good point," Shawn said.

"And if he really is crazy, then . . ." Gus trailed off, unable to bring himself to finish the sentence.

"Then it's possible that he's the one who killed Clay Filkins," Shawn said. "And we've helped a murderer flee the country."

Gus let that horrifying thought bounce around his brain. There had to be a way out of this disaster. There had to be. He just couldn't begin to think of one. "What are we going to do?"

"Plead guilty," Shawn said.

Chapter Thirty-seven

If Shawn and Gus had ever been in a situation that called for a complicated plan to get out of, this was it. They were ten thousand miles away from home with no passports, with no return ticket, and suspected of helping an accused murderer escape justice. To make matters worse, those suspicions were almost certainly correct.

Unfortunately, there was no time to formulate a complicated plan. During the few moments before Kitteredge emerged from the lavatory and the plane began its final descent, they might have been able to rough out the basics of a simpler one. But Gus' mind couldn't focus on planning because something else had driven everything else out.

"You've believed all this time that Kitteredge was crazy," Gus said, checking to make sure the professor hadn't stepped back into the main cabin.

"You didn't?" Shawn said.

"You know I didn't," Gus said.

"Well, here's a handy hint, then," Shawn said. "When someone comes up to you in the supermarket and says that all those jars of Best Foods are actually alien eggs, and one day they are all going to hatch into ferocious monsters that will explode out of refrigerators across the West Coast—the East is safe because labeling them Hellman's destroys them—and kill everyone, and he's the only one who knows, you want to err on the side of assuming he's not operating at one hundred percent."

"Professor Kitteredge never said anything about mayonnaise," Gus hissed angrily.

"It's not the condiment that matters," Shawn said. "Unless you're making a turkey sandwich, and then you really want the sweetness you only get in Miracle Whip. The point is, whenever you hear that magic phrase 'and I'm the only one who knows,' it's time to head for the hills."

"But you let us follow him," Gus said.

"I let *you* follow him," Shawn corrected.

"You're in the same private jet I am."

"True," Shawn said. "And wearing the same clothes as you, too. But this was your case, so I thought we should do things your way."

Gus glared at him, the truth only now hitting home. "You're saying this is all my fault?"

"I hadn't actually thought it was necessary for me to use those exact words, but if you'd like me to, all right," Shawn said. "This is all your fault."

"I didn't hear you presenting an alternative plan," Gus said.

"I had an excellent alternative, which would have wrapped up our role in this case ages ago."

"And you didn't think it might be a good idea to mention it to me?" Gus said.

"I begged, I pleaded, I urged," Shawn said. "But no matter what I said, you refused to call off your doomed trip to the museum and come with me to the C. Thomas Howell Film Festival."

Gus was momentarily struck speechless. Even when he regained the use of his tongue, he found it impossible to do anything but restate the obvious. "You allowed all this to happen just because you didn't get your way."

"Sometimes words aren't enough," Shawn said. "You need to give a concrete example so the lesson is learned. Next time, you'll listen to me."

"What next time?" Gus said. "We'll be lucky not to spend the rest of our lives in jail."

"But if we don't, when I tell you that the Ralph Macchio Film Festival starts next month, you'll be first in line for tickets."

Before Gus could respond, the lavatory door opened and Kitteredge shambled his way back to his seat. "I want to thank you gentlemen for accompanying me on this adventure," he said as he buckled himself in. "I know we're not arriving in ideal circumstances, but soon we will be heroes to the world. We do have some work to do first."

"Yeah, fifty years of it," Gus said glumly. "Breaking rocks."

The meaning of Gus' words seemed to fly right over Kitteredge's head as he leaned over to pick up a small notebook that had slipped out of his pocket. He flipped through the pages until he found the one he was looking for. "It's just one more puzzle, and then we'll have our answer. We simply need to understand the meaning of this phrase: 'Let not my rusting tears make your sword light! Ah! God of mercy, how he turns away! So, ever must I dress me to the fight.' Any thoughts?"

Gus had one, but it wasn't going to be much use. He turned away, hoping to hide his rapidly approaching panic attack, and saw that the ground was rising even more quickly. But it wasn't like any airport approach he'd ever seen. The countryside below was a patchwork of varying shades of green, each one bordered by darker green hedgerows. He couldn't help but compare it to the gigantic corn and wheat fields he'd flown over when he traveled across the United States and think that it looked magically antique, as if their flight had gone off course and they were landing in the outskirts of Fairyland.

But if they had been landing in an enchanted place, there would have been some mystical way to put the plane on the ground. Right now, Gus would have been thrilled to see the few clouds in the bright blue sky form into a giant hand that would snatch the jet out of the air and set it down.

Because there didn't seem to be any place for their plane to land. There wasn't a field that stretched longer than a few dozen feet before it was broken by a hedge-row, and the roads barely seemed wide enough for a compact car, let alone the jet's wingspan. Gus tried to comfort himself with the thought that it looked like this only because they were so far up in the air, but if that was the case, then the sheep grazing below had to be forty feet tall.

And then he saw it—just what Shawn had predicted. A long, unbroken stretch of field bisected by a straight road that led to an oversize barn.

"We'll be landing in just a minute." Malko's voice came over the intercom. "Please make sure your seat belts are securely fastened. This may get bumpy."

Gus braced himself for a hard landing, but Malko was apparently a much better pilot than he gave himself credit for. The wheels touched down with a whisper, and the jet braked easily as it traveled down the asphalt road. It purred down the tarmac and then through the wide doors into the barn.

Kitteredge had his seat belt off and was standing by the door as soon as the engines shut down. Gus was rising to follow him when Shawn grabbed his arm and pulled him back into his seat.

"Do you have a plan yet?" Shawn said.

"I'm working on it," Gus said, which was technically

true as long as panicking over not having a single idea could be considered a kind of work.

"Keep working," Shawn said. "That way, if you come up with one, you can compare it to the one of mine we will already have used."

It took Gus a moment to work through the logic behind the grammar. "You have a plan? What is it?"

"Watch and learn," Shawn said, then reclined his chair and closed his eyes.

Gus didn't want to watch. He didn't want to learn. What he wanted was to wake up in his seat in the Bijoux Theatre to discover that he'd fallen asleep in the middle of *Dangerous Indiscretion* and there were only three more features to go before the festival was over. But since that didn't seem likely, he waited in his seat, wondering what it was he was waiting for and if there was any chance it wouldn't make everything even worse than it already was.

He didn't have to wait long. After a moment, the cockpit door swung open, and Malko went over to Kitteredge.

"I hope you enjoyed the flight, Professor," Malko said.

"Your flying is even more graceful than your minuet," Kitteredge said, and Gus was surprised to see a tinge of red coloring the hunchback's cheeks.

Malko reached past Kitteredge and hit a few buttons on a console. There was a thunk as machinery whirred into gear. The cabin door swung open, and a flight of stairs extended into the darkness of the barn's interior. Kitteredge squeezed Malko's outstretched hand and then disappeared down the steps.

Malko waited by the open door until it became obvious that Shawn and Gus were not going anywhere. Then he turned and walked heavily back to their seats.

"End of the line," he said. "Everybody out."

"That's true in so many ways," Shawn said, cracking one eye open but refusing to raise his seat back. "Just not in the one you're thinking of."

Malko lifted his lip in a sneer, and Gus thought he was actually going to growl like a dog. Instead, he spoke clearly and forcefully. "Both of you, out of the plane now."

"Listen, Malk," Shawn said. "Mind if I call you Malk? Mal? Ma?"

"Out." This time it was less a word than a bark.

"I understand that you're fond of the professor," Shawn said as if he hadn't noticed the hostility coming from the other man or remembered how handy he was with a shotgun. "But there's something you've got to understand. He's nuts. Absolutely stark raving insane. I'm pretty sure your master doesn't realize this, or he never would have sent us all off like this, but—"

"My *what*?" Malko said. To Gus' ears it sounded less like a question than a death threat.

"That's the guy," Shawn said. "Your master. You know, the one who orders you around and shoves torches in your face when you don't obey."

"Flaxman Low is my employer," Malko said quietly, but with an undercurrent of bloodlust in his throat. "I was hired through a top-flight recruiting agency and work under union contract."

"And I'm sure he's a great boss," Gus said quickly, before Shawn could ask if Malko had answered a want ad specifically asking for someone to dig up dead bodies for parts. "He's also a great friend to Professor Kitteredge. I'm sure he doesn't want to see any harm come to him. And that's what this is all about."

Gus glanced at Shawn, hoping that this was indeed what it was all about. He was beginning to have a glimmer of Shawn's plan, and while it was pretty flimsy, it wouldn't get any stronger if Gus cut its legs off.

"Exactly," Shawn said. "We've all been wrong about

the prof. He's seriously sick, and he needs help. We need to take him back to Santa Barbara and get him into a hospital for observation. Once the doctors rule that he is mentally ill, his lawyers can get him a deal. But we need to get him back home first."

Gus watched Malko's face carefully as he listened to Shawn. At first it looked like the hunchback was simply going to order them off the plane again. But as Shawn went on, Malko's features began to soften.

"I have to say I was worried about the same thing," Malko said. "Mr. Low gives him the benefit of the doubt when he talks about this Cabal, but I studied psychology in college, and I recognize the symptoms of paranoid schizophrenia. It pains me to see him this way."

"Then you'll help us?" Gus said. He couldn't believe it was going to be this easy.

"I've got to refuel the jet, and that's going to take a little while," Malko said. "That gives you two some time to come up with a story that will get him to agree to return. If you can do that, I'll do whatever I can."

"Thank you," Gus said.

"I'm doing it for Professor Kitteredge," Malko said, and turned to walk to the door.

Gus undid his seat belt and waited for Shawn to do the same. "That was your great plan?" he said. "To ask for help?"

"It's not the complexity of the plan, but how well it works," Shawn said. "Besides, I like to keep the tactic of sincerely telling the truth in my toolkit. It isn't the right thing very often, but once in a while it comes in handy."

Gus led Shawn to the jet's door and then down the short flight of stairs into the darkened barn. He peered into the gloom but couldn't see Kitteredge anywhere.

"Professor?" he called.

There was no answer.

"Professor Kitteredge?" he said again as Shawn stepped down next to him. "Langston?"

"I'm afraid Professor Kitteredge can't talk right now," a man's voice said from somewhere in the darkness.

"Did that sound like Malko to you?" Shawn said. "Because I don't remember him speaking with an English accent."

"Who's out there?" Gus called. "Where's Professor Kitteredge?"

"Who I am is of no importance right now," the voice said, sounding much closer to James Mason than to Malko. "As for the professor's whereabouts, you can see for yourself."

A row of fluorescent lights across the barn's ceiling flickered on. Gus blinked against the sudden illumination, then opened his eyes. They were standing in what appeared to be a traditional wooden barn, aside from the substitution of the private jet for a stack of hay bales. One wall was covered with farm tools hanging from hooks, and the other was hidden behind a series of stalls.

It was the nearest of those stalls that caught Gus' eye. Because Professor Kitteredge was standing in its doorway. And behind him was a man in a pinstriped, three-piece suit. A man whose face was completely covered by a black ski mask.

And he was holding a gun to the professor's head.

Chapter Thirty-eight

Lassiter was shocked at how easy it had been to get in to see Hugh Ralston, the museum's executive director. He and Henry had spent twenty minutes talking about what to do if they were asked to produce a badge, and the closest they got to an answer was a mutual agreement to improvise.

But Ralston's secretary didn't ask for any identification. She took one look at the men standing across from her desk and hit the intercom to let her boss know that there were two police detectives to see him.

If only the next part of the interview had gone as well. Not that Ralston wasn't cooperative. He seemed almost desperately eager to please.

It was just that he didn't know anything. They'd started out by asking standard questions about Clay Filkins—friends, enemies, home life, financial troubles. All the things that Juliet O'Hara had undoubtedly already asked in the course of the official investigation. Ralston didn't have any objections to answering them again; he just didn't have any information to give the police. They'd worked together for a couple of years, and Ralston had held Filkins in the highest regard professionally, but they'd never spent any time together outside of work, and all their conversations in the office had been strictly business. Not that they objected to speaking personally; it was just that there was so much about the museum they both found fascinating that there was never a need to change subjects.

"What about the deal with the painting?" Henry asked. "That sure sounds funny to me."

"It sounded funny to everyone here," Ralston admitted. "But some things are too good to question too closely. Clay insisted it was legitimate, and his word was sacred around here. So we took the deal, even with the strict rules about anonymity."

"I'm sure you can see how those rules can't stand anymore," Lassiter said. "Your donor's instructions matter much less than a human life."

"I agree entirely," Ralston said. "I'd break the confidentiality in a second if I could."

"If you could?" Henry said, his face reddening. "My son is being hunted by the police because he's trying to clear Langston Kitteredge's name. If you have information that can help him, I won't leave you alone for a second until you hand it over."

Ralston threw up his hands defensively. "I'm sorry; I said that badly," he said. "I mean I would give you any information I had. I just don't have any. I went into Clay's office, I broke into his private files, and I dug out everything he had on this picture. This is it."

Ralston picked up a file and handed it across his desk. Henry flipped it open. It was empty. "Somebody stole his files?"

"Or he never kept any paperwork at all," Ralston said. "Or he hid it at his home. I have no answers. I have nothing."

"Come on," Henry said. "There must be some other way of tracking down this donor."

"No, you don't understand," Ralston said, his voice

close to cracking. "I have *nothing*. All I've ever wanted was for this museum to thrive. Because it's so much bigger than I am. I couldn't even make my ex-wife happy, but this institution can touch the lives of generations. And look what I've done for it. Thanks to my brilliant financial skills, we've lost two-thirds of our endowment in the markets. Now one of the best people who ever worked here has been murdered in one of our galleries, and the painting he spent his last months acquiring for us has been stolen. Could I have done a worse job?"

If there was one thing that Henry—and every cop Henry had ever known—hated, it was whining. When you saw as many terrible things as a rookie saw in his first year, it was just too hard to listen to anyone moaning about how tough he had it. Henry would never tolerate it from Shawn, and he hated when he heard it in an interview. He glanced over at Lassiter to confirm that the detective shared his disgust. But to his shock, Lassiter seemed to be listening sympathetically. And there was something bright and shiny in the corner of his eye, which—if Henry hadn't known better—he would have sworn was a tear.

"It's the hardest thing in the world," Lassiter said, "to love a job, to love an institution, and to know you've let her down."

"Yes!" Ralston said in a voice that was perilously close to sobs.

"When you'd do anything in the world for that place and those people, and all you bring them is shame," Lassiter said.

"Oh, God, yes," Ralston said.

"And you think there's nothing you can ever do to wipe that stain away," Lassiter said, his voice taking on a dreamy, distant quality. "Sure, for a while you want to crawl into a hole. You want to disappear and never show your face to the people whose trust you've violated. But you keep on going. Do you know why?"

"Why?" Ralston choked out.

"Yes, Carlton," Henry said. "Tell us all."

"Because that's what a man does," Lassiter said. "He takes the beating, he makes his mistakes, but then he gets up and keeps working. Because if he's a real man, he knows it's not about him. It's about the institution he's sworn to protect. And if he's failed her once, then it's up to him to work twice as hard to make sure he never lets her down again. And to be proud he's been given a chance to serve."

Ralston looked at him, tears streaming down his face. "Do you really think so?"

Lassiter reached across the desk and gave his hand a firm squeeze. "I know so," he said. "It's what we do."

"Thank you," Ralston said. "Thank you."

For a moment, the three of them sat in silence. Then Henry got to his feet. "If you come across anything you think might be useful in the interrogation, you be sure to let the police know."

Ralston nodded wordlessly. Henry walked to the door, Lassiter right behind him. Neither man spoke until they were out of the museum.

"That was a waste of time," Henry said as they walked down the steps to the street.

"Really?" Lassiter said. "I thought it was tremendously useful."

"He had no information," Henry said incredulously. "We didn't learn a thing."

"I don't know about you, but I feel like I've learned a lot from this experience," Lassiter said. "And now if you'll excuse me, we need to take up this investigation some other time."

"Some other time?" Henry sputtered. "What about right now?"

"I can't right now," Lassiter said. "I have an appointment with a kindergarten teacher. And I think I just learned how to tie my shoes."

Chapter Thirty-nine

Gus pulled against the ropes that bound his hands behind his chair. He'd seen so many movies in which the hero was able to stretch them just enough to slip his wrists through. But all that was happening to Gus was that the rough cord was scraping the flesh off his bones.

"Keep it up," Shawn whispered. "If you keep bleeding, maybe you'll make the ropes slick enough you can slip them off."

If Gus could have twisted his head around to shoot a killing look at Shawn, he would have. But Shawn was behind him in the stable, tied to his own chair. Gus had seen two more masked men, less well dressed in workers' coveralls, tie him there while the suited man held the gun on him. Then it was his turn.

"We've got to save Professor Kitteredge," Gus said, hoping that this was indeed still the case. After they'd been captured, they'd heard noises from another stall that sounded like unspeakable things being done to human flesh, accompanied by screams from the professor. In the past few minutes, though, the sounds had stopped.

"Save him from what?" Shawn said. "I thought you said all this conspiracy stuff was insane."

"You said that," Gus said, feeling an additional surge of outrage. "You essentially said I was an idiot for ever taking him seriously."

There was a long silence from behind Gus.

"Oh, right," Shawn said. "I knew it was one of us. But just because I said something, that doesn't mean you're supposed to listen to me."

Gus knew that was as close to an apology as he was ever going to get from Shawn, so he chose to accept it.

"Besides," Shawn said, "we have no idea who these guys are. Just because some thugs in black masks take us hostage when we step off the plane, that doesn't mean they're part of a centuries-old global conspiracy."

"It seems like a pretty good sign to me," Gus said.

"Think it through," Shawn said. "This might not even have anything to do with the professor, or with the painting, or with us."

"Mighty big coincidence if it doesn't," Gus said.

"Really?" Shawn said. "The plane belongs to the world's biggest smugglers of looted artworks."

"Now Low's the world's biggest?" Gus said. "Where do you get that from?"

"His henchman has a union contract," Shawn said. "Do you have any idea how much that must cost over standard hunchback myrmidon pay scales? And that's not even including benefits."

Gus filed that away with a million other things he meant to argue about later. Right now there was something more important to discuss.

"Okay, fine, he's the Donald Trump of smugglers," Gus said. "So what?"

"So a guy like that is going to make a lot of enemies," Shawn said. "And then there are his friends. I mean, how can he ever know if they really want to be his BFF because they like him, or because they're waiting for him to accidentally mention the location of the barn in England where he ships all his best stuff out of? I think we've all had that kind of problem before."

Despite the hopelessness of their situation, Gus began to feel a little better. Particularly about Professor Kitteredge. If these men were really after Low's treasures, the awful noises he heard were much more likely to have come from Malko. Not that he wished the man any harm, but he was clearly a lot tougher and more accustomed to violence than Kitteredge. And as Low's pilot he was undoubtedly involved in the smuggling scheme, which made him much less of an innocent victim than a soldier in a war between criminals.

"Do you really think it's possible that these are just smugglers or crooks?"

"You have to ask yourself, which sounds more likely?" Shawn said. "And if you find yourself answering 'an international conspiracy with tentacles reaching into every area of life led by some mysterious unseen figure with a name out of a Tintin book,' you're listening to too much talk radio."

Gus did ask himself, and the answer made him feel much better. "So if these guys are just crooks, what do we do next?" he said.

"Criminals are a superstitious and cowardly lot, so my disguise must be able to strike terror into their hearts," Shawn said.

"What?" Gus said.

"Look around," Shawn said. "Do you see anything that looks like a giant bat costume?"

If Gus had been able to find a giant bat, he would have hit Shawn over the head with it. "That's not helping."

"Ask the citizens of Gotham City," Shawn said. "I think you'll find they disagree."

Gus was about to answer when there was a sound from across the barn. After a moment Malko appeared in the entrance to the stall, accompanied by the man in the pinstriped suit. Gus studied Malko closely but could see no signs that he'd been abused in any way. It was still possible that he'd been beaten in places that wouldn't show bruises, but that didn't seem likely. What did was that Shawn's hopeful theory was completely wrong, and they were in the hands of the Cabal.

"What am I supposed to do with these two?" Pinstripe said.

"The one in back is some kind of psychic," Malko said. "He helped figure out the clue in the painting. If Kitteredge won't talk, he may be able to help you."

Pinstripe man ignored him. "And the other one?"

"He might be even more useful," Malko said. "He's an old and dear friend of Kitteredge's."

There was a time when that description would have made Gus' day. That was back when friendship meant getting together for lunch every now and then, not submitting to unspeakable torture as leverage to force the professor to talk. "More of an acquaintance, really," Gus said. "Former student, dropped out after a couple of weeks."

"Who was willing to risk his own life to save Kitteredge from the police," Malko said. "It might be worth your while to see what the professor would be willing to give up to save him."

"You don't have to torture anybody," Gus said. "We'll tell you everything we know."

"Which won't take long, fortunately," Shawn said. "Then we can all go on our separate ways."

Pinstripe turned toward Shawn and raised his gun. "Perhaps we won't be needing this one after all."

Gus struggled frantically against his ropes. If he could get one hand free, he could bat the gun out of the masked man's hands—if he could also free his feet so he could cross the space separating them. But if the rush of terror was sending a jolt of adrenaline through Gus' body, it wasn't enough to give him the kind of super-strength he needed.

Gus squeezed his eyes shut and waited for the gunshot that would end Shawn's life, grateful at least that he wouldn't be able to see it. But instead of a gunshot, he heard a strange moaning coming from behind him.

"The tears!" Shawn wailed. "Tears of rust. Flow my rusty tears."

Another two seconds passed with no shots. Gus opened his eyes. Pinstripe still held his gun on Shawn, but he was staring at Malko. "Does he know what it means?"

"Maybe the spirits told him," Malko said.

Shawn wailed again. "I see the tears," Shawn cried. "Rusty tears. Red tears. Tears for fears. Tears in baseball—oh, wait, there aren't any."

"This is his process," Gus said quickly. "He gets messages from the spirits, but they're vague at first. Sometimes it takes a little while before he can understand the precise meaning."

"Tears of a clown," Shawn wailed. "As tears go by. Summer kisses, winter tears."

The gun in the man's hand wavered for a moment; then he lowered it. "We'll take all three of them," he said. "There might be some use to him." He turned toward the back of the barn and called loudly. "Leonard! Chip! We're going now."

"Chip!" The name burst from Gus' mouth before he could call it back. The only Chip he'd heard of in the past few days was the one who had been Kitteredge's student. Chip Polidori. Which meant that everything the professor had told them was not a paranoid delusion, but was hideously, horribly true.

If Pinstripe noticed that Gus had spoken the name, he didn't show any signs of it. He waited silently until a windowless van pulled up around the plane and the other two masked men got out.

"We're taking all three of our guests back to London," the leader said. "Load them in the van."

The two men started to move into the stall, but Malko stepped into the stall entrance, blocking their way. "I allowed you to question them for free," he said. "But if you've decided to complete the transaction, I'm going to need my payment now."

"When we have the sword," Pinstripe said.

"You don't understand me," Malko said. "I don't work on consignment. I have betrayed not only my employer but a man who considers me a friend. For that, I expect to be paid exactly what I deserve. And to be paid in full. Now."

Pinstripe seemed to think that over, then nodded slowly. "When you put it that way, I can't disagree," he said.

"Good," Malko said.

Pinstripe raised his gun and fired three times. Three tightly grouped red spots appeared in the center of Malko's chest. Then he crumpled to the ground.

The well-dressed man shoved his gun in his jacket pocket. "Let's hurry this up," he said. "We've wasted too much time already. Arthur's sword is waiting for us."

Chapter Forty

The trip in the windowless van was a smorgasbord of pain. First, one of the masked men had cut off Gus' ropes, and the blood flowing back into this veins seemed to be made of Liquid Plumber. Then his arms and legs had been retrussed, and with no furniture to absorb some of the ropes' pressure, he could feel his flesh being flayed from his body. The three were gagged and blindfolded and tossed onto the bare metal floor of the van, where they bounced around helplessly for what felt like hours. The only positive was that every once in a while Gus would be bounced across the van and roll against Shawn or Kitteredge, and both of them responded with grunts of pain. So at least all three of them were alive and conscious.

After a journey that felt longer than the plane flight, the van slowed and stopped. Gus could hear the front doors open and close, and then he felt a blast of cold, fresh air as the back was thrown open. Four hands grabbed him and pulled him out, then steadied him on the ground.

"If you try to escape, you'll be dead before your second step," an English-accented voice said in his ear. "Is that clear?"

Since he was gagged, Gus assumed the speaker didn't need him to answer with anything but obedience, but he nodded anyway. He felt himself being led a few feet from the van and then through a door. After a few more feet, one of the men shoved him hard, and he fell backward. Fortunately there was a chair to catch him. He could feel his bonds being adjusted, and he knew he'd been tied to this chair, too. At least it was padded, which was a huge relief after the van's floor.

After a minute, Gus heard scuffling footsteps, and then the sound of a body falling into a soft chair. Then he felt hands touching his face, and his blindfold fell away from his eyes, followed seconds later by his gag.

He looked around quickly to see that Shawn was on one side of him and Kitteredge on the other. To his huge relief, the professor didn't seem to have been beaten too badly. There were bruises on his face and a small trickle of blood from his lower lip, but compared to what Gus had imagined he might have just come back from a spa.

"Are you all right?" Shawn whispered.

"I'm fine," Gus whispered back. "Professor?"

"Nothing a couple of Band-Aids and some lidocaine won't fix," Kitteredge said. "Fortunately, Polidori's men don't seem to have studied much of the history of torture. If they had, they might have tried some of the more arcane techniques, such as the Black Lady of Monmouth or—"

Gus was vaguely aware that Kitteredge was still talking, but he'd stopped making sense of the actual words after the professor said the name "Polidori." Even after all that had just happened, he couldn't believe he was actually at the heart of a conspiracy that had existed for hundreds of years, if not longer.

If it was really true, the conspirators had certainly found the perfect spot for their headquarters. An enormous warehouse, it was crammed full of what must have been the fruit of centuries of looting. There were statues in marble and bronze, stacks of paintings in gold frames, and furniture from every period of history scattered around the floor. There were so many pieces, each one of unimaginable historical and financial value, that there was hardly a square foot of unoccupied floor space.

"Want to put money on this?" Shawn said quietly to Gus.

"On what?" Gus said, glancing over to see that Kitteredge was still lecturing on the history of torture.

"Who comes in to question us," Shawn said.

"You already know," Gus said. "It's Polidori. The man you said was a hallucination."

"Of course he's going to call himself Polidori," Shawn said, ignoring the fact he'd denied the man's existence only hours before. "That's got to be the code name. Like James Bond's boss. You don't really think they keep finding people who are named M to run the spy agency, do you?"

"What makes you think that isn't his name?" Gus said.

"First of all, if you're running a global conspiracy, you probably don't want to put your own name on the letterhead," Shawn said. "More importantly, it would violate the rule."

Part of Gus wished a heavy statue would fall on Shawn before he could finish. But another part welcomed this discussion as one last bit of normalcy before they became the Cabal's latest victims. "Which rule?"

"Think about it," Shawn said. "Have we met anyone named Polidori throughout this whole case?"

"One of the masked guys was called Chip," Gus said. "I assume he was Professor Kitteredge's former student, Chip Polidori."

"If they're masked, they don't count," Shawn said. "But since you seem to be so unclear on the concept, the answer is no. No, we haven't met anyone named Polidori. Which means that it's a fake name used by someone we've encountered along the way. The most obvious choice would be Flaxman Low, but any idiot could have figured that out ages ago. It could be that Hugh Ralston guy from the museum. But what would be really cool is if it turned out to be Lassiter. No one would ever see that coming."

"Because it wouldn't make any sense," Gus said. "Lassie is not the head of a secret, worldwide conspiracy."

"Don't be so quick to judge," Shawn said. "Have you ever seen him and this Polidori in the same room together?"

"I've never seen Polidori at all," Gus said. "And neither have you."

"We'll see about that," Shawn said. "Very soon."

Across the warehouse, a door opened and three figures stepped in. Gus tried to make out their faces as they came through the maze of furniture and artworks, but there was always something in the way.

"Last chance," Shawn said. "Ten bucks says it's Lassie."

Gus ignored him as he tried to peer through the dusty air to see the faces that were approaching them. Even Kitteredge seemed to have realized that he was not in a classroom and had given up the lecture. For a moment the only sound in the warehouse was the shuffling of feet around furniture.

And then three men stepped from behind a Second Empire armoire. The two in back were clearly the subordinates. They were barely out of their twenties and looked comfortable in their workers' coveralls.

It was the man in front Gus stared at. He had a round face with a pronounced nose and ruddy cheeks. A bowler hat sat jauntily on his head, and his immaculate, pinstriped suit now had a carnation in its pocket.

He looked like he was well past fifty, but he had been so well tended, it was difficult to tell.

Gus quickly catalogued the other details he could see—the folded umbrella under one arm, the briefcase in the other hand, the blue-and-red tie done in a perfect Windsor knot.

But all the details were swept away by the most important fact about this man: Gus had never seen him before.

"Good afternoon, gentlemen," the man said, his posh accent accentuating his cheerful smile. "I am Charles Polidori, and I'm very pleased to welcome you to my establishment."

Chapter Forty-one

Gus heard a gasp from the chair next to him.

"It is you, Polidori," Kitteredge said. "After all these years."

"Surely it hasn't been so long," Polidori said. "It seems only yesterday young Chip went off to university. Imagine, I tried to talk him out of going to the States. We have far better institutions here, I said. Imagine how foolish I felt afterward."

"Who are you again?" Shawn said, peering closely at Polidori's face.

"I apologize if I didn't speak clearly enough," Polidori said. "Charles Polidori. This is my son, Chip"—he turned to his left to introduce the taller of the other two, and to the right for the other—"and this is my assistant, Leonard Goldstone."

Shawn squinted. "Are you sure we didn't catch you embezzling from Aunt Kitty's Soul Food last year?" Shawn said hopefully.

"I can't say I know what that is," Polidori said. "But I'm certain I've never been accused of embezzlement."

"Nothing that trivial," Kitteredge growled. "Only crimes against humanity."

"I prefer to think of my enterprise as bringing un-seen antiquities to a new audience," Polidori said. "In today's case, it is to be Excalibur, the sword of King Arthur. As soon as you provide me the final clues to its location."

Shawn closed his left eye and studied Polidori with the right. "You weren't the guy who stole the ponies from the petting zoo, were you?" he said.

"I haven't set foot in the United States in twenty years," Polidori said.

"Except to murder Clay Filkin," Gus said. "And frame Professor Kitteredge for the crime."

"I assure you, our only previous meeting was in that barn," Polidori said. "Although it's understandable you might not recognize me. I am a completely different person when I trade my chapeau for a ski mask. I do hope you won't force me to reintroduce you to that other chap."

"And so the Cabal will claim another victim," Kitteredge said. "I have only one request. And that is you let me see *The Defence of Guenevere* one last time before I die."

Polidori exchanged puzzled looks with his helpers. "We don't have the painting," he said finally.

"You don't?" Shawn said.

"We thought Professor Kitteredge stole it," Polidori said. "It was all over CNN International. We assumed he'd destroyed it to keep anyone else from finding the clues."

"I would never destroy a great work of art," Kitteredge said, sounding like the accusation had wounded him more than the beatings.

"It's true, Dad," Chip said. "I tried to tell you."

Polidori waved him off. "Yes, yes, you never tire of telling me how you knew him first. You are the great genius in the family."

Shawn looked from one Polidori to the other, a

light dawning in his eyes. Gus knew that look. It meant
Shawn had figured out a large part of the puzzle—or
at least thought he had. Gus thought back to the last
few moments of the conversation and tried to figure out
what he'd picked up on, but aside from a not-so-thinly
veiled threat to start torturing them if they didn't talk,
he couldn't spot anything of significance.

But Shawn wasn't waiting for him to figure it out.
"The tears!" he cried. "The rusty tears!"

The three standing men leaned in toward Shawn. Kitteredge would have, too, if he hadn't been tied down.

"I see tears," Shawn said again. "Rusting tears."

"We've heard this part," Polidori said.

"What is that you say, O spirits of the poem?" Shawn
chanted to the ceiling. "Take the sword to the tears?"

"What is that supposed to mean?" Polidori said.

"No," Shawn moaned. "Not to the tears. At the tears.
The sword lies with the tears!" Shawn's body went limp
as he slumped in his chair. Then he bounced back up
again, or at least as much as he could while tied down.
"What did I miss?"

Polidori gazed at him suspiciously. But Kitteredge
was already working.

"The sword lies with the tears," Kitteredge said.
"What is a tear? It is water that runs from an eye."

"Yes, obviously," Polidori said. "But what does this
mean? Whose tears? And how can they still exist a century and a half later?"

"It has to be a metaphor," Kitteredge said. "It's a location, after all."

"Professor, what are you doing?" Gus said. "You're
helping Polidori find Excalibur!"

A wave of shame passed over the professor's face. "I
have to know," Kitteredge said. "Don't you see? Even
if it means aiding my direst enemy, I have to see that
sword just once."

"He killed your friend Malko," Gus said, outraged at

this betrayal. "Murdered him in cold blood. He'll do the same to all of us."

"Our lives are but flickers of a candle flame," Kitteredge said. "I would trade all my remaining years for one glimpse of the thing I've been hunting for so long."

"And ours, too," Gus said.

"Give it up, Gus," Shawn said. "Excalibur is the only thing he's cared about. He's not going to give it up for you or me."

Kitteredge looked away from him, ashamed. "We are looking for a place where water runs from an eye in London."

The assistant named Leonard shot his hand in the air. "That's it, sir!" he said. "The London Eye. It sits on the banks of the Thames."

There was a long moment of silence. Polidori looked like he was trying to stop himself from hitting his head on the floor. "My sister's boy," he said apologetically. "Nice kid, but not really cut out for this line of work."

"What?" Leonard said.

Chip smacked the back of his head. "The London Eye was built in 1999, almost one hundred and fifty years after the poem was published."

"Maybe there was an earlier version of the Eye," Leonard said stubbornly.

Chip was going to smack Leonard again, but Polidori waved him off. "The first Ferris wheel was constructed in 1893, still far too late to be our answer," Polidori said. "William Morris had many talents, but I've never heard anyone claim he had psychic abilities. Unlike our friend here."

"It would have saved him lots of trouble if he did," Shawn said.

"So now that we have ruled out one eye, what is left to us?" Polidori said.

"Maybe it's not a literal eye," Chip said. "Could it be a famous observation point? A lookout of some kind?"

Polidori thought that over for so long that Gus thought his carnation was going to start wilting. Then his face lit up. "An observation point overlooking water is far too vague," Polidori said. "But there is another kind of eye—and I know of one in London. One which stands by the water, and has stood there for almost two centuries."

Kitteredge stared at him, trying to make sense of the puzzle. "It can't be . . ."

"It must be," Polidori said. "And I'm going to do you the supreme honor of allowing you to come along to watch me uncover Excalibur before your unfortunate death."

Chapter Forty-two

Gus had hoped to be able to keep track of the turns in the road from inside the back of the windowless van, so he could reproduce the journey should they manage to get away from Polidori and find a policeman.

Two minutes into the trip, though, Gus was hopelessly lost. It wasn't just the fact that they made some kind of turn every twenty feet, or that they seemed to drive around every roundabout four times before choosing an exit. It was that he kept being distracted by the gun that Leonard was pointing at him.

Gus tried to console himself with the thought that having a gun trained on him was better than being tied up again. The ropes had been sliced off back at the warehouse, and after several minutes of agony, his arms and legs even felt normal again. Of course, the advantage to being tied up was that if the van hit a pothole, the rope was much less likely than Leonard's pistol to go off and put a bullet in his head. But he supposed that being shot couldn't hurt any more than Kitteredge's betrayal.

Shawn didn't seem bothered by any of it. He sat on a wheel well and tried to engage Leonard in conversation. "I guess all the smart people get to ride up front," Shawn said.

Leonard just glared at him and shifted the gun in his direction.

"No, I get it," Shawn said. "The Polidoris would rather ride with someone who understands the same things they do. Gus has the same problem."

"I do?" Gus said.

"Imagine what it's like for poor Gus, being the only nonpsychic member of a psychic detective agency," Shawn said. "He must feel like he's left out of everything. You thought he was pathetic back in the warehouse when Kitteredge sold him out for a glimpse at an old sword? That's what it's like for him every day."

Another betrayal, Gus thought. First Kitteredge, and now, for reasons he couldn't begin to understand, Shawn was turning on him, too. But even as the notion crossed his mind, he rejected it, realizing that only his exhaustion allowed him even to entertain the idea. Shawn was planning something. Gus just didn't understand what.

Then he caught a flicker of sympathy in Leonard's eye. And Gus got it. "You keep telling yourself that," he said defensively. "Not everybody cares about all your precious psychic stuff."

"Not everybody," Shawn said. "That's my point. When I want to talk psychic stuff with my colleagues, you'd just be bored. It's better if you don't come."

"Like when you and your psychic buddies decided to pool your powers and pick the winning lottery numbers?" Gus sulked. "I wouldn't have been bored by that."

"But you couldn't have contributed, either," Shawn said. "So it wouldn't have been fair to the others."

"You could have taken my money and given me a share of what you won," Gus said.

Shawn shook his head wearily and turned back to Leonard. "He just doesn't understand that people with a higher understanding naturally want to be together," he said. "I'm glad you do."

"They're pumping the professor for information," Leonard said, although a touch of uncertainty had entered his voice.

"That's the spirit," Shawn said. "They're your friends, no matter what."

Leonard stared down at his gun. Time for stage two, Gus thought.

"Are you going to let them do this to you?" Gus said.

"Do what?" Leonard said.

"Cut you out," Gus said.

"No one's cutting Leonard out of anything," Shawn said. "They're just having a nice chat about history and things like that."

"Yeah," Leonard said dubiously. "I mean, they're pumping him."

"Then why were they so quick to dismiss your idea about the London Eye?" Gus said.

"Because it's only been there for a few years," Leonard said.

"I didn't hear them mention what might have been on that spot before," Gus said. "And whether it was called the London Eye, too."

Leonard's eyes narrowed suspiciously. "Was it?"

"Don't ask me," Gus said. "I'm not a historian. But they sure changed the subject fast. And I didn't hear anyone say where we were actually going, did you?"

"Stop it, Gus," Shawn chided him. "I'm sure the Polidoris only have Leonard's best interests at heart."

"Sure," Gus said. "Just like you did when you cut me out of your psychic investment club because it was just too confusing for me. And then told me you'd lost all my money, even though the rest of you made a fortune."

"I told you, we were doing what was best for you," Shawn said. "And when there's something you need to know, we'll tell you. Until then, you need to keep out of things you can't understand."

Leonard looked like he was about to ask a question when the van pulled to a stop and the engine switched off.

"I guess we're here," Gus said. "Wherever here is."

After a moment, the back doors swung open. Chip grabbed Shawn and pulled him out, gesturing for Leonard to do the same with Gus. Behind him, Gus could see Polidori holding on to Kitteredge's arm.

Gus let Leonard lead him out of the van. They were parked on a busy street, and the traffic hurtling past seemed louder and faster than any Gus had ever seen before. Also, it all seemed to be going in the wrong direction, but Gus assumed that he was merely suffering from jet lag or van lag or tied-up lag.

Fortunately Gus didn't have to worry about crossing the street. Leonard pulled him away from the curb and down a tree-laden path that led away from the traffic.

"Where are we going?" Gus whispered to Shawn as Leonard came closer to Chip.

"Not to the London Eye, that's for sure," Shawn said loudly. "No one actually believes that's where the sword is."

Chip cuffed Shawn across the back of the head with his free hand. "Shut up."

Gus glanced up to see that Leonard was eying Chip suspiciously. But before he could stoke that particular fire further, the path rounded a curve and they found themselves at their destination.

At least Gus assumed it was their destination, because the path ended at the banks of a wide gray river that even he knew to be the Thames. And because both Polidori and Kitteredge had stopped and were staring up at an enormous tapering pillar of reddish granite that sat on a huge marble base. The obelisk towered at least six stories above them, covered on all four sides by ancient hieroglyphics. Bronze sphinxes watched it from either side.

"What is that?" Gus whispered to Shawn.

"Looks like a big rock to me," Shawn whispered back. "Aside from that, your guess is as good as mine."

"But you made them bring us here," Gus said.

"Did I?" Shawn said.

Gus thought back on the conversation in the warehouse. What had Shawn said? As Gus played it back he realized that Shawn hadn't actually said anything specific. He'd restated the words in the poem, and Kitteredge and Polidori had filled in the blanks.

"I can tell you what it isn't," Shawn said loudly. "And that's the London Eye. Because that's over there." Shawn pointed across the river, where a gigantic Ferris wheel towered over all the surrounding buildings. "Clever of them to bring us here where they can keep an eye on it—and still keep you away."

Leonard looked longingly at the wheel until Chip shoved him toward the stone pillar.

As Shawn and Gus were led up to the pillar's base, Polidori and Kitteredge were already deep in speculation.

"Is it possible?" Kitteredge said in wonder. "Have we finally uncovered the mystery of Excalibur?"

Shawn glanced up at the pillar. "If that's the sword, Arthur must have been a pretty big guy," Shawn said.

"This is Cleopatra's Needle, you fool," Polidori said.

"So the sword is even bigger?" Shawn said. "Because a sword's got to be bigger than a needle."

"Professor Kitteredge!" Gus tried to rush to him, but Leonard held him back. "This man is your mortal enemy. Stop now before it's too late."

"It's already too late," Kitteredge said sadly. "I know he's going to kill me after this, and he will have the sword. But he is letting me finish my life's work first."

"Do you think he might do us the same favor?"

Shawn said. "Because I've always seen my life's work as dying at ninety-three."

"I am sorry that won't be possible," Polidori said. "But at least you have the privilege of seeing one of the world's great mysteries solved first."

Chapter Forty-three

Gus tried to pull away from Leonard. He wanted to run to the professor and shake some sense into him. But he couldn't get free, and even if he could, he knew all the shaking in the world wouldn't do any good. Kitteredge was in the grip of an obsession, and it would never let him go. Gus knew that because it had dragged him in, too, and if he'd spent any more time on it, he might not have been able to escape, either.

"It's the sword's resting place," Polidori said. "It has to be. It fits the poem perfectly: 'Let not my rusting tears make your sword light! Ah! God of mercy, how he turns away!' Can't you see it?"

Shawn and Gus looked up at the pillar.

"I see a big rock," Shawn said.

"It was you who gave us the final clue," Polidori said.

"That was the spirits," Shawn said. "They didn't bother with subtitles."

"We should have seen this all along," Polidori said. "The obelisk was erected in 1877, just five years before Rossetti painted that last picture."

"But decades after the poem was written," Kitteredge said. "That was what kept me from understanding the truth. The fact that the verse itself was not written to be a clue to the puzzle, but that Rossetti and Morris chose to construct their clue out of an existing work."

"Well, sure, if you'd just said that before, we all would have gotten it," Shawn said.

"Tears are water that runs down from the eye," Polidori said. "In this case, that has to be the eye of the Needle. Tears that appear to be rusty because of the red granite it's made of."

"Of course, that could have meant so many things," Kitteredge said. "But the next line is what seals it. 'Ah! God of mercy, how he turns away!' That could be no place but here."

"Uh-huh," Gus said.

"Look at the sphinxes," Polidori said. "They should be guarding the obelisk, but instead they seem to be looking at it. That's because they were installed backward— they turn away!"

"Which would mean nothing, unless you know that the golden cherubim on the biblical Mercy Seat are actually believed to be sphinxes," Kitteredge said. "This has to be the place."

"It all seems to fit," Shawn said. "Except for one thing. What about the eye?"

Polidori stepped up to the obelisk and rapped on the marble pedestal it sat on. "In here," he said. "The eye of the needle. It has to be."

"When the obelisk was erected, they put a time capsule in the base," Kitteredge said. "It contained all the usual things you might find in such a container—the day's newspapers, a Bible, a portrait of Queen Victoria."

"And the sword of King Arthur?" Gus said.

"You'd think someone would have noticed," Shawn said.

"When Rossetti's wife, Lizzie, died, he placed the manuscripts of his most recent poems in the casket with her," Kitteredge said. "Several years later he was desperate for money, and his only prospect was the publication of those poems. So he sneaked into the graveyard in the middle of the night, dug up his wife's grave, and took the papers back."

"Is it such a stretch to believe he and Morris would repeat that stunt with the sword?" Polidori said.

"If you've stretched things this far, why not?" Shawn said. "So what do we do next? Steal the pillar?"

"This is the point at which our destinies diverge," Polidori said. "Professor Kitteredge, Chip, and I are going to wait here until long after dark, at which time we will attempt to find the mechanism to open the time capsule. I'm afraid that you will be going with Leonard to a slightly less scenic spot."

For the first time since they had left the warehouse, Kitteredge seemed to be aware of the reality of the situation. "There's no reason for that," he pleaded. "Let them stay—at least until they see the sword."

"You can describe it to them when you see them in heaven," Polidori said. "Leonard."

Leonard took the van keys out of Chip's outstretched hand and dropped them in his pocket, then grabbed Shawn's arm with one hand and Gus' with the other.

"I have a better idea," Shawn said. "Why don't you just have Leonard hit us over the head and dump us into the river right here?"

"Thanks for the suggestion, but I'd prefer not to bring the police down to this particular spot," Polidori said.

"What police?" Shawn said. "Put rocks in our pockets; no one will ever know."

"Except all the tourists lined up for the boat tour below," Chip said. "Nice try."

"Then let Chip take us," Shawn said. "Leonard can stay here."

"Yeah," Leonard said. "I'd like to see the sword."

"Chip's been my partner in this for years," Polidori said. "He deserves to be here when we retrieve it."

Leonard looked unhappy. He didn't move.

"It's okay, Leonard," Shawn said soothingly. "I'm sure they'll still be here when you get back. It's not like they're going to wait here until you've gone, and then make a dash for the real hiding place."

Gus felt Leonard's grip loosen on his arm a little. "Sure—they already told you there's no way the sword's at the London Eye," Gus said. "They wouldn't lie about something like that."

"Not to you, Leonard," Shawn said. "You know how much they think of you."

For a second, no one moved. Then Leonard let go of Shawn and Gus. His hand dug in a pocket and came out with a pistol. He leveled it at Chip.

"Chip takes them," Leonard growled. "I wait for the sword."

"Put that away, you fool," Polidori hissed. "Don't you realize where you are?"

"I'm not up front with the smart guys. I know that," Leonard said.

"That's because you're not smart," Chip snapped. "Now put that gun back in your pocket."

"It's a little too heavy," Leonard said. "Stretches out the fabric. Maybe if I lightened it a little. Just by the weight of a couple of bullets."

He kept the gun and his gaze aimed straight at Chip. Which meant he didn't see Polidori reaching into his own pocket and pulling out his own pistol.

"I told you to put that away," Polidori said. "I should kill you right here. But there's no more time. We have to move—now!"

Chip pushed past Leonard's gun and grabbed Gus' arm.

"What's going on?" Gus whispered to Shawn as Chip started to pull him away. "What happened?"

"Nothing yet," Shawn said. "But there's a funny thing about England. It's—"

Something hit Gus in the back and knocked him to the ground. He threw out his hands to protect his face as he fell, landing hard on his palms. He tried to turn around to see what had struck him, but before he could move, someone grabbed his wrists and whipped plastic cuffs around them. He lifted his head, but all he could see was a swarm of black uniforms and yellow Windbreakers.

"—the biggest surveillance state in the world," Shawn said as he was cuffed. "You can't go anywhere in public without the police seeing you."

Chapter Forty-four

If it had occurred just a day earlier, Gus would have thought the flight back to the States was the worst thing that had ever happened to him. Handcuffed to his seat, accompanied by a uniformed U.S. marshal, he knew that everyone who walked by his row was staring at him and wondering what he had done. But compared to the ride in Polidori's van, this was better than the luxury flight in Flaxman Low's private jet.

And spending ten hours flying back to Santa Barbara was definitely preferable to ten years in an English jail, which was what their arresting officer had originally threatened them with. That threat began to ease when it became obvious that neither they nor Kitteredge was carrying a gun, and that there seemed to be little with which to charge them. When a routine search of their names turned up the California warrants, the English government was only too happy to turn them over to American officials.

That wasn't the case with the Polidoris. They would be going away for a long time, especially once the police started to inventory what turned out to be multiple warehouses of stolen antiquities. It seemed that a certain division of Scotland Yard had long been suspicious of Polidori and Son Antiques, and now planned to devote substantial resources to uncovering every illegal transaction in the firm's long history. That task would prove to be substantially easier once Leonard started talking about everything he'd been involved with, starting with directions to the barn containing Malko's body.

"Do you realize what this means?" Gus had said to Shawn while they sat in a holding cell waiting for the marshal to transport them to the airport. "They're going to break up the entire Cabal."

Shawn stared at him. "Maybe you want to join Professor Kitteredge in the other cell," he said. "This one is reserved for sane people."

"What?" Gus said. "You can't still be denying the Cabal exists. They nearly killed us."

"An antiques dealer nearly killed us," Shawn said. "Which, by the way, is nothing to brag about if you happen to tell this story to that blond sales rep at next year's Christmas party."

"He wasn't just an antiques dealer," Gus said. "He'd spent his life searching for the sword, just like Kitteredge said."

"Yes, just like Kitteredge said," Shawn agreed. "Because that's where Polidori heard about it. Or, more precisely, his son heard about it from Kitteredge in class. And Chip told Daddy. And the hunt was on."

Gus was about to object, then stopped to think it through. "You mean, this entire thing started with Kitteredge's obsession? And that's all there ever was to it?"

"What did I tell you about the third kind of conspiracy theorist?" Shawn said. "They're the ones who are dangerous to themselves and others, because they're smart enough to invent theories that are so plausible and compelling they can make otherwise sane people believe them."

Gus thought that over. There was still one problem. "But that means the poem wasn't really a clue," he said. "Or the painting. That fifty-five on the two shields. Why was that there?"

"It wasn't," Shawn said. "Unless you chose to look at it that way. There were a couple of animals on the shields. Everything else came from Kitteredge, with some help from Low."

Gus still couldn't let go. "But it led us to the Needle. You led us to the Needle."

"I didn't lead us anywhere," Shawn corrected him. "I made up some nonsense about a line of poetry, and they invented meanings for every word. It's what Kitteredge has been doing for years."

Gus still wasn't convinced. There had been such an elegant complexity to Kitteredge's theories that he hated to give it all up for the sad reality of coincidences and misunderstandings. But the more he worked it through, the less persuasive the evidence became, and by the time they were halfway across the Atlantic he thought back on his belief in the Cabal with the same sort of embarrassed nostalgia that accompanied memories of his once firm faith that Phil Joanou would eventually surpass Steven Spielberg in the directing hall of fame.

But there was still one piece to the puzzle that Gus couldn't figure out. He'd mentioned it to Shawn in the cell, but the answer he got back didn't make him feel any better.

"So if there's no Cabal, and Polidori is just a crook with an antiques business, who killed Clay Filkin?" he said.

"It's still possible it's Kitteredge," Shawn said. "He did have the bloody murder weapon in his pocket. Although our lives are going to be a lot easier if he didn't do it. I don't think the penalties are quite as harsh for helping an innocent man escape."

Gus had been so busy assuming he'd never see his

home again that he'd forgotten what was waiting for him there. "I'm sure he didn't," Gus said. "Someone must have framed him. And whoever it was must have stolen the painting as well."

"I hope you're right," Shawn said. "And I hope we can figure it out before we get back to Santa Barbara. Because if we can't, we're going to have to blame it on the Cabal. And I don't think anyone else is going to buy that."

Gus groaned. "If only that picture hadn't been stolen," he said. "If Kitteredge had been allowed to look at it for as long as he wanted, we never would have gotten involved like this."

Shawn was about to respond, but then he stopped himself. A smile spread over his face. "We kept thinking it was the Cabal that stole the painting."

"But there was no Cabal."

"So who had a reason to steal it?" Shawn said.

"I don't know," Gus said. "Anyone who wanted a painting worth millions of dollars."

"Maybe," Shawn said. "Or maybe it was someone who didn't."

Chapter Forty-five

Gus had always liked this courtroom. When he'd been here before, either as a witness or as just a spectator, he'd always taken time to admire the high beamed ceiling, the bright white plaster walls, the oaken benches, and the murals of Santa Barbara's founding painted on the back wall.

But now that he was sitting at the defendants' table, waiting with Shawn and Kitteredge for their arraignment to be over, he couldn't remember why he'd been so enthusiastic about it. All he wanted was to get out as quickly as possible.

Whether that was going to happen would be determined in the next few moments. They had been brought straight from the airport to the courthouse for their arraignment. The district attorney had offered them some time to meet with their state-appointed attorney first, but Shawn had merely slipped him a list of names and sent him away. Gus had expected Kitteredge to say something, but he'd been completely silent since they'd been arrested in London. It was as if learning that the Cabal had never existed had sucked all the life from his body.

Now the courtroom was packed with the people Shawn had asked the lawyer to fetch. Lassiter was sitting right behind Gus, his badge gleaming brightly on his belt, flanked by Henry Spencer and Chief Vick. It took Gus a moment to recognize the thin man sitting a few rows back, because he'd seen Hugh Ralston, the museum's executive director, only that one night. But Flaxman Low he spotted right away. And there were two uniformed officers he thought were the ones who'd wanted to hire them for the bachelor party.

Gus had sat silently through the first parts of the proceedings except for the moment when the white-bearded judge came in and he was ordered to rise. He'd only half listened as the prosecutor, a sharkish young woman named Sarah Willingham, had laid out the charges against them, although that half was enough to convince him that they'd all be going away for a long time.

Now it was all coming to an end. The judge would ask them a simple question, they'd claim innocence, and the prosecutor would request that they be sent to jail until trial. Since they'd already proven themselves flight risks, the judge would grant her request. And then his life would be over and he could die. At least he'd be able to change into a comfortable prison jumpsuit. The tuxedo was now so filthy and sweaty that it had hardened into an armor Tony Stark would envy.

The judge pulled his attention away from the prosecuting attorney and turned it toward the defense table. "How do the defendants plead?"

Their lawyer started to stand up, but Shawn put a hand on his shoulder and pushed him back down, then leapt out of his chair. "That's a very complicated question, Your Honor," Shawn said.

Gus looked up at Shawn. What was he doing? Why would he want to drag this out any longer than necessary?

"No, it's not," the judge said. "It's a simple binary. Yes or no. Up or down. Guilty or not guilty."

"But who among us can be said to be truly innocent?" Shawn said. "I say, none of us. Certainly not her," he added, jerking his thumb at Sarah Willingham.

She jumped to her feet. "Your Honor, I object."

Shawn glanced at her, and he *saw*. Saw the sealed Wet-Nap sticking out of her jacket pocket. The spot of barbecue sauce on the sleeve of her white silk sleeve. And, sitting in her open purse, a small bottle of hand cream—the kind placed in hotel bathrooms. Then he glanced at the judge. And saw a small red spot in his otherwise meticulous white beard.

The judge gaveled for order. "She is not being charged with any crimes. You are. How do you plead?"

"Your Honor," Shawn said. "At this time I'd like to call my first witness."

"Objection!" Willingham said. "This is an arraignment. You don't call witnesses at an arraignment."

"In that case, I'd like to send out for some lunch," Shawn said, staring at the judge. "You don't happen to know a good barbecue place, do you?"

The judge's face reddened under the white beard as he banged his gavel. "The defendant will sit down."

"Okay, don't tell me," Shawn said. "I'll ask around. I'm sure *someone* saw you having lunch today."

Gus sank his head in his hands. He was pretty confident that the judge at an arraignment couldn't actually sentence them to death, but Shawn seemed to be doing everything he could to find out. After a long moment when the judge hadn't spoken or gaveled, Gus looked up again.

The judge was glaring at Shawn. Sarah Willingham was glaring at the judge. And the defense attorney was desperately trying to figure out what was going on. Apparently, whatever Shawn had seen was something he wasn't supposed to.

The judge banged his gavel again.

"One witness," the judge said. "And then a plea."

"Your Honor, I object to these proceedings," Willingham said.

"If you'd done that before lunch, I wouldn't be getting away with this," Shawn said sweetly, then turned to the courtroom. "Ladies and gentlemen of the jury—"

The judge gaveled again. "Once again, there is an arraignment, not a trial. There is no jury here."

"Fine, whatever," Shawn said. "Ladies and gentlemen whose opinion means nothing to this court, I'd like to introduce you to my first witness."

Shawn tapped their lawyer on the shoulder, and the man produced a small metal and plastic rectangle. Shawn took it and held it up for the onlookers to see. "I present to you Izzy the iPod," Shawn said.

"Your Honor, this is ludicrous," Willingham complained in a voice that suggested she knew he wouldn't do anything about it.

"Now you may be wondering what a simple iPod has to tell us about the terrible crimes we're accused of," Shawn said. "Let's find out. I'm going to put Izzy in shuffle mode." Shawn worked the central wheel, then looked at the screen. "What have we got? 'Killing Me Softly.' 'Innocent Bystander.' 'Run Like a Thief.' 'Magical Mystery Tour.' 'The Hunter Gets Captured by the Game.' 'Free the People.' Do you see what it's saying, aside from the fact that my lawyer apparently doesn't own any songs recorded after my birth?"

"Who cares?" Willingham said.

"It's trying to tell you something," Shawn said. "About a murder, and the innocent bystanders who were caught up in it. How they had to flee to England where they caught a group of murderous smugglers, and now they should be set free."

Gus still wasn't sure what Shawn was doing, but he

noticed that the judge seemed to be intrigued. At least he did until the prosecutor spoke.

"Your Honor, that's a list of songs generated at random by a computer algorithm," Willingham said. "Any meaning we might find there is simply a product of the human brain's need to find patterns in any set of data."

"Exactly!" Shawn shouted. "Which is exactly what my former client Langston Kitteredge spent the past decades doing. Only he's smarter than we are, so he didn't do it with iPod songs. He took bits and pieces from all sorts of books and paintings and kept messing them around until they fit in a pattern."

"And he became so enamored of this pattern he let it replace any sense of reality," Willingham said. "That's called paranoid schizophrenia, and if the professor wants to claim it was this mental illness that caused him to murder Clay Filkins, he only has to enter the plea. And this would be a good time to do it, since we're in the middle of his arraignment."

For a moment, Gus had been feeling pretty good about what Shawn was doing. He hadn't had any idea what it was all about, but it definitely seemed to have a direction. Now it looked like he had played right into the prosecutor's hands. Because if Kitteredge did plead not guilty by reason of insanity, that still left Gus and Shawn guilty of accessory and obstruction and who knew what else.

"No pleas just yet," Shawn said. "I'd like to call my first witness."

"You just called your first witness," Willingham said. "That iPod."

"An iPod can't be a witness," Shawn said. "That's ludicrous. Now if it were a Walkman, maybe. At least there's a person in there."

"Your Honor," the prosecutor said.

"I'll allow it," the judge sighed.

"I call Flaxman Low to the stand," Shawn said loudly.

Chapter Forty-six

Low stood up and strode to the docket, where he took a seat. Gus glanced over at Kitteredge to see if he'd acknowledge his old friend, but he just stared down at the table.

"I remind the witness he is still under oath," Shawn said.

"What oath?" Willingham said. "He never swore an oath."

"I solemnly swear to tell the truth, the whole truth, and nothing but the truth," Low said. "Can we get on with this now?"

"*Now* I remind the witness he is still under oath," Shawn said. "Mr. Low. May I call you Flaxman?"

"If you'd like," Low said wearily.

"Really?" Shawn said. "How about Flax? Or Man? If I were you, I'd go with Man. It doesn't sound like something you'd eat to boost your fiber."

"Your Honor!"

The judge didn't even bother to overrule Willingham but just waved at Shawn to continue.

"So, Flaxy, you've known the defendant Longbow Crispirito for a long time," Shawn said.

Behind him, Gus heard the sound of a hand slapping a forehead and wondered if that was Henry or Lassiter. Maybe both. It had taken all of his self-control to keep from doing the same thing.

"I've known Langston Kitteredge for many years," Low said.

"And you've known about his belief in a conspiracy involving King Arthur's sword, and some artists no one has ever heard of?" Shawn said.

"We have had many discussions about his belief that William Morris and Dante Gabriel Rossetti had found Excalibur, and that a secret organization had been searching for it ever since," Low said.

"Would you say he was convincing?" Shawn said.

"I wouldn't have spent so much time on the subject if he hadn't been," Low said. "I believe you've had the experience yourself. Once he started weaving facts together, it was impossible to see where he was wrong. And while you may want to claim that this was nothing more than your iPod hypothesis, a search for patterns in unrelated data, I don't see that anyone has disproved his main thesis."

At this, Kitteredge did look up briefly, then returned his gaze to the tabletop.

"So if the professor said he had proof that Rossetti had painted a final picture and it had all these great clues in it, people would believe him, even if no one had ever seen the thing," Shawn said.

"He's the authority," Low said.

"Which means that if someone else painted that picture, but Kitteredge said it was the real thing, whoever had it could sell it for jillions of dollars," Shawn said.

"It's hard to imagine a forger good enough to fool my friend Langston," Low said.

"Even if he was only allowed to see the picture for a few minutes before it was stolen?" Shawn said.

"Your Honor." Willingham didn't even bother to get

out of her chair this time. "What does this have to do with the defendants' plea?"

"What does barbecue sauce have to do with hotel sheets?" Shawn said. "It's one of life's mysteries."

The judge banged his gavel. "Just hurry it up."

"Yes," Low said. "Langston's word would be enough to establish the piece's provenance. But if you're suggesting that he was used to artificially inflate the value of a forgery, you're forgetting the fact that the picture was never sold. It was donated to the museum by an anonymous donor who received nothing in return."

"But if something happened to the painting, Kitteredge's pomegranate would still stand," Shawn said.

"Provenance, yes," Low said. "Which means the whole world can mourn the loss of this masterpiece, knowing it exists."

"Excuse me," a voice said from the audience. Gus turned to see that Lassiter was standing now. "Carlton Lassiter, head detective for the Santa Barbara Police Department. I wonder if I might ask the witness a question."

"I object again!" This time Willingham did get out of her chair. In fact, she seemed to have been propelled out by jets of rage. "This man is not a lawyer."

The judge pointed at Shawn. "And this man is? If it will get us any closer to a plea, come on down."

Lassiter sidled over the chief's legs, then walked through the low gate to the stand. "Mr. Low," he said. "As you know, our English colleagues have been going through the records of Polidori and Son, and they've discovered that you sold the firm some several extremely valuable Pre-Raphaelite paintings."

"I have been fortunate in my dealings," Low said.

"I'd say you've been extremely fortunate," Lassiter said. "Because you were able to sell some paintings that actually existed simultaneously in Japanese bank vaults, owned by corporations that had squirreled them away as investments. Scotland Yard will soon be retrieving the pictures you sold, and will be able to prove they were forgeries. So you might want to cooperate now if you hope to head off extradition."

"I'm delighted to cooperate, but even if I had painted this picture, what gain would there have been for me?" Low said. "It was donated. Given away. No money changed hands."

Gus noticed that Kitteredge was looking up at Low now, staring at him in acute betrayal. Then he lowered his gaze to the table again.

"Your Honor?" Shawn said. "I'm looking out in the audience, and I think someone else would like to ask a question. Dad?"

Shawn gestured, and Henry rose uncomfortably. "Sorry, Your Honor," Henry said. "I'm Henry Spencer. SBPD, retired. I know this isn't exactly the way things are done."

"Everybody else is doing it," the judge said wearily. "So jump on in. Ask Mr. Low your question."

"Actually, I'd like to ask someone else," Henry said. "Hugh Ralston, executive director of the Santa Barbara Museum of Art."

"Hugh Ralston, come on down!" Shawn shouted.

Ralston looked like he'd just been shot. He stood weakly, then came down the aisle. At a gesture from the judge, Low got out of the witness box and held the door open for Ralston.

"Hugh, I remind you that you are still under the oath the last guy swore," Shawn said.

"Is that real?" Ralston said in a quiet voice.

"Frankly, I'm not sure any of this is real," the judge said. "I sincerely hope to wake up on the couch in my chambers within the next five minutes. But until then, proceed as if you are sworn."

"Your witness, Dad," Shawn said.

"Thanks, son," Henry said. "Nice tux, by the way. Formal's a good look on you." He turned to the witness box. "Mr. Ralston, you told me you loved the museum."

"It's my life." Ralston's voice barely rose above a whisper.

"You told me it was more important than your life," Henry said. "Because you could touch only the lives of the few people you were close to, but the museum could give joy to generations."

"That's true," Ralston said.

"So if you found a way to protect the museum, to keep it open despite its financial difficulties, you would do it even if it weren't strictly legal?" Henry said.

Ralston nodded, tears in his eyes.

Shawn clapped Henry on the shoulder. "Good work, Dad. We'll take it from here." He turned to Gus. "You want a shot at this?"

Gus worked furiously to put together all the pieces Shawn and the others had been laying out. How could a museum profit from a forgery, especially one it had possessed for only a few days?

And then he knew. He stepped up to the witness box as Henry headed back to his seat. "So, Hugh, after Flaxman Low came to you with the idea of this forgery, how much did you decide to soak the insurance company for?"

Ralston's mouth was moving to speak when the courtroom doors burst open. A small, swarthy man marched down the aisle, two police officers chasing after him.

"Those two!" the swarthy man shouted, pointing at Shawn and Gus. "They are the ones who robbed me! I demand that they be arrested for grand theft!"

Chapter Forty-seven

"You have to admit: Things could have turned out a lot worse," Gus said. "For one thing, these orange jumpsuits are much more comfortable than the tuxedoes."

Shawn didn't even waste a glare on him but just turned back to his hard labor.

"Okay," Gus said. "I admit it. This was my fault. I got us into this, and you are paying the penalty for my mistake. But at least we've got the sun on our backs."

A car tore by no more than five inches from Shawn's foot, kicking dust in their faces as it sped down the 101 freeway.

"And don't forget the fresh air," Shawn said. "Lots and lots of fresh air."

Gus lifted his stick and speared a cigarette butt from among the succulents, then dropped it in his shoulder bag. "Considering what we were charged with, it could have been a lot worse."

It certainly could have been if Shawn hadn't managed to put it all together. As soon as Ralston had been confronted on the witness stand, he broke down and confessed the whole thing.

Not all at once, and not coherently at first. Because he kept breaking into sobs and pleas to be forgiven. He'd taken part in the scam only to help the museum. He'd never dreamed that anyone would get hurt.

The plan had been Flaxman Low's, of course. He'd been listening to Kitteredge obsess about that nonexistent painting for so many years he had half decided to paint it himself just as a prank. But once the idea was in his head, he realized it could be so much more lucrative if he took it beyond the level of practical joke.

Low knew how much financial trouble the Santa Barbara museum was in, so he went to Ralston with a proposal. He would arrange for a lawyer to contact curator Filkins and offer the museum *The Defence of Guenevere*. Of course Filkins would leap at the chance, especially since the only condition of the bequest would be that it remain entirely anonymous, even to all museum personnel. Then they'd get Kitteredge to declare it a masterpiece, thus establishing its provenance. And then the painting would be tragically "stolen," never to be seen again, and incurring an insurance payout in the tens of millions.

And it was all going so well until the day of the painting's official unveiling. Filkins had never been completely comfortable with the anonymous gift, and he'd been studying the picture closely. That day he told Ralston he suspected a forgery, and took him into the gallery to show him what he'd discovered. That's why the surveillance cameras had all been turned away—Filkins hadn't wanted to alert anyone to his suspicions until he'd shared them with Ralston.

Panicked, Ralston told Filkins the truth, hoping to enlist him on his side. But the curator was outraged and vowed to go to the museum board and have Ralston fired. The executive director claimed his memory was fuzzy on precisely what happened next, but there was a scuffle, and when it was over Filkins was dead and Ralston was holding the bloody knife.

There was no way he could hope to transport the body through the museum. He knew he was going to be caught, and he was prepared to turn himself in. Then he had an idea. Thanks to Kitteredge, there was a mythology about a conspiracy surrounding this painting. Why not make it look like the Cabal had killed Filkins? He found a sword in the museum's archives that was a fairly close match to the one in the picture and ran the corpse through with it.

But as the premiere drew closer, Ralston began to panic again. How could he hope that sane people— police detectives—would believe a ridiculous fantasy about a global conspiracy? They'd be much more likely to assume that anyone spinning such a tale was insane. And thus came the idea to slip the murder weapon into Kitteredge's pocket when the professor hugged him on the museum steps. After that, all he had to do was cut the forged painting out of its frame and make sure it was never seen again.

During Ralston's entire sobbing confession, Kitteredge barely looked up once. His spirit seemed to have been completely broken, either by the revelation that his decades-long obsession had been ridiculous or by his guilt over how it had led him to betray the people who'd tried to help him. After he had been cleared of all involvement in the murder, and the escape charges had been dropped as a matter of justice, the professor had taken a leave of absence from the university and checked himself into a mental hospital.

That should have completely cleared Shawn and Gus as well. After all, they'd done nothing but try to help an innocent man clear his name. But in doing so they had accidentally committed an act of theft, and their victim demanded that they face justice. Not only had Shawn and Gus stolen two tuxedoes; they had taken them out of the country. And by the time the tuxes were recovered, they were so disgusting that they couldn't be cleaned and had to be destroyed.

Which is why they were spending four days in orange jumpsuits picking up trash from the freeway median. Right under the sign reading "This stretch of freeway maintained by Sami's Formal Wear."

"Clearly," Shawn said, "this is a time to revisit our rules."

"I know, I know," Gus said. "No cases that require formal wear."

"That's never going to be a problem," Shawn said. "I'm sure we're on a national tuxedo blacklist and we'll never be able to rent again. No, I've got other rules in mind. Lots and lots of other rules."

Gus braced himself. Whatever Shawn had come up with now was going to be big. And after getting them involved with Kitteredge, Gus would have no choice but to go along with it. "Let's have them."

Shawn leaned forward, bracing himself on his stick. He opened his mouth to speak. And then closed it again. He smiled. "You know, I think we've had enough of rules for a while."

Gus stared at him suspiciously. "How long a while?"

"I don't know," Shawn said. "When's lunch around here?

Acknowledgments

At the risk of disillusioning those readers who are in the process of booking their flights to London, I have to confess that, as far as anyone knows, William Morris and Dante Gabriel Rossetti never engaged in a search for Excalibur or gave any thought to claiming the throne of Britain. If it seems like a terrible calumny to suggest such a thing even in a work of fiction, I can only remind you—SPOILER ALERT for those three of you who read the acknowledgments first—that the entire theory was crafted in the mind of a crazy person.

That said, I have drawn on some aspects of Morris' and Rossetti's real lives. And as is so often the case, their true story is much more fascinating than any fictional account. If you are interested in learning more about their odd Arthurian triangle, you can't do better than Fiona McCarthy's *William Morris: A Life for Our Times*. It is unaccountably out of print but well worth searching for.

Rossetti's painting of *The Defence of Guenevere* is as fictional as his search for the sword, but the poem is real and can be found in its entirety online.

There is a real Santa Barbara Museum of Art, but it in no way resembles the one portrayed here, which is purely a fictional creation, as are all its employees and benefactors.

And I'm almost positive that the sword of King Arthur is not hidden in the time capsule beneath Cleopatra's Needle in London.

About the Author

William Rabkin is a two-time Edgar-nominated television writer and producer. He has written for numerous mystery shows, including *Psych* and *Monk,* and has served as showrunner on *Diagnosis Murder* and *Martial Law*.

Also available in the new series based on
the hit USA Network television show!

PSYCH
A Mind Is a Terrible Thing
to Read

by WILLIAM RABKIN

After the PSYCH detective agency gets some top-notch
publicity, Shawn's high-school nemesis, Dallas Steele,
hires him to help choose his investments. Naturally,
their predictions turn out to be total busts. And the
deceptive Dallas is thrilled that he has completely
discredited and humiliated Shawn once and for all—
until he's found murdered.

But the police have a suspect—found at the scene with a
smoking gun. And she says Shawn took control of her
mind and forced her to do it. After all, he is a psychic…

And don't miss
Psych: Mind Over Magic
Psych: The Call of the Mild

Available wherever books are sold or at
penguin.com

OM0025